PENGUIN

Two I

P. J. Tracy is the pseudonym for the mother-and-daughter writing team of P. J. and Traci Lambrecht. They are the authors of the award-winning and bestselling thrillers *Live Bait*, *Dead Run*, *Snow Blind*, *Play to Kill* and the Richard and Judy Book Club pick *Want to Play?* All five books feature detectives Gino and Magozzi and maverick computer-hacker Grace MacBride. P. J. and Traci both live near Minneapolis, Minnesota.

Two Evils

P. J. TRACY

PENGUIN BOOKS

PENGUIN BOOKS

Published by the Penguin Group
Penguin Books Ltd, 80 Strand, London WC2R 0RL, England
Penguin Group (USA) Inc., 375 Hudson Street, New York, New York 10014, USA
Penguin Group (Canada), 90 Eglinton Avenue East, Suite 700, Toronto, Ontario, Canada M4P 2Y3
(a division of Pearson Penguin Canada Inc.)
Penguin Ireland, 25 St Stephen's Green, Dublin 2, Ireland (a division of Penguin Books Ltd)
Penguin Group (Australia), 707 Collins Street, Melbourne, Victoria 3008, Australia
(a division of Pearson Australia Group Pty Ltd)
Penguin Books India Pvt Ltd, 11 Community Centre, Panchsheel Park, New Delhi – 110 017, India
Penguin Group (NZ), 67 Apollo Drive, Rosedale, Auckland 0632, New Zealand
(a division of Pearson New Zealand Ltd)
Penguin Books (South Africa) (Pty) Ltd, Block D, Rosebank Office Park,
181 Jan Smuts Avenue, Parktown North, Gauteng 2193, South Africa

Penguin Books Ltd, Registered Offices: 80 Strand, London WC2R 0RL, England

www.penguin.com

First published as *Off the Grid* in the United States of America
and Canada by G. P. Putnam's Sons 2012
First published as *Two Evils* in Great Britain by Michael Joseph 2013
Published in Penguin Books 2013

001

Printed in Great Britain by Clays Ltd, St Ives plc

ISBN: 978-1-405-93131-1

www.greenpenguin.co.uk

MIX
Paper from
responsible sources
FSC www.fsc.org
FSC™ C018179

Penguin Books is committed to a sustainable
future for our business, our readers and our planet.
This book is made from Forest Stewardship
Council™ certified paper.

Acknowledgments

Heartfelt thanks to Christine Pepe, our brilliant editor at Putnam; to the president of G. P. Putnam's Sons, Ivan Held; and to our agent, Ellen Geiger. This trio of wonderful, talented people all exercised extraordinary forbearance with us during some very difficult personal times, and their support meant more to us than they will ever know.

1

Sometimes the water was glassy and still, and the boat sat on it like a piece of paper on a flat table. Motionless, utterly silent. Other times, particularly when they were tied up in port, the tide would push in a wave that made the boat hump over the water like a roller coaster topping the big hill. But on the rarest of nights, the ocean off the Keys was like a cradle, and on those nights it was safe to anchor a few miles offshore where the gentlest of swells rocked you to sleep and the water made kissing noises against the hull. Grace MacBride liked listening to that. It reminded her of the sounds Harley's koi had made when they took food from your fingers, before they'd all been butchered by some serial killer raccoon.

There were no human serial killers in the Keys that she knew of, and the proof was evident. She'd been living here for months now, without benefit of riding boots, black jeans, black duster, or a gun on her hip, and here she was, still alive. The heat and the humidity had sent her to a boutique on her second day here, put her in a sundress and sandals for the first time in over a decade, and something about that change of outfit had changed her head, gobbled up the fear she'd lived with forever, as if bare toes and legs were the one antidote to paranoia she'd never thought to try.

Poor Magozzi. The Minneapolis Homicide detective

was the only man she'd ever opened her heart to, if only just a tiny bit – and he'd worked so hard to get her to the point where she could walk outside her house without a gun, and, as it turned out, a sundress accomplished the goal in a single day. You can't wear a shoulder harness with a sundress. It just looks bad.

Grace MacBride hardly knew what to make of this new life, where the elements ruled and people simply went along for the ride. There was no choice but to cede control when a sailboat was running in front of the wind, and at first that had terrified her. For all her life, control had always been the key to her survival; excruciating attention to every detail of her surroundings had been the only security. Sailing had taken all that away. There were no startling noises out here; no muggers, no killers, no sudden movements caught in the corner of your eye that made you want to run for cover. Just the endless expanse of water and sky and the constant smell of salt on the wind.

She wakened every morning without a single thought of the myriad dangers she would face simply by leaving her house, and fell into a dreamless sleep in her tiny berth belowdecks each night, untroubled by nightmares of terror and murder and blood flowing down the bare legs of innocent women. John Smith had given this to her, this exotic experience of living without fear, as if she were a normal person living a normal life.

He was FBI, twenty years her senior, a solitary, humorless agent who lived for the job and little else. Three months ago he'd been assigned to work with Monkeewrench, Grace's computer software company, and the Minneapolis PD on a series of Internet murders.

They hadn't bonded in any serious way; even defining each other as friends would have been a stretch at that point. And yet when John had asked her out of the blue to go sailing with him in the Caribbean, Grace had said yes. To this day, she didn't fully understand why she had done that. The way he'd delivered the invitation hadn't even been particularly persuasive.

I have a boat . . . When I get back to DC, I'm going to get on the boat and just sail away . . . You want to come along?

It had been a ridiculous question. What kind of person would walk away from her life and sail off with someone she barely knows? And yet the moment he asked it, one of the very few happy moments she'd had in an otherwise frightening childhood popped into her mind: the night when a weary, distant foster mother had relented long enough to read a bedtime story to her.

The Owl and the Pussy-cat went to sea in a beautiful pea-green boat . . . They sailed away, for a year and a day, to the land where the Bong-Tree grows . . .

To an unhappy child, the image of sailing away from her life had been magical. Maybe it still was. Maybe that was why she'd said yes to John.

Sometimes when the waters were gentle and the world was quiet, Grace let herself miss what she had left behind. Not Minneapolis in particular, but certainly her partners in Monkeewrench. They'd made a fortune in computers, writing educational software, crime-solving programs, and a game that ended up getting a lot of people killed. But that work was salvation for Grace and the surviving three partners who were her family.

The great thing about computers was that they were

utterly predictable. You entered the correct information and the results were consistent. Two plus two equals four. Always. It never worked that way with people. She missed the certainty of the work, but mostly she missed her partners. Fabulous fashionista Annie Belinsky; Harley Davidson, massive, bearded, tattooed, and lamb-gentle; and rail-thin, tenderhearted Roadrunner, the living embodiment of the scarecrow from *The Wizard of Oz*. Geniuses all. She missed Magozzi, too, but she tried not to think of him too often.

Tonight the boat was a cradle rocking, gently rocking, and the sailcloth overhead made a sound like sun-dried sheets billowing on a midwestern clothesline. Charlie was snuggled up to her leg in the narrow berth, breathing doggy breath against her skin, snuffling a soft snore that was music in itself, and all these sounds and movements started to put Grace to sleep, as they always did.

And then she heard the noise that didn't belong.

Grace bolted up in bed, her ears straining to the point of numbness. She could hear the gentle baffling of the sails and the rattle of fittings in the breeze, but she could also isolate soft, stealthy footsteps. Too many of them for John Smith, unless he'd grown a few extra legs in the hours since they'd parted company and retired to their sleeping quarters.

She and John were no longer the only two occupants on this boat, and Charlie knew it, too, because he rose from his sleep curlicue of canine joy, stuck his nose in the air, and let out a soft growl.

Within an instant, Grace's quiet heart rediscovered the blazing sear of an adrenaline push she'd been so happy living without. Now it was business as usual; no thoughts in her mind, just instinct and the action of her body as she rose to a crouch and peered out the porthole.

It was black out there, as black could only be when you were out at sea, and the scope of her vision was limited by the tiny window. But still, she could see there was something out of place in the shadows she'd come to know so well. Something that looked like a rope, fastened to the railing with a makeshift knot no sailor worth his salt would ever tie. It hadn't ever been there before, and it shouldn't have been there now.

She felt her heart kick in a few extra beats, and the skin on her face start to prickle with heat. Goddamnit, for three months she'd been safe, unafraid, almost feeling like a normal person for the first time in her life, and oh God, she'd licked that up like a child tasting her very first Popsicle. And now, in the space of a blink, it was all gone, taken away by whoever was up there, whether their intent was innocent or evil.

Grace ducked back into her berth. Charlie had gone from vigilant to frozen, and she could see even in the darkness that his black lips were curled back. 'Stay, Charlie,' she whispered in the dog's ear, then grabbed her Sig Sauer off the miniature, boat-scaled nightstand.

As she silently crested the few short steps to the top deck, she briefly wondered what she was up against, or if it really mattered.

Sea legs. It had sounded like a menu item the first time Grace MacBride heard the phrase, but now, months later, she knew what it was, and she knew she had them.

She was standing on the teak deck in almost total

blackness, bare feet spread wide for balance, because even the gentle swells could throw you off a little if you weren't used to them. Lucky her, steady on her practiced sea legs, invisible to them because they weren't used to starlight. The idiots had brought flashlights, which served nicely to illuminate their intentions, but kept Grace hidden in the darkness beyond the circles of artificial light as long as she didn't move.

They hadn't heard her pad up the steps from belowdecks, hadn't even searched the boat for another passenger, so they didn't know she was there. That was good; excellent, in fact, since there were two of them, and she'd need the advantage of surprise to handle them both.

Clothes had always been her first line of defense; always black, always covering her from toe to neck, cloaking her body and her fear. And yet here she was in bare feet, bare legs, and a shortie nightgown, still and quiet and utterly unafraid. What an amazing feeling that was.

She watched them for a few seconds to make sure they weren't innocent door-to-door salesmen who just happened to be making a call on a boat ten miles from shore in the dead of night. And then she saw them grab John, saw the flash of a knife blade at his throat, and the time for watching was over.

Charlie the Wonder Dog bounded up the steps at the sound of the first shot, in spite of her earlier command to stay. He breached the deck with his teeth bared around a growl, but by then she'd pulled the trigger on the big Sig Sauer for the second time, and both men were making a mess of the pretty teak deck with their blood.

'It's okay, Charlie.' She laid her hand on the dog's wiry

head and felt the tremors of fear she would have shared not so long ago.

John Smith was using his hands to push himself to his feet, and once he was standing he had to grab the rail to remain upright. Grace had to get close to see the spot of blood on his neck where the knife had started to go in. She touched it with her finger. It looked black in the starlight. 'Just a prick. Sorry about that.'

He was breathing through his mouth, too fast and shallow, and his neck was clammy and cold under her finger. 'Jesus Christ, Grace.'

She slid her hand down to his chest and felt the pounding there. 'Deep breaths. Slow it down. You're going to have a heart attack.'

'Yeah, well excuse me. No one's ever tried to slash my throat before. Jesus Christ.'

'Sit down.'

'No.'

'Sit down before your legs give way. What were you doing up here anyway?'

'Meteor shower.'

'Oh brother.'

She picked up one of the flashlights rolling on the deck and shone it down at the faces of the two men. 'You know them?'

John looked at the two men, both dark-skinned, black-haired, and absolutely unfamiliar. 'No.'

'What do you think? Pirates?'

John dropped his head, fighting back nausea, still breathing hard. 'Sometimes . . . sometimes the Mexican drug cartels highjack boats for drug running, kill the occupants.'

Grace dropped to her haunches, looked at the two dead men carefully, then started going through their pockets. She pulled out their wallets, checked the IDs and a few scraps of paper she found inside, then tossed the wallets over to a place on the deck that wasn't bloody. 'These aren't Mexicans. They're Saudi nationals here on student visas.'

John shrugged. 'The cartels and the terror groups are working the drug trade together now. Hezbollah's turning into a big player in Mexico. So is al-Shabaab out of Somalia.'

Grace shook her head at a world gone mad, then continued searching the men's pockets. The only other thing she found was a folded sheet of paper. She opened it and put the flashlight to it. 'Oh my God.' She rocked back on her heels and looked over at John.

'What is it?'

'It's a photograph of you.'

'What?' His hands trembled as he took the picture and stared at it. Gradually, the paper stopped rattling in his hands and his breathing slowed while thoughts raced through his head like rats in a maze. 'Good Lord. I'm a target.'

Grace looked down at the two men she'd just killed. 'They're assassins?'

'Looks that way.'

'Who wants you dead, John? What the hell have you been doing?'

'I don't know who wants me dead. It has to be a mistake.'

'Did you have any cases involving the cartels that might be coming back to haunt you?'

'Never.'

'How about organized crime or counterterrorism?'

'No, Grace. I was strictly cyber crimes, a desk jockey, bored out of my mind for most of my career. The first time I ever saw any action in the field was when I came to Minneapolis to work with you and MPD on the Internet serial case last summer.' He paused and smiled a little, as if at a blissful memory. 'Great.'

Grace almost rolled her eyes. John had ended up in a gunfight on a golf course with a psychopath. Only a man would consider that a career high point. 'These men found you in the middle of the ocean, John. The only way they could do that was tracing your computer through the satellite link.'

He shook his head firmly. 'Impossible. The Bureau insists on Federal firewalls, even on our personal computers. No one gets through them.'

Grace snorted softly. 'Except the Chinese, the Russians, and probably a dozen others just getting warmed up. So let's assume that's how they tracked you. There's no other explanation. So now the question is, what have you been doing on your computer that would make you a target?'

He shook his head helplessly. 'Nothing. I've been using the Monkeewrench software you gave me to monitor jihadist websites. Even though the Federal firewalls may be vulnerable, Roadrunner said the ones you put on that software are impenetrable.'

'They are. What do you do with the information?'

'If I find something suspicious, I send it on to law enforcement.'

'Are you still on the job?'

'Definitely not. But counterterrorism is spread paper-thin after all the budget cuts. We don't have enough agents keeping eyes on terrorist communications, so I help out. Anonymously.'

She raised her brows in a question.

'I wasn't certain how the Bureau would react to a retired agent having access to that software, and I didn't want it to come back on Monkeewrench. Anyway, we have thousands of agents monitoring these websites every day, and no one is trying to kill them . . . Jesus, Grace, what are you doing?'

She was using a bare foot to move the body of the one who'd held the knife at John's throat. 'Burial at sea.' One more push and the man rolled under the rail and splashed into the water. The second one was heavier, and she had to use her hands.

Charlie was sitting next to John now, shoving himself under a limp arm, and both of them were looking at her as if she were a stranger. 'You can't do that, Grace.'

She had a bucket over the side now, hauling up seawater, splashing the blood on the deck over the side. 'You want to take these bodies back to report what happened? Then you might as well rent a billboard that says you're still alive.' She untied the dinghy the men had arrived in from the rail and watched it bob away over the swells to become someone else's mystery.

2

The girls huddled together in the back of the van like a litter of frightened kittens. Aimee was in the center, her long arms stretched to pull the others close, partly for warmth, partly for comfort.

They hadn't moved them before, so this rushed, dead-of-night trip in the cold metal box terrified her. Where were they taking them, and what waited there? The others were too drugged to care, and for the first time, she thought maybe that was a good thing.

They'd been locked in a windowless, lightless room for a full week. You got used to the room, to the dark, to feeling your way along the filthy floor to the toilet that sometimes flushed and sometimes didn't. After the first few days, the room started to feel safe for all its putrid smells and blinding darkness, because no man touched them there.

One had tried, stealing in alone and grabbing Little Mouse by the hair, and then there had been a brief light from a cracked door and others dragged him out, doing something to him that made him scream.

It took her a long time to calm down the other four girls that night, hugging them all, whispering meaningless words of comfort she didn't believe, because at fifteen, she was the eldest and the others were her responsibility.

She'd stopped eating on the third day. They were given

a bowl of some kind of gruel twice a day. They'd scrambled for the foul-tasting mush, shoved through a hinged panel in the bottom of the door, partly because they were starving, and perhaps partly because it pushed them into forgetful sleep where terror receded. Only Aimee suspected that it had been drugged to keep them quiet, but she couldn't convince the others not to eat it. They were so young, so frightened. Better to live in the blurry oblivion of artificial sleep than to face their new reality.

Aimee knew why they had been taken. The tribe had warned them time and again about the smiling men who lured at-risk Native girls off the reservation with wonderful promises, only to sell them on the streets of Minneapolis or in the port city of Duluth. But no one had warned them, no one had ever suspected that they would come to the reservation and snatch little girls off the road as they walked home from school under a blue October sky. Elizabeth, twelve years old; Taka and Winnie, both eleven; and sweet Little Mouse, who had just turned ten.

Every moment of that day was burned into her memory. She could still hear the shrill screams of terror, she could still see Taka's skinny legs and arms flailing as the man who held her pressed the cloth over her little nose and mouth, and she could still feel that burst of grim satisfaction when her own fingernails bit deep into the muscular arm of the man holding her, drawing blood. One of the men was Native; the others were something else, but she would remember all their faces for the rest of her life.

Aimee didn't know if they were being taken to a final destination, or simply to another house to confound the police and whoever else was searching for them. The FBI, of course, and certainly all their parents, perhaps the whole tribe.

Oh God. Poor Mama. Poor Daddy. She saw them in her mind all the time, imagining them half crazed with fear, hearts clenched with hurt.

She imagined them talking to the Tribal Police, to the FBI, maybe even on television, choking out tearful pleas that the kidnappers would probably never hear.

Aimee hated these people. She didn't care who they were, what nationality they were, what their motives were – only that they were breaking the hearts of loving parents and terrorizing the tender children whose hands she held on the way to and from school. She hated them with a fire that burned inside her, obliterating the innocence of her fifteen years forever. She wanted to kill them.

It was hard to push that rage down, but she had to; she had to be clearheaded and ready, because this would be the best chance she had. Maybe the only chance. None of them were bound anymore, nor were their mouths duct-taped. The drugs had made that unnecessary. And the men didn't know she had been flushing her gruel for the past four days. The van would stop eventually, and that would be her moment.

It came sooner than she had expected. The van made several sharp, fast turns, then backed up. Within seconds, the double back doors were opened. Two men with large knives dragged the drugged girls from the van, saying nothing but keeping the knives visible. They pushed the girls toward the back of a house and they shuffled in a mindless, obedient line, as compliant as the zombies they had become.

Aimee got out last, eyelids drooping, shuffling like the other girls. One of the men opened a gate in a chain-link fence, and Aimee knew if she passed through that gate, there was no hope for any of them.

Why couldn't they hear her heart pounding? How could they not notice that every muscle in her body was tensed and ready? Two steps away from the gate, she spun and bolted out to the street.

Her legs were weak from inactivity and hunger, but she ran for an entire block before she heard the footsteps of the man chasing after her. She told herself she was younger, faster, and that sanctuary was surely just ahead. But the streets were empty and dark in an unfamiliar place where half the streetlights were out and there were no lights in the windows of the shadowed buildings around her.

She closed off the sound of the heavy footsteps pounding behind her because they were so terrifying. Instead, she concentrated on the strong slapping of her tennis shoes against the asphalt as she pumped her legs harder and harder.

Why is this happening to me? Is he still back there? Is he getting closer, and why isn't he yelling at me?

And then she understood that he was silent because he didn't want to call attention to the life-and-death race on the streets beneath the darkened windows. Maybe there were people up there. Maybe they were asleep.

And so she started screaming, running down the middle of the street, her arms held high as if she could take flight, her voice echoing against the mute brick walls of the buildings around her.

Aimee's chest hurt. Every pull of good, clean air felt

like fire in her lungs, as if she were being burned to death from the inside out. But then she saw her own shadow on the street ahead of her and knew it meant a car was behind her.

It's the van, she thought, actually feeling the headlights on her back. She risked one look over her shoulder just for a second and saw a yellow cab. And then, because she was finally saved, she started to sob, the tears streaming from her eyes and blurring her vision.

She couldn't remember getting into the backseat of the cab, but she felt the forward thrust as the driver stepped on the accelerator. She didn't have to say anything, which was a good thing, since her throat was sore from screaming and there was no air left in her lungs. But the driver knew she was in trouble, and he was taking her farther and farther away from the man who had been chasing her. She felt the soft cushion of vinyl seats and leaned her head back, eyes closed, smelling cigarette smoke and spicy sausage.

I did it, Mama. I did it, Daddy. I'm coming home.

Finally her heart and breathing slowed, and she found enough air to whisper desperately, 'Police.'

'Yes,' the driver said, and her brown eyes opened. She looked forward into the rearview mirror and caught her breath as she saw the face of the man who had grabbed her on the reservation, who had pressed the acrid-smelling cloth over her face as she'd walked home from school under a blue October sky.

3

Leo Magozzi stared out his living room window at the deep carpet of dried autumn leaves in his yard. They were pretty, he had to admit, all mixed together like a good fall stew – the deep reds and russets of oak, the pumpkin-orange sugar maple leaves, and a smattering of chromium yellow courtesy of a couple birches in his neighbor's yard.

And that was the problem. None of these leaves were his, because he had no trees in his yard. They'd blown in on the winds of last night's storm from the adjacent neighbors' comparative urban forests. And he was bitter and angry about it, as a man who'd consciously chosen to live a life of tree celibacy, looking now at cleaning up other people's messes. He did enough of that during his day job.

He had options, of course. The first was to pull his trump card and threaten all his neighbors with a leaf rake, his sidearm, and possibly their lives. *Minneapolis Homicide. Clean up my yard now or suffer horrible consequences.* But that probably wouldn't look good in the psych evaluation that would quickly ensue.

The second option was to suck it up and waste a perfectly good day off raking, then spend the next five days with ice packs on his shoulders.

The third, and most rational, option was to ignore the

leaves. The only problem was, he'd been watching too much cable TV lately; had been lulled to sleep by too many quiet, mindless home-and-garden shows. Shows that apparently all had the same insidious and evil agenda: be a good grass steward, rake your lawn in the fall, or else you will have absolutely no value as a human being and others will shun and despise you without relent.

Magozzi hated cable TV, mostly because it was something he'd never relied on, but couldn't live without anymore, thanks to his not-girlfriend Grace MacBride. If she hadn't been flitting around these past few months, tanning her toes somewhere in the Bahamas with a geriatric Fed-cum-sailor, he wouldn't have had all this free time to melt his brain in front of the idiot box, developing completely irrelevant complexes.

Yes, his leaf anxiety and cable dependency were all Grace's fault, he firmly decided, cleverly exonerating himself from all personal responsibility for his actions and well-being. Psychological contortion didn't get much more brilliant and useful than that.

He turned away from the window and grabbed the nearest phone. Important decisions required sage counsel. 'Gino.'

'Hey, buddy, happy Sunday! Man, am I glad to hear from you.'

Magozzi could tell by the tone of his partner's voice that he was, in fact, very happy to hear from him. And then he registered a lot of female voices and the drone of general melee in the background. 'Did I catch you at a bad time?'

'Not on your life. I hope you're calling with a homicide, because we're on Annual Garage Sale, Day Number Two. And let me tell you that garage sales aren't about clearing out junk you don't need, it's about a bunch of neighborhood women getting together and giggling for eight hours straight. Plus, Angela sold my Wheaties box with the Twins on it from the '87 World Series. I'm so distraught I could spit. So, you got a body for me?'

'No, but I have leaves. And questions about leaves.'

'Good enough for me. I'll be right over.'

Magozzi was waiting on the porch when Gino pulled up a half hour later, styling in their MPD loaner Cadillac – a seriously fast, supercharged, bells-and-whistles piece of automotive glory that they'd had the great pleasure of driving on the job ever since Narcotics had confiscated it in a drug bust earlier in the year. Gino had secured the somewhat unconventional loan of those sweet wheels for their use while they waited for their new, standard, unmarked piece of junk to be delivered to the car pool. And yet, for some reason, the standard unmarked was taking its sweet time in arriving. Magozzi suspected it had something to do with more behind-the-scenes negotiating on his partner's part, because Gino loved that Caddie like it was his own flesh and blood. But who was he to question? He loved the car, too.

Gino hopped out, opened the trunk with the key fob, and pulled out a couple of rakes, a handful of black lawn bags, and a six-pack of beer, which he brandished with purpose. 'The ladies have been sucking down mimosas since noon, so I figured we boys deserved some adult beverages to sustain us while we're doing our manly raking chores.'

'You serve booze at your garage sales?'

'It's a critical element. Sober people don't buy your old, worthless crap. Buzzed people, on the other hand, will pick up that holey, sweat-stained GETTING LUCKY IN KENTUCKY T-shirt, think it's kitschy and charming, and pay five bucks for it.'

'Wow.'

'Yeah. Angela's a marketing genius.' Gino held out a rake. 'Come on. Let's get this over with.'

Magozzi ignored the rake, popped the caps off a couple beers, and regarded his yard with ambivalence. 'Here's the thing – why should I rake the leaves? I mean, Mother Nature's been dropping leaves for a million years, and what's wrong with that? Neanderthal Man did not rake his yard and the world did not end.'

Gino took a pull on his beer and settled into the creaky old glider opposite his partner. 'No, but Neanderthal Man didn't have a yard, either.'

'Neither do I. My yard is shit. My grass is shit. What do I care if it molds over the winter?'

'Obviously you don't. So don't rake. I'm totally okay with that. I came here ready to help you out, but I'm just as content to keep this pathetic excuse for outdoor seating warm while I nurse some of Milwaukee's finest.'

'That's exactly what I needed to hear. Screw raking.'

Gino made a sweeping gesture with his beer bottle. 'Yeah. Screw raking. And I'll tell you exactly what I told Angela last weekend – some dead leaves on the lawn over the winter might actually be good compost.'

Magozzi considered for a moment. 'Did she buy it?'

'Hell, no. But it was worth a try.'

After a comfortable silence spent sipping beer and gazing victoriously at a yard full of defiantly unraked leaves, Gino took a deep, audible breath – the precursor for an awkward, compulsory inquiry about Grace, Magozzi was certain. Not that Gino ever pursued any deep conversation about it, he just didn't avoid the subject. In his mind, as much as he'd grown to like Grace personally, he'd never considered her a viable pairing for his best friend and partner. He'd actually been relieved when he'd gotten the news of her sudden, unexpected flight. *'I'm here for you, buddy, but let me tell you something – this is a best-case scenario for the both of you. I don't care how big your sword is, you ain't never gonna be able to slay her dragons. Nobody can. That's something she's gotta figure out for herself.'*

And as often as Gino was wrong about lots of things, he had a decent track record of being right, too, especially when it came to the fairer sex. He'd managed to stay happily married to one of the greatest women on the planet for almost two decades, so he obviously had some insight.

But Gino surprised him, never mentioning Grace.

'I've got some really bad news, Leo.'

Magozzi's heart stuttered a little. No, it stuttered a lot. That was a really ominous preface to any conversation that instantly launched an inner litany of dreaded words like cancer, divorce, death, and teenage pregnancy.

Gino let out an anxiety-ridden sigh before delivering the ending. 'The Caddie's going up on the block at the MPD confiscated property auction next week.'

Magozzi was so relieved, he actually started laughing. 'Buy it, Gino!'

'Are you kidding? Two more years, I'm looking at college tuition . . .'

'Shut up and buy it. Life is short. And in our business, life can be shorter. You work hard, you saved your money, you have a great pension, what's to worry about?'

'Are you kidding me? I'm worried about my anatomy. If I bought that thing, Angela would be serving a whole different kind of meatballs for dinner.'

'Not necessarily. You've been driving the same crippled Volvo now for, what, ten years?'

'Longer.'

'So you need a new car. What if the Caddie ends up going for two grand on the block and you miss out?'

'I'd probably kill myself.' Gino's gaze gave the Caddie a wistful, loving caress. 'You *can* get deals at those auctions sometimes.'

'Yes you can. So get yourself an auction paddle. That's free.'

As Gino considered a bright, new vehicular future sans a broken-down Volvo station wagon, Magozzi's cell phone suddenly burped out a very specific call tone, completely ruining the magic moment.

'Oh, hell,' Gino groaned. 'That's your Dispatch ring, isn't it?'

Magozzi nodded and flipped open his cell. 'Magozzi here. Hang on, I have to get a pen.' He went to the kitchen and scrambled for a pen and paper. The best he could do was a nearly dry Sharpie and a supermarket sale flyer advertising two pints of raspberries for the price of one.

Gino followed him inside, then watched as he scribbled down an address and a few other things in hieroglyphics before clicking off with Dispatch. 'So where are we going?'

'Barrington Industrial Park on the edge of Little Mogadishu. Female vic, found in the vacant lot in front of that deserted warehouse.'

'Needle city.' Gino sighed. 'Another dead junkie.'

'Probably.'

4

Gino looked out the passenger window as they headed toward Barrington Industrial Park, passing through the neighborhood known as Little Mogadishu. It had gotten the moniker in the early nineties when the Lutheran Brotherhood and Catholic Charities brought in thousands of Somali refugees fleeing the famine in their own country. Minnesota still had the largest concentration of Somalis in the country, and, like any other immigrant culture, the first few generations tended to settle close together and keep to themselves.

Crime Scene was already crawling all over Barrington by the time Magozzi pulled up to the curb. Jimmy Grimm was about thirty yards into the weed-choked lot, decked out in his disposable whites and booties. He held up a hand when he spotted the Caddie, holding them back. Apparently Crime Scene hadn't yet cleared a path to the body.

Gino and Magozzi got out of the car and started pacing the street just outside the yellow tape tracing the curb, enjoying the terrific view of spent needles, syringes, and liquor bottles strewn across the broken concrete slab that had once been parking for a bustling manufacturing district. Twisted metal and chunks of cement added to the depressing tableau, probably harvested from the vacant, graffiti-covered warehouse just a few yards in the foreground – remnants of a time when this part of the city had been vibrant. Now it was a magnet for crime and a derelict civic sore that should have been razed long ago. Magozzi would never understand the logic of city planners who worked so hard to maintain Minneapolis's pristine image of health and butter golden goodness, while letting wounds like this fester.

In the near distance, a car-sprinkled freeway overpass lifted into the blue sky, the occupants oblivious to what lay below as they passed. Lucky them, Magozzi thought, feeling the ground beneath his feet buzz from the faint aftershocks of the traffic, listening to the ambient murmurs of a city full of life while he and Gino dwelled in death.

'God, this place is a dump.' Gino summed it up tidily. 'It's going to take Jimmy's team about a thousand years to sift through all this trace.'

Magozzi nodded, watching as Jimmy finally approached. He was the king of the BCA's Crime Scene Unit, and every detective on the force was always happy to see him on a site.

'You guys are late,' Jimmy greeted them.

'And you look like the Pillsbury Doughboy,' Gino shot back.

'You always say that.'

'You look good to me, buddy,' Magozzi said. 'What did we do to deserve the big gun today?'

'You may have the big gun, but I'm working with the B team here. Most of these kids are interns or fresh grads who haven't seen a body since *Nightmare on Elm Street.*'

'Where's the A team?'

'Over on Dupont at a domestic with five dead. That's

where I was, too, until I got the ID on this vic, and I came running.'

Gino raised a brow. 'You already ID'd her?'

'I didn't.' He jabbed his thumb over his shoulder at a big Native American man in blues who looked like he was carrying all of Magozzi's childhood cannoli in his gut. 'That's Officer Bad Heart Bull, first responder. He and I go way back, and the minute he recognized her, he called me on my cell.'

'Who's the victim?' Gino asked.

Jimmy looked down, then pulled a sheet of paper off the clipboard hooked to his belt. 'Sorry. I guess you didn't get the word yet. Chief Malcherson put a serious squelch on this when he heard the first call-in, which explains why the media isn't crawling up your shorts right now. Sure, a five-kill domestic is big, juicy news – lots of body bags, lots of crying people – but this is bigger.' He drew a circle on the paper and passed it to Gino. 'That's her. Aimee Sergeant. Somebody slit her throat, at least that's what I got from a quick first look. Choked on her own blood, probably.'

Gino looked down at the same Amber Alert flyer every cop in the state had been carrying around all week. The photos of five missing Native American girls, kidnapped from Sand Lake Reservation in northern Minnesota, stared up at him with smiling, innocent eyes. The youngest was ten; the oldest, fifteen. 'Goddamnit,' he muttered, handing the paper to Magozzi. 'Any sign of the other four, Jimmy?'

Jimmy shook his head. 'Not so far, and thank God, because that means they might still be alive, maybe even still in the area. Aimee was the oldest one at fifteen, so I was thinking that when she finally got a chance to run, she risked it.'

Which hadn't paid off, Magozzi thought, feeling his stomach take a nasty acid bath. Suddenly, there didn't seem to be enough air in the world, and Magozzi and Gino both sucked in a few deep breaths of unusually warm October air. It was like inhaling July in a concrete graveyard. 'We have to tear this place and this city upside down fast.' Magozzi stated the obvious. 'We lost one, but what the other four might have in store for them is just as bad. Young girls get kidnapped without ransom demands for one reason, and one reason only, and that's to turn them out in the sex trade, either on the streets or on the Internet for cash money.'

Jimmy looked down and angrily kicked at a tiny shard of glass that shimmered in the October sun beside his right foot. Magozzi figured he was probably thinking about his own sweet kids, who loved to ski and skate and play soccer – things Aimee Sergeant would never be able to do again.

'It's the goddamned gangs,' Jimmy finally muttered. 'They're the ones running girls.'

Gino looked up at the freeway overpass and shot out a quick breath, trying not to think of all the horror stories he'd heard from the Vice guys about human trafficking.

By now, Officer Bad Heart Bull was approaching, looking like a carved piece of oak on the move. Jimmy looked over his shoulder at him and another man in a white jumpsuit who was hanging back a little. 'I'll get back to it while you talk to Bully and get his take. You know him?'

Magozzi shook his head. 'I don't think I'd forget him.'

'Yeah. He's a big one.'

Gino looked the man up and down. 'Big? He's a building on legs.'

'Well, cut him some slack today, will you? You know how it is. You can't get mushy at a scene, so you just get mad, and let me tell you, that is one seriously pissed-off Indian.' Gino watched Bad Heart Bull drawing closer and heard all the sound effects of Godzilla literally making the earth move under his feet. 'Are we allowed to call them Indians?'

Jimmy shrugged. 'Bully doesn't much care what you call him. If he doesn't like it, he'll just fist your head into the ground and walk away. But he's Ojibwe, just like the girls, and I think he knows some of the families. He's just this side of losing it.'

Magozzi squatted and pulled a piece of dead, brown grass out of the parched soil. 'We'll take it easy on him.'

'He's a good cop.'

'I'm sure he is.'

'And after you get his take on it, talk to that squirrelly-looking kid in whites, name's Donnie Marek. He's pretty shook up, barely out of the womb, but he's got promise. He'll take you to the body on the path we cleared.'

'Thanks, Jimmy.'

Bad Heart Bull had his notebook out and his mad face on. 'Afternoon, Detectives.'

'What do you have for us, Officer?'

'Nothing but bad news. I've been walking this beat for fifteen years, but today tops anything I've seen on these streets. Normally, this place is hopping with all the scumbag dirtballs who hang in that warehouse, shooting up. I clean up a couple dozen losers off this lot every morning, but today it was deserted, which was weird, so I took a closer look. That's when I found the little girl.' He took off his cap and rubbed at a blue-black brush cut, a gesture that took Gino back to his own days on the pavement. Man, he'd hated those caps, especially on hot days like this one. They made your head sweat, then itch, and by the time you finished a patrol, you were scratching like a dog with fleas.

'So no witnesses,' Gino said.

'Hell, no. Those head cases either saw the murder, or found the body and split, which means they'll be back. I know these people, and some of them took off without their kits. So what I was thinking was that I'd get some backup and just park our butts down here until they show up again, and haul them all in so you guys can beat them with a rubber hose until they talk. Think you can get the okay for something like that?'

Magozzi nodded. 'Absolutely. So these are your streets. Any thoughts on what particular brand of dirtball we should be looking for?'

Bully nodded solemnly as he looked over at the tight rectangle of double-strung tape surrounding the body. She was in a scrappy nest of weeds that screened her from view at this distance, and he was grateful for that. One look had been enough. 'Yeah, I got some ideas, but you're not going to like them. This is a big problem in the Native community lately, our girls getting lured down to the cities and then into prostitution. Usually, it's the homeless and at risk who get preyed on. But this is the first time we've had them kidnapped from their own reservation. And we've never lost any as young as these five girls. Christ, this is bad.' He'd been talking fast, like he could hardly wait for the words to get out of his own head and into someone else's, and now he had to stop for a couple deep breaths before continuing.

Magozzi gave him a minute, then asked, 'Who's doing it?'

'Native mob, for one. They take the girls, pump them up with drugs, then turn them out to work the docks up in Duluth or on the streets down here. The whole setup got a lot worse when the Native mob hooked up with the Somali gangs down here. There's big money for virgins in the Middle East, the younger the better, and the Somalis have the connections. The Feds are seeing this kind of thing more and more. Apparently, it's one way the radicals are financing their terrorist agenda these days. Buy the girls on the cheap, sell them at a big profit.' He slapped his cap against his pants, leaving a circle of dust. 'Goddamned media puts out an hour special on making kids wear helmets on the playground when a white kid gets a bloody nose falling off a jungle gym, but never cover Native girls getting pumped into the sex trade slime bucket. The white kid with the bloody nose is a victim. The little Indian girl teetering on five-inch heels is just another drunk Indian hooker. Why do you think the Somalis are targeting us? We're not just marginalized; we're invisible, goddamnit . . . oh, shit, did I really just say that to a couple of white detectives?'

Gino found a little smile. 'I didn't hear anything. But I gotta say, the media's been all over this kidnapping.'

Bully snorted. 'Yeah, for now, but just wait. If Lindsay

Lohan gets another DWI, those little girls are going to disappear from the screen in a heartbeat.' He stopped abruptly, wiped at his head again, and slapped his cap back on. 'Sorry. I'm way out of line. I'm just scared to death whoever's got the other four girls will get them the hell out of here before we get a chance to put the heat on, especially after what happened here. This was a mistake. She got away somehow. For a while, at least.'

Magozzi nodded. 'We won't be sitting down on this one. We'll tap into Gang Task Force and Vice and have them pull in the likelies from the Native mob and Somali lists before noon.'

Distant sirens pierced the air and they were getting closer fast. 'That's my canvass crew,' Bully said. 'I'll get it started.'

'Spread it wide,' Magozzi said. 'I want those Amber Alert flyers wallpapering Little Mogadishu. Door-to-door the whole neighborhood.'

There were a lot of flies. And a lot of blood. It was matted in Aimee Sergeant's hair, streaked on her gray flesh and torn clothing, and sprayed on the tall scrub grass that surrounded her. But even in the very worst ugliness of death gone cold, you could still see that she'd once been a very pretty young girl – at least before some sociopath asshole had butchered her in a shit hole vacant lot before she'd even had the opportunity to legally drive.

Magozzi took a shallow breath against his gloved hand and tried to calm his blood pressure, which was mounting exponentially along with his fury. There was no worse crime scene than one where the victim was a child, except for one like this, when the child had been discarded like trash in a place already littered with it. 'Not a body dump,' he finally mumbled, his tongue feeling like a thick, woolen sock in his mouth. 'Too much blood, and the spray on the grass screams arterial. She was killed here.'

Gino nodded woodenly and knelt down to prod her gently. 'A while ago. Blood is way dry and rigor came and went already.'

Donnie Marek, their mostly mute and nervous cub CSI escort, stepped in a little closer, his eyes blinking as fast as a frog's in a hailstorm. 'That's what I thought,' he offered timidly. 'Decomposition is in the early stage, even with this heat. I calculated time of death between four and five o'clock this morning. But we don't have a body temperature yet . . .' His voice trailed away as he looked down at the ground. 'The ME should be here soon,' he finished weakly.

Magozzi raised a brow at him. 'You don't need the ME to tell you what you're seeing. What do you think about her missing shoe?'

Donnie Marek looked up tentatively, almost hopefully. 'I saw a bloody blister on that bare heel. I think she got away and was running from her captor or captors, just like Jimmy figured. Lost a shoe along the way, and she finally got brought down here.'

'Good thinking so far, so think about this – every time Aimee's foot slammed down, the impact sent some blood splatters flying. Not a lot – it's just a blister – but maybe enough to track. There's a blood trail out there somewhere, so get out the blue lights and trace it to its terminus, and close down the streets all the way to Iowa if you have to. And get us that missing shoe. It's out there, and maybe it won't bring us to the source, but it'll get us closer.'

Marek nodded exuberantly and made tracks toward his supervisor, who was in a huddle with a few other techs.

Gino stood slowly, puffed out a breath, and looked around, wondering how far she'd run, and how you got that brave at the age of fifteen. 'Damnit, Leo. This makes me want to go home and microchip my kids.'

'If I had kids, I'd feel the same way.' Magozzi pulled out his phone. 'I'll call the Canine Unit and get some dogs down here. That's our best chance to track any further than her shoe, if the kid finds it.'

'I'll check in with the FBI up in Duluth, since they've been handling the kidnapping angle from the beginning. Maybe they have some info or persons of interest that can put us on a track down here.'

Half an hour later, Donnie Marek found the shoe four blocks away. They had three scent dogs coursing the street, but every one of them returned to the shoe and sat down next to it. The trail died there.

5

Joe Hardy sat in the single chair with an innocuous blanket wrapped around his bare legs as if he were a passenger on the deck of an early-twentieth-century steamer crossing the cold Atlantic sea. This was how he'd spent every single morning of the past twenty days, and he wasn't happy about it. Hospitals should close down on Sundays so people could watch the Minnesota Vikings lose another football game, or stay home and celebrate their birthday. Thirty-two years old today, Joe Hardy, and for your very special gift, we have another round of chemo.

They'd put him in the same room they always put him in. A slot, really, only as wide and long as an average man was tall, with no door – just an opening that looked out on a broad hallway, where healthy people passed on their way to the coffee station or the exit doors, pointedly looking straight ahead, so as not to see the doorless room or its current occupant. Maybe they slapped a sign on the wall outside after they dumped him. NO CONTACT. NO NOTICE. IGNORE THE MAN IN THIS ROOM IN CASE WHATEVER HE HAS CAN BE SPREAD WITH A GLANCE.

'Now you just make yourself comfy for a few minutes until someone comes to collect you,' the nurse always told him, making him feel like a can on the curb on garbage day. His isolation was only broken when the next nurse would inevitably come in with a big smile and a pink plastic upchuck container. 'Shall we go?' she would always say brightly.

But they'd left him alone in the small room too long today, because now he was beginning to think bad, rebellious thoughts, thoughts like anyone who would willingly go anywhere that involved an upchuck container was flat out of his mind. What had he been thinking? Letting them wheel him away all these months to a place where they shot poison in his veins and then let him throw up? Maybe he'd had enough. Maybe, by God, today he'd finally take his life back. He'd smile brightly right back at the nurse and say, 'Gee, thanks for the invitation, but you know what? I've decided to skip chemo today. Just don't feel like it.'

Yeah. That's what he was going to do, because big bad Joe was finally, finally tired of fighting this particular fight.

When the next nurse came in she was wearing a little frown, as if she'd heard his naughty thoughts. She surprised him by saying, 'There's been a change of plans, Mr Hardy. Dr Pierce would like to see you first. Would that be all right with you?'

The great thing about Tom Pierce's office was that it didn't look like it belonged in this building. Come to think of it, that was the great thing about Tom, too.

'Who decorated this place?' Joe asked him. He was sitting in the leather chair across from the desk, feet propped on a matching ottoman and his hands laced together behind his head, elbows akimbo.

Tom leaned back in his chair and pumped it around in a circle, gazing at the walls. Paneling everywhere, a life-sized skeleton on a pole in the corner that looked like it was smiling, and a twelve-pound walleye mounted on the back wall. 'You don't like it?'

'I like it fine. I just can't believe they let you get away with it. The paneling's all wrong. So's the dead fish on the wall and the rug under my chair. Very unsanitary.'

Tom shrugged. 'They cut us some slack in this wing. All of us are kind of cutting-edge brilliant.'

'Really. If you were so cutting-edge brilliant you'd design better gowns. You remember that old board game, Operation? The cartoon guy with the red lightbulb on his nose that lit up when you killed him had a better-looking gown than this.'

Tom was close to the ugliest man Joe had ever known. He had a wandering eye, a nose he had broken repeatedly in high school hockey, and a nowhere chin that slid right down into his neck. But when he smiled, he looked like God had just touched him or something. 'Oh, man, I totally forgot that game. Used to love it, even though my little brother always beat my socks off. Don't think I ever won, but I sure loved lighting up that bulb.'

Joe's brow lifted. 'Great. My surgeon never won a game of Operation. You could have told me that before you sliced me open the first time.'

Tom's smile didn't exactly disappear, but it changed. He sighed, pulled a decanter and two glasses from the bottom drawer of his desk, and loaded them up with something that looked expensive.

Joe made a face. 'Oh God. Now I get why you pulled me out of chemo today. You want to cut into me again, don't you?'

'No more surgeries, Joe. And you don't need any more of this particular treatment. It was the last session anyway. I think we can skip it.'

Joe's breath caught in his throat as if a hairball of hope he'd been holding under his tongue for months had finally slipped out. Swallow, or spit? That was the question. 'The tests came back?'

'They did.'

'And they're that good?'

Tom didn't say anything for two seconds that felt like a hundred years to Joe. 'Don't leave me hanging, Tom. Are we celebrating here, or is this the first drink at my own wake?'

Tom took a breath. 'There are a couple of new experimental drugs out there. Houston's starting a blind study next week on something that looks promising . . . it's a chance, Joey.'

Funny. When you finally heard the words you'd been terrified of hearing for so long, they weren't all that terrifying anymore. In a strange way, it was almost a relief.

Joe took a sip from his glass, then gave Tom a little smile, because the man deserved it. They'd been friends for a long time.

He'd parked on the ramp that was a skyway away from Tom's office. Halfway across the glass bridge he had to stop and catch his breath. He stood for a minute, looking out over the heat waves rising from the parking lot below. It was going to be a hot walk.

He stopped at the car and picked up the little cooler to carry along with him. His wife, Beth, always packed bottled water and juice and a few bland snacks for him on chemo days. Today she'd thrown in a celebratory candy bar because it was supposed to have been the last day of this treatment round. He wolfed the candy bar and drained the juice, figuring he'd need the energy, but left the rest of the goodies inside.

He walked out of the hospital complex ramp into the blast furnace of the hottest October day on record. Not that Joe put a lot of stock in that statistic. Pick a day, any day out of the whole damn year, and in this stupid state you were always breaking some record or other. Hottest, coldest, rainiest, whatever.

Riverside Hospital wasn't in the best neighborhood. Maybe he'd get real lucky and someone would shoot him in the head for his wallet so he wouldn't have to think about how to tell Beth.

His dad had brought him down here a lot when he was a kid, mostly because the only decent place to eat happened to be a bar with a kid's menu, which meant you could call it a restaurant. *Took Joey down to Seven Corners today, Marsha. Bought him the cheeseburger plate you and I used to have when we went to the U, remember? Told him what you looked like in those wooden beads and that fringe vest you wore without a blouse.*

His dad had been way past cheeseburgers by then, fulfilling his daily carbohydrate quota with as many frosty beers as he could fit into an hour, excusing his transgression with the cover of old memories. Impromptu street dances without a permit, hamburgers that dripped red juice down your chin, and onion rings fried in pure animal fat. Bell-bottoms and belly buttons and an impossible image of Joe's mother dancing on asphalt, twirling, holding a tambourine in one hand and a joint in the other.

What's a joint, Daddy?

Just a cigarette, son.

Mom smoked?

Only every now and then, and only at Seven Corners.

Wow. I can't believe Mom smoked.

The memories had been sharp and clear to a father who had blanked out the rest of his life, as if Seven Corners had been the last thing he held in his mind, and everything that came after had been erased like a dusty blackboard. His father had died at thirty-five years old, arms slit and bloody from the wrist to the elbow, in the hospital Joe had just left, and today he was feeling the irony.

He walked all the way down Riverside Avenue to Washington Avenue, seeing the pictures his dad had painted instead of what was really there. On the way back, the hippie era faded and all he saw was cramped markets and coffee shops with exotic faces behind yellow, smoke-stained glass. Still pissed him off that the only place you could get away with smoking in this city was in a neighborhood where immigrants never had to consider the law, because the city fathers were constantly tripping over their dicks trying not to offend other cultures.

Still, he liked walking this street, liked the spicy aromas coming from the cafés and the jangle of a dozen different languages. There were some bad types down here – gangbangers of every nationality and some seriously angry people who could hate you with a look. Those were the ones that took him right back to Baghdad in those worst of days, when you kept your eyes out for that look of pure hate, because it usually meant somebody was about to take you down. But there were also shiny-faced university students, giggling kids darting around like energy was air, and tall, amazingly beautiful Ethiopian women in native dress that made everyone else look drab and ordinary. Mostly lambs afoot in a field with a few really bad snakes.

Most people were sheltering inside the air-conditioned shops today, but those few who passed him on the sidewalk looked at him curiously. He was getting used to that by now. The chemo had whittled his six-foot frame down to one hundred and fifty pounds, his head was bald, his skin sagged gray, and by now the sweat was dripping off him. One woman had even stopped to touch his arm. 'Are you all right, sir? Do you need help?'

Joe stopped for a breath and mopped his forehead. The woman was wearing a long, bright red scarf with little beads all over it, and he thought that was terrific. 'I'm fine, thank you, just a little overheated, but it was kind of you to ask.'

You walk out of a hospital where people are afraid to make eye contact and bump into a stranger concerned enough to touch your arm and ask after your welfare. That lifted him up, just a little, and he picked up his pace.

Halfway back to the hospital he came to the side street and took a left. The sweat was running into his eyes now, and his legs felt like overcooked pasta, but he kept going, down two blocks, over one, and there was the house with the unpainted porch, the wheezing, rattling window air conditioner, and the cheap venetian blinds pulled down tight. *Look out,* he said to himself. *Pay attention.*

He walked up onto the porch like he belonged there,

opened the door, went inside, and closed it behind him. Two startled men jumped up from a sagging couch when he walked in, then hesitated, looking at him closely.

'You sick?' one of them asked.

Kindness again? From these two? It almost stopped him. Almost.

Joe gasped and nodded, leaning against the doorframe, then reached into his cooler for the empty water bottle jammed over the barrel of his weapon.

Two quick, accurate shots, one in each forehead, and the men crumpled. The first shot had been barely audible; the second was louder, of course, with the bottle pierced, but the window air conditioner covered the sound nicely.

The walk back to the parking ramp took longer, partly because he was exhausted, partly because he wasn't in any particular hurry to get home and tell Beth what the doctor had said.

6

Detective Magozzi had cleared the door-to-door canvass with Bad Heart Bull's sergeant, a twenty-four-year man who was happy to delegate as much responsibility as possible to his underlings while he coasted the few months to his pension.

Your beat, Bully, your canvass. Carve out the grids and I'll get you the people you need.

Bully had picked a baby cop with less than a year under his belt to partner with on the back streets butting up to Riverside Avenue, mostly because he looked friendly and harmless. Dealing with the bad guys in this neighborhood, you wanted to look mean and dangerous, but when you were trying to get information from frightened Somali women who thought all cops were monsters, friendly and harmless worked better.

Brady Armand was the perfect choice, with his youthful good looks and ready smile, which made the door-to-doors easier than if it had just been him on his own – his dark, pockmarked face and imposing stature scared the hell out of most people when they saw him on their doorstep.

Trouble was, not many in this neighborhood spoke English, and even if they did, they rarely talked to anyone outside their ethnic group. Bully had a double whammy against him because he was a cop and an Ojibwe, and the Somalis trusted Native Americans least of all. The two factions had been competing for housing and resources ever since the North African population had jumped from a sprinkle to the clear majority, and to Bully's way of thinking, his people had gotten the raw end of the deal. The friction was right out there in the open, but of course you never heard about that on the news, either, just like you never heard about the Native mob and the Somali gangs hooking up to share commerce in the sex trade.

And maybe that was a lesson – two warring tribes would never smoke the peace pipe, but they'd tolerate each other if there was money involved.

All the do-gooders kept preaching about how great it was when cultures mingled and interacted. And maybe that kind of thing would happen given enough decades. It was the time in between when they didn't interact that got scary, when they crossed the street to avoid people with a different mind-set. It really hurt here in the heart of the Midwest, where people hugged strangers, smiled, and talked to everyone. You could only hang on to that sense that all people could come together for so long. You could only face so many rebuffs before it wore you down.

Brady stopped under the shade of an old elm tree, consulted his clipboard, and pointed to a ramshackle little box of a house. 'This is our last house on the search grid,' he said despondently.

'Let's do it,' Bully said, taking long strides across the badly cracked walk that was more weed than concrete. But his pace faltered when he saw the front door hanging open. His hesitation wasn't exactly based on sound reasoning, it was more a gut feeling. But if you were a cop and didn't follow your gut, you could end up a dead cop.

He stopped abruptly and put his hand on the butt of his gun, scanning the yard and the front windows, which were all closed tight and covered by dirty venetian blinds. An old air-conditioning unit wheezed in one of the windows.

'What's wrong?' Brady asked, stopping beside him.

'The door's partially open.'

Brady frowned. 'So? It's a nice day.'

'You see an open door at any of the last fifteen houses we visited?'

'Uh . . . no. I guess not.'

'That's because people don't leave their doors open in this neighborhood, especially with the windows closed and the air-conditioning running. I don't like it.'

Brady's demeanor changed fast, and he was doing a poor job of trying to look like he wasn't scared. Funny how a little thing out of place like an open door that should have been closed could make your blood run cold.

'Let's take a look, Brady. Take it slow, keep your eyes sharp.' He glanced over his shoulder at the young officer, who looked like his shoes were glued to the sidewalk. 'Come on, kid. This is what we do.' In the old days, he would have said that and meant it; now it sounded like false bravado, even to him.

Fifteen years ago, Bully had still been bench-pressing his own weight, he'd had abs like stone steps carved into flesh, and he wasn't afraid of anything. But now the stone steps had softened into a wheelchair ramp of fat and inside he was shaking like a girl, although he'd never let Brady see that.

He hesitated at the open door, knocking on the frame, then took a breath, hating his sagging gut and the years of deep-fried onion rings that had probably turned his blood into Crisco, softening him too much for this job. He knocked again.

Silence.

'This feels wrong,' Brady whispered, 'and something smells funny.'

Brady was young yet, fit as a fiddle, and now genuinely terrified that all his hours in the gym might not save him from whatever was on the other side of this open door. Funny how this new generation jogged and ate lettuce and thought this would let them live forever. Maybe in this case, Bully was the lucky one. You got to a certain age, watched your body start to deteriorate, then something inside with those spiny teeth that hung on to life so hard finally, finally let go. You didn't know you'd figured it out until you felt the acceptance seeping into your soul. One day you'd stand in front of an open door like this one, knowing in your gut that something real bad was on the other side, and you took that first step inside anyway.

The interior of the house was dark, but you could still see the lifeless bodies slumped on the floor in front of a debilitated sofa. Bully aimed a flashlight at the human wreckage. Two young Somali men, each with a single bullet hole in the forehead. He squatted down, felt the carotids to make sure they were dead, then pushed himself to his feet. 'Call it in, Brady. Then we've got to clear the house.'

Adrenaline had a way of warping your sense of time and space, and even though the house was little more than a small box, it seemed to Bully that he and Brady had been walking for hours back-to-back, through a never-ending maze of rooms with ominously closed doors that could conceal any number of deadly threats. The one he worried about most was a hidden perp who would have nothing to lose by killing a couple cops in order to flee the scene.

As they methodically cleared each room, Bully felt sweat bursting from every pore in his body, dripping down his torso and soaking his uniform. He didn't know what kind of shape his heart was in, and didn't much care to know, but right now, it felt like a wolverine was trying to claw its way out of his chest.

Don't die of a heart attack now, you fat fuck. One last room, one last closed door. It'll be over soon. And maybe you're not so ready to die after all.

He signaled Brady, and they flanked the door, guns drawn. 'Minneapolis Police!'

They waited, listening for movement, their chests heaving in fearful synchronicity. After a few moments of silence, Bully finally nodded and Brady tried the knob. He shook his head.

Shit. Bully banged his fist on the door, announced himself again, but still no sound. It was time to go in.

In the split second it took for him to take a step back, rotate his shoulder, and shift his weight to turn his body into a battering ram, happy memories from his childhood he hadn't recalled in years suddenly came flooding back: catching his first walleye on Elbow Lake; his first wild rice harvest; the elaborate regalia of the jingle dancers, and the hypnotic rhythm of drums and chants at his first powwow. He had a fleeting thought that this was a premonition of his impending death, the last gift of his own history before he took his final breath, and suddenly his fear left him. He didn't know what was on the other side of that door, but the moment his shoulder hit, he felt the calming sense that he was ready for it.

But he'd been dead wrong about that, because crashing through that door was a stunner, the kind of moment that hammered into your soul and captured your breath; the kind of moment that would eventually coalesce into the most pivotal, important memory you'd ever keep. Life, not death, was on the other side, and it was so unexpected, Bully thought he might pass out.

He moved his flashlight beam across the small, putrid space where four little girls sat clustered together on the floor, barefoot, hands bound, hair matted. Their brown eyes squinted up toward the light, disoriented and terrified.

'We need two buses, Brady. Fast,' he whispered over his shoulder, then walked into the room with the flashlight trained more on his own face than the girls', so they could see he wasn't a faceless monster behind a blinding light – they'd seen enough monsters in this past week.

'Hello. My name is Bully. I'm a police officer and everything's going to be all right.' He crouched down in front of one of the girls, a child, really, and gave her a gentle smile. 'What's your name?'

The girl recoiled a little, but some of the white around her eyes receded.

'Can I take these plastic ties off your wrists?'

She nodded warily, then started to cry. Bully's throat tightened and he swallowed hard as he used his pocket-knife to cut the stiff white bonds that were biting into her wrists, then moved back to give her space.

She rubbed at her eyes and nose and looked up at him. 'I'm Taka,' she finally choked out. 'Are you here to save us?'

He cleared his throat and tried to answer, but all he could do was nod.

7

Elbow Lake was still this mild Sunday morning, its glassy surface scattered with pink diamonds from the rising sun. This was the quiet time, when only the water spoke, in hushed burbles that gently woke the world around it.

A V-shaped flock of migrating geese was the first to break the early-morning silence, honking overhead, looking for a place to rest their wings after flying the red-eye on their way south for the winter. A loon uttered a haunting cry from Spider Bay, calling its brethren to do the same before the weather turned.

This was the one place on the reservation Chief Bellanger always came to when the world threatened to suck all the peace right out of him.

It was maybe the worst thing about being Chief of Tribal Police. He got all the bad news long before anyone else, and there was a large loneliness in that. The first call this morning had come from Bully Bad Heart Bull. They weren't close, exactly, but the Chief had given him a training slot on the Tribal Police Force back when he'd been rejected by every branch of the service because of a skin condition. Bully had been a gawky, tall kid then, subject to boils, and damn near suicidal because he couldn't enlist with the rest of his friends to become a modern warrior for his tribe and his country.

Within a year, the boils were gone, he'd filled out some,

got some policing experience under his belt, and the Minneapolis PD was willing to look at him. As a Native American, he was an ideal liaison for the tribal community clustered in the city, and he was there still. He'd never forgotten the boost up the ladder Chief had given him; thus, the call. But it wasn't a good one.

I found one of the kidnapped Sand Lake girls this morning, Chief. Aimee Sergeant. She was murdered.

Chief had just closed his eyes and tightened his grip on the phone while he listened to the gruesome details. *Did you call Sand Lake?*

The Feds took care of that, and MPD. They don't like beat cops spreading that kind of word. But I remembered you were tight with the Sand Lake Chief. Thought you might want to give him a call.

Thanks, Bully.

There's another thing. The BCA lead thinks Aimee ran to save the others.

A little warrior.

Yeah. Something Sand Lake can hang on to.

And so, Chief had made his condolence call and then gone to the lake, where things made a lot more sense than a little girl ending up dead in a vacant lot.

His canoe cut soundlessly through the water, along the margins of tall grass near the shore. He was pleased to see some of the seed heads swelling with wild rice. It would be prime for harvest in another week, when he would enlist his cousin Moose to paddle while he knocked the ripe grain into the bottom of the canoe.

His 'Old Woman,' as he affectionately called his wife of thirty-two years, would then weigh and bag the rice to sell to the two local gas stations, the scant tourist roadside stands, and the casino on the northern border of Elbow Lake Reservation. Their share of the proceeds would be their mad money for the year, never much, but enough to blow without guilt on a nice dinner and a few games at the Golden Eagle Bingo Hall.

Not that they hurt financially. But if you were an Indian who'd grown up on the rez fifty-some years ago – and both of them were – you learned the prudence of frugality pretty much from weaning. You also learned the importance of continuing tradition, whether the motivation was sheer practicality or cultural pride and preservation.

Chief dipped his paddle and created a whirlpool of resistance in the water that slowed and finally stopped the canoe; better to see the pink diamonds of sunrise transform to a flawless chromium white as the sky lightened. He absently reached into the thicket of rice to pull the seeds for closer examination, and smiled when a few long, pale gray *mahnomen* sifted into his open palm. It was going to be a good ricing year.

Rice had always been such a prominent part of his life – the best and the worst – a source of joy for him, from boyhood on, the worst part coming a little later. Those bad memories didn't ever taint the happiness he felt with the coming of each season, but ricing time was also the one and only time of the year he ever thought about the war, so many decades in his past now. He'd tried to separate his experiences, but had finally given in to the fact that they were inextricably linked. Good always came with bad, and as the sun lifted high enough to warm his shoulders, he was transported back in time and place.

His spirit guide was a bear – Mukwa in his native language –

and Mukwa suddenly visited him in a dream on a September night under a full moon – a Wild Rice Moon, his people called it – in the middle of a rice paddy on the way to Khe Sahn. It seemed meaningful, appropriate, even though the rice in Vietnam wasn't even remotely related to his native grass.

Mukwa didn't stay long before he disappeared back into his dream, just long enough to tell him that there were many roads to the High Place. Upon waking, he made the decision that he didn't want to go to the High Place. Not yet. And he didn't want his friend to go there, either. It wasn't their time, and this wasn't their road.

He poked the man dozing at his side. 'Claude.'

But Claude didn't wake up; he just grunted and rolled over in the wet, composted mash of their foxhole.

'Hey. Chimookman. White man. Wake up.'

Claude still wouldn't rouse. No surprise – when he slept, you could bash him over the head with an oil barrel and you'd be lucky to see his eyes flutter.

So he grabbed his weapon and furtively made his way up to the berm and out into the jungle, because the way he had been taught, your spirit guide didn't talk to you unless you had a job to do . . .

Chief was startled back to the present when a tasty-looking cluster of fat mallards flushed skyward from the reeds, damn near next to him. He should have thought to bring his bird gun.

When he pulled into his driveway shortly after noon, Old Woman, whose given name was actually Noya – a nod to the distant Inuit Eskimo roots on her mother's side that had probably sprouted during the Alaska Gold Rush – was already up and busy in the garden, harvesting the last of the fall crops. She was hacking down tall stalks of Brussels sprouts, tossing them next to a pile of winter squash she'd already picked. The woman loved to garden, and she was good at it. Unfortunately, that meant another healthy meal on the lunch table today.

When she heard the truck, she straightened and waited for him to come to her. If you wanted to talk to Noya, you went right up to her and did it face-to-face. There was no hollering from room to room because you were too lazy to get up and walk the distance, and certainly no raised voices out in the yard where others might overhear and mistake it for anger.

Chief hadn't understood that in the early days of their marriage – why walk ten yards when you could just call over the noise of the TV to ask when dinner was ready? It had taken her less than a week to train him, simply by refusing to reply until he was standing right in front of her, and then, she rewarded him with her magical smile that instantly righted all things wrong in the world. It was a smile worth much more than ten yards – it was a smile worth a walk to the moon and back.

And she was smiling at him now, which seemed a little strange considering the bad news they'd received about Aimee. 'Bully called again. He found the other four girls alive.'

Chief shoved his hands in his pockets and looked down at the frost-nipped plants in the garden. It was hard to find happiness in your heart when a little girl was dead; and hard not to when four others had been saved. Good and bad, he reminded himself, feeling Noya's firm hand on his arm.

'Come in the house,' she said gently. 'I'll make you Brussels sprout soup to make you feel better.'

Now he could smile, just a little. He hated Brussels sprouts, and she knew it.

As they walked arm in arm toward the house, Noya asked, 'What time are Joe and Claude coming?'

'Later this afternoon. I'll head to the cabin after lunch and get things set up, but you know they won't give me the time of day until they see you first, so expect some visitors.'

'I'd be furious if they didn't stop to see me first.'

Chief looked over at his wife. Her long braid danced across her back in time with her gait. It was still mostly black, unlike his own braid, which was mostly gray, but he did notice some pale hairs shooting out through her long, carefully done plait. 'Now tell me what's really for lunch, Old Woman.' He nudged her in the spot just under her rib cage that always made her burble out a cute giggle – the same one she'd always had, since way back in elementary school. Funny how every single thing about a human aged as time passed, except for the laugh. It made Chief think that the Creator, if there was one, had a damn fine sense of humor.

'You're getting a boneless, skinless chicken breast today, old man.'

Chief wasn't fat, but he was very large in stature, and he suffered the same post-middle-age paunch most men of his vintage did. 'You trying to deflate these Chippewa air bags or something?' he asked, patting his belly.

Noya tipped her head, her lips curling into that smile, which made him happy. Oh yes, he'd charmed her yet again, even after all these years. It was one of his greatest pleasures in life.

8

Magozzi got the call from Bully just as he and Gino were leaving the vacant lot where Aimee Sergeant had died. 'Good news,' he said to Gino as he hung up. 'Bully found the other four girls alive, locked in a back room in a house over on Camden Street.'

Gino let out a relieved sigh. 'Are they okay?'

'As okay as they can be, considering what they've been through. They're on their way to the hospital. But the two men who were holding them are dead in the house – somebody shot them – so we're not done with Little Mogadishu just yet.'

Gino grunted. 'Even better news. Two flesh trade gangsters just got eliminated from the petri dish. And when we find out who did that fine civic duty, we'll roast them, too, because they're part of the same bad protoplasm.'

Magozzi lit up the tires on the Caddie as he pulled away from Barrington Industrial Park and headed east down Riverside toward Camden. It was a weird crime scene. The yellow tape was strung around the house and yard, but other than a single squad parked at the curb, the site was deserted. No rubbernecking neighbors, no media, no patrols rolling in with sirens and lights.

They pulled in behind the squad, where Officer Bad Heart Bull sat sideways in the open passenger door, sweating in his blues, wiping at his face with a big white handkerchief.

He braced a hand on the squad's roof and pulled himself to his feet with some effort, handing Magozzi a blank sign-in sheet.

Gino cocked a brow at him. 'You okay, Officer?'

Bully nodded. 'Yeah. It's just the heat – I was getting used to October, then it turned back into July.'

Gino nodded sympathetically. 'I hear you. Plus, it's been kind of a rough day so far.'

Bully sighed and looked down at the ground. 'Yeah, it has been. I gotta tell you, those girls really got to me. Christ, they were just babies. Was the world always this ugly, or am I just burning out?'

'The kids always hurt,' Magozzi said, remembering a few of his own past scenes that had made him seriously question his career choice. He scribbled his name on the top line of the sign-in sheet and changed the subject. 'We're here first?'

'Yes, sir. I put the call out for backup and Crime Scene. They should be rolling in soon, and then we'll start canvassing neighbors. But don't get your hopes up. The people who live around here don't sit out in their lawn chairs watching the neighbors; they spend most of their time holed up in their own places. Hear no evil, see no evil kind of thing. In the meantime, I've got the kid I partnered with for the house-to-house covering the backyard.' He mopped at his forehead again and gestured them toward the house. 'Come on, I'll take you in before things get crowded.'

From the outside, the house was in tough shape – not unusual for this part of town – and decades worth of previous occupants' paint choices were flaking off the weather-beaten siding, revealing a rainbow of colors, from white to brown to yellow to Porta Potty aqua. But the wear and tear seemed entirely organic. There wasn't the standard exterior damage of a gang drive-by, which was the general assumption in this neighborhood. No multiple bullet holes in the structure, no shattered window glass.

Gino looked over at the air conditioner rattling in a front window. 'That thing sounds like a jet engine. Loud enough to cover up the sound of gunshots, if we're talking small caliber.'

'I think we are,' Bully contributed. 'I'm no expert, but I would guess a .22 took out those two inside. And Dispatch never got a shots-fired call – I checked.'

Magozzi and Gino walked up to the open door for a look, taking turns, since they couldn't stand abreast in the narrow doorway, and the splintery frame could have snagged a ton of evidence they didn't want to mess up. Magozzi asked Bully, 'Was this door open when you got here?'

Bully nodded. 'Just like it is now. No signs of B and E. They kept the girls in the back room with the shattered doorframe – I had to bust through it. That's the only thing we touched.'

'Thanks, Bully.'

'You got it. Give me a shout if you need anything.'

Magozzi and Gino entered and walked straight to the bodies on the floor just in front of a sofa, and Magozzi trained a flashlight on the two dead men. Clean shots to each forehead. Precise shots. The minimal damage of a small-caliber weapon, just like Bully had figured. There were no other weapons in sight.

Gino slipped on a glove and dropped to his haunches for a better look and a tentative prod. 'They're not fresh, but they're not too old, either. What do you think, Somalis?'

'Good guess, from what Bully said about the gangs running girls. Besides, it's the neighborhood demographic. Any IDs?'

Gino prodded some more, then shook his head. 'No wallets on them.'

Magozzi took a cursory glance around the room, then returned his gaze to the position of the bodies. 'Somebody surprised them,' he said. 'They were sitting on the sofa, somebody came in, they stood up and went down for the count. Didn't even have time to take a step.'

Gino nodded. 'It's a clean scene; there was some purpose here. No excessive blood, no signs of struggle, no stray bullets shredding the hell out of everything.'

Magozzi looked down at the dirty carpet beneath his feet and saw glittery shards of what looked like plastic. He pointed it out to Gino. 'Water bottle silencer?'

Gino stared at the plastic for a moment. 'Like I said, there was some purpose here. Whoever it was came here with killing in mind.'

'The shooter knew them.'

'Yeah. Probably some kind of gang-related beef.'

Magozzi turned his attention to a small table next to the sofa. It was littered with old newspapers, plastic cups, and paper plates smeared with dried food. There was a newer laptop resting in sleep mode, a Koran, and disorganized stacks of papers with weird writing that could have been Chinese, Russian, Arabic, or Hebrew, for all of Magozzi's linguistics expertise.

Gino paused at the table, bent at the waist, and stared at one of those tiny, mass-produced calendars businesses gave out for free. 'We can assume these guys were Muslim, right?'

Magozzi moved up behind him. 'Well, yeah, probably. There's a Koran right there. Why?'

'Well, I'm guessing that Muslims don't celebrate Halloween, but they've got about a hundred red circles around the thirty-first of October.'

Magozzi shrugged. 'Maybe that was the pickup date for the girls. Maybe it was a dentist appointment. It's just a date, Gino.'

In the kitchen, they found a knife in the sink. Magozzi thought about Aimee Sergeant, how in her last moments after running for her life, she'd felt her throat being slashed, and wondered if he was looking at a murder weapon.

On the surface, the rest of the house showed them nothing but ratty carpet, bare, flimsy walls with nothing on them, and two naked mattresses without bedding on the floor of one bedroom. No personal items anywhere. The place had a very temporary feeling. They finally got to the last room where the girls had been kept and wished they hadn't.

Crime Scene showed up a lot faster than they'd been expecting, given the fact that they'd had five bodies at the earlier domestic, Aimee's scene, and now these two. While Gino made a call to Hennepin County to track down the property owner, Magozzi took Jimmy Grimm on a walk-through, briefed him on the backstory, and pointed out salient things like the knife in the sink, the paperwork and computers, and the room where the girls had been kept. It didn't take long before his team was crawling all over the house – with Jimmy, you always knew the job would get done, and get done right.

Gino finally got off the phone. 'Hennepin County doesn't have a record of this house being a rental property.'

'Who owns it?'

'You're gonna love this – a retired Lutheran minister with Alzheimer's. I talked to his niece – she said it's been vacant and on the market for almost three years.'

Magozzi looked at the two dead men. 'So they were squatting.'

'Looks like it.'

'We need IDs on these vics, Jimmy. There's got to be something here – passports, ID cards, driver's licenses. We can't even see a cell phone anywhere.'

Jimmy pulled out a notebook and sketched out a few notes in big, loopy cursive that seemed so old-fashioned in these days of LOL and IOMW. 'You got it. We'll print them right away, too.'

'Thanks, Jimmy,' Magozzi said, suddenly feeling the strain of the day start to establish painful roots in his back. 'We'll light a fire under Tommy Espinoza and get him down here for the computer forensics. Whatever's in that computer might not just solve our homicide, it might bust up a seriously ugly vice ring.'

An hour later, Magozzi and Gino were sitting on a bench in a city park, not far in distance from their two Little Mogadishu crime scenes, but a universe away as far as atmosphere. They were happily bolting down rubbery hot dogs near the shore of an idyllic pond where ducks and geese floated gracefully. An elderly couple on the other side of the pond was tossing in chunks of bread and stuffing the birds silly.

'Man, that's the life I want,' Gino said wistfully. 'Hang out in a park with Angela all day and feed ducks. Can it get any better than that?'

Magozzi pondered the scene for a moment. 'Hell, I hope so.'

Gino actually eked out a small chuckle – no mean feat after the day they'd had so far. 'Yeah, maybe I'm setting my standards a little low. Two weeks of this, and I'd probably do something really crazy, like take up macramé.'

Magozzi looked down at his second, half-eaten hot dog, dressed with neon green relish and raw onions that were hot enough to fuel a Formula One car. 'This is not a Chicago hot dog. It doesn't even have casing. It's like those sad, limp things you get off the rolling steamer at a gas station.'

'Totally agree with you, buddy, but it's food, and I'm starving,' Gino mumbled, shoving the last half of his second dog into his mouth. 'At least they got the relish right.'

Gino's cell suddenly blatted out a scream – literally. Magozzi gave him a quizzical look, and Gino shrugged. 'It's almost Halloween.' He answered, listened for a few minutes, then said, 'Okay. Thanks, Jimmy.'

'What?'

'No IDs in the house. Their prints eventually popped, but in Canada, not the United States. They entered Toronto with Somali passports and did a little border jumping.'

'So they were illegal.'

'Yeah. Tommy has the computer, and he's trying to round up a translator.'

Magozzi stood up and tossed the rest of his hot dog in the trash. It was time to get back to work.

9

Claude Gerlock looked like Texas, or at least the idea of Texas that Hollywood had created. Tall, broad-shouldered, and long-muscled, with a rocking gait and a permanent squint. In his youth, nearsighted women had told him he reminded them of Gary Cooper, which was dumb and no way true because the man was just too damn pretty. As he aged, people started comparing him to Robert Duvall in that *Lonesome Dove* movie, which wasn't half bad, except that the actor was almost a foot shorter than Claude and in no way a Texan just because he played one on TV.

Texas wasn't just a look and an easy way of talking; it was a mind-set, and Claude Gerlock was as true a Texan as God had ever created, from the oil wells to the cattle herds to the home arsenal he kept, which served to keep his five-thousand-acre ranch clear of varmints of all species, including the Homo sapien type, if any ill-intended chanced to trespass. He'd been through the hell of war, been gored almost to death on a wild boar hunt, and had even once survived a month alone in the Odessa desert on rattlesnake blood and cactus paddles, just to see if he could do it.

But it always took a while to accustom himself to this claustrophobic, conifer-studded terrain – there were too many pine trees up here and the whole place reeked like a car air freshener. And you couldn't see a thing through all the goddamned foliage and tree trunks, which brought him right back to a Vietnamese jungle. He didn't think of those jungles much anymore, which was a mercy, but the memories were like an old splinter that hadn't ever completely worked itself out of the skin.

He paused at the base of a big spruce in a small clearing, braced the butt of his rifle against his shoulder, and squinted down the scope at the man who'd been stalking him for some time. 'I hear you, Chief,' he said with a smile. 'And I got you in my sights.'

'Bullshit you heard me, you deaf old shit kicker,' a distant voice filtered through the pines.

'I did, louder than the bells of St Mary's on Easter morning, half a click back. What's all this about Indians being silent and stealthy?'

'I left my moccasins in the teepee, Chimookman.'

A minute later, Chief Bellanger stepped into the clearing, his heavy-soled boots crunching on the dried pine needles. He smiled, his sun-cured brown face creasing like a geisha's fan. 'You see anything worth shooting yet, Chimook?'

'Just you.'

'Likewise.' Chief braced his own rifle against a tree trunk and moved in to give Claude a grizzly bear embrace.

The hugs were a recent thing – probably an old man thing – and neither one of them were very good at it. Warriors didn't run around hugging each other all the time, and at their core, both men were still warriors even though those days were far behind them.

'You got the place ready?' Claude asked.

'Don't I always?'

'Reckon you do.'

'Got the last of our supplies in my truck back at the lodge. Some Indian fry bread, along with some of that fancy foreign jet fuel you like to drink.'

Claude smiled. 'Then your truck is where I want to be. Fuck the bread. Just throw me in the back with the booze.'

The two men walked single file down the narrow deer trail that led back to the lodge, and for the entire walk, neither spoke. Not because they didn't have anything to say, but because this was how their relationship had begun, and the habits that kept you alive in war lasted a lifetime.

If there was one thing Claude remembered about the majority of missions in 'Nam, it was the silence. A line of men moving through the jungle on paths as narrow as this one, rattling belts held still by sweating hands, forearms straining to hold M-16s steady and quiet. He and the Chief still watched the ground beneath each boot step, looking for trip wires that had never existed in the northern forests of Minnesota.

It didn't take Claude long to slide into the good feelings that came right along with putting his boots on this land. If there was a place on earth he loved as much as Texas, it was right here on Elbow Lake Reservation. He loved the Ojibwe people, their native legends and lore, the spirit stories, the pranks, and the good-natured prejudice of a people who believed absolutely that every single other culture on the planet was inferior to theirs, because that was a damn fine survival skill. This from a tribe who had once lived in broken-down trailers without a pot to piss in and ate government cheese rations.

When Chief first brought him up here after the war,

about two dozen men sat him down at a fire that smelled like burning cow dung, sliced the inside of his forearm with a dull knife, and told him it was a ceremony honoring him because he'd saved the life of one of their own.

'Am I a blood brother now?' he'd asked, because he'd read about that in a comic book.

All the Indians had rolled over laughing. 'Hell, no, that's just what you white folks think we do. You're just a dumb Texan who sat there and let us cut your arm open.'

Then they gave him horrible whiskey in a Mason jar, dubbing him some Indian name he couldn't pronounce. It was years before he learned that the name translated roughly to Cowboy Who Fucks Dogs, and by that time he was way past taking offense.

He'd been here every year since to hunt with Chief, watching the transformation of the reservation, tickled by it, becoming a part of their history he knew would be passed down through the generations. Gave him a prickly sense of belonging somewhere he didn't belong at a time when the rest of the country looked at him askance and made him hide his dress uniform in the very back of his very large closet as if it were some kind of leper's sore.

After a time the trees started to thin and Claude saw the resin-ambered logs of the lodge, the gravel parking area, and his rental SUV hitched to a trailer that held ten shiny, new canoes with ELBOW LAKE YOUTH CAMP stenciled on them.

Chief stopped when he saw the canoes and his face went still. Damn fool always had to act stoic when something really touched him, as if emotions were the enemy. 'What the hell is this, old man?'

'I was up here last year when you opened that camp. Sorriest damn sight, seeing all those poor little Indian kids trying to figure out how to paddle in that beat-up piece of junk that makes up your entire fleet. Indians should know their way around a canoe.'

'City Indians,' the Chief explained. 'That's mostly what we get up here for camp. A lot of 'em don't know a canoe from a giraffe.'

'Well, now you can teach 'em all how to paddle proper.'

After a long silence, Chief nodded. '*Migwich*, my brother. Thank you.'

Claude redirected his attention and let his gaze drift into the rich green blur of pine that surrounded the lodge. 'Car's coming.'

'Gotta be our boy.'

They waited and watched, and finally a car crunched up on the gravel and parked beside Claude's rental SUV and his gift of canoes.

'Holy shit,' Claude breathed when a skeleton emerged from the car. Joe was over thirty years their junior, but he looked like an old man. The disease had done some ugly work. 'Man, he looks bad.'

'Real bad.'

'I heard that,' Joe Hardy called out as he walked toward them. He was moving real slow, and Chief felt himself wincing as he watched every labored step. 'Goddamned Indians and Texans, you've both got the manners of a hog at a trough. Now say something nice.'

Chief snorted a laugh. 'GI Joe, you dumb fuck, get your ass out of the open before the vultures see you and pick what's left of you clean!'

'That's better.' Joe grinned as Chief walked to meet him halfway, grabbed his bony shoulders, and probed for meat. 'Son of a bitch, kid, they sucked the flesh right off you. Told you, white man's cures are worse than the disease. What you need is a little Indian medicine.'

'And what's that?'

'Liquor and food, in that order.'

'Sounds good.' Joe looked over at where Claude was standing, holding back. This would be harder for him. The three men had met when Joe brought Claude's only son, Grover, home from Afghanistan in a coffin. Their bond had formed over their mutual loss – for Claude, a son; for Joe, the best friend he'd ever had and tried so hard to save during that mountain ambush. He still carried metal fragments in his shoulder from the shells he'd taken carrying Grover out of the line of fire and over to the chopper. 'Get over here, you big pussy Texan. I won't bite.'

Claude didn't have the stoic thing going. He should have, as a big bad Texan, but Joe canceled that out like a bad check. Always had. He walked over slowly, almost afraid to get there, and this time the hug felt right and real around the deflated bag of skin and bones that barely resembled the man he remembered from just a few months ago and loved like a son. 'Think you can still heft a gun with those puny little arms?'

'You bet your scrawny ass I can still hold a gun. I've been practicing.'

Part of Joe wanted to tell them what he'd done, about the dark little house and the two lifeless bodies bleeding on the floor. The temptation was strong, almost irresistible.

Some twisted need for a legacy, he supposed. But he couldn't do that. They wouldn't understand.

'You know your problem, Joe?' Claude was trying to fight the dark moment and his own emotions, just like the Chief always did. 'You fought in the wrong war. If you'd had to go through what we went through in the 'Nam, you'd be a little tougher. Probably could kick this little illness you got right to the curb.'

Joe grinned. 'Wrong war, my nowhere ass. You two slapped mosquitoes. Big deal. You should try living through a sandstorm when it's a hundred and twenty degrees. A day of that and you're crapping windowpanes the next morning.' He chuckled a little, then went serious. 'I still think of Grover, Claude. Every day.'

Claude nodded and slapped him on the shoulder. There would be a large bruise there later. 'So do I, son.'

Joe looked down at the gravel beneath his feet, remembering what death felt like in that medevac helicopter over the mountains of Kandahar. He'd been holding Grover's hand, never noticing the blood pouring out of his shoulder, never noticing the medics who were frantically tending to them both.

You're gonna be okay, G-Man. Hang on, we're almost there.

Where?

Back to base. We'll shoot some pool after they put a couple Band-Aids on us, okay?

Where are we now, Joey?

Coming down out of the mountains. Just a few more minutes.

Grover had smiled then. *Closer to God,* he'd murmured, and then Joe felt Grover shudder, felt his hand seize up, as if a valve had been switched off and all the juice that made a person a person had suddenly evaporated into thin air. Joe had known in an instant.

He finally looked up and lifted his nose to the air, drinking in the piney scent he'd come to love these past few years, after Claude and the Chief had brought him into their fold. 'So are we shooting today or what?'

10

Harley Davidson's historic Summit Avenue mansion had been home to the Monkeewrench offices ever since they'd shuttered their Minneapolis loft space almost two years ago. There had been a lot of blood on their last day there, the dead bodies had been real, and none of them wanted to go back ever again.

The mansion was an old, imposing structure, crafted from local red stone, encircled by a wickedly spiked wrought-iron fence. Even at the peak of summer, when the perennial flower gardens exploded into full color and the fountains burbled cheerfully, it still seemed menacing.

But now, as Halloween approached, the menace of the place had entered an entirely new dimension, thanks to some overzealous decorating. The antique French gargoyles Harley had recently installed hadn't helped matters, but the overblown Halloween decorations he was putting the finishing touches on now sent it straight over the top.

In the front yard, there was a vintage Shelby Mustang convertible with two life-sized skeletons dressed as bride and groom, along with a makeshift cemetery with real granite headstones engraved with movie monsters' names. The tableau was augmented by a choreographed light show of ghouls on remote-controlled zip lines, outdoor audio playing sound effects, and several fog machines strategically placed around the property.

'What do you guys think?' Harley called down to Annie and Roadrunner, his massive body teetering on a ladder as his black ponytail whipped in a freshening breeze. He draped the last of the cobwebs over the portico. 'More?'

'Enough!' Annie snapped, steadying the ladder. 'Now, get down off that thing before you fall and kill yourself. And by the way, who gets real granite tombstones for their front yard?'

Harley chuckled and clambered down, his jackboots about five sizes too big to manage the ladder rungs with any kind of grace. 'I do. And stop complaining. You love this, Annie, you know you do.'

'I love this? Are you kidding me? I've got some really expensive white stiletto heels sinking down into your grass right now, trying to save your sorry and big behind. Roadrunner, give me a hand.'

Roadrunner had been squatting like a praying mantis over one of the troublesome fog machines, but he quickly unfurled his six-foot-seven frame and helped steady the ladder. 'Sorry, Annie.'

'Don't be sorry. Just help me get this idiot down alive.'

Once Harley had landed safely, he folded his arms across his broad chest, the leather of his biker jacket creaking like a haunted house door. He looked around his elaborately dressed grounds, which were now wreathed in fog thanks to Roadrunner, then gave a satisfied nod. 'Brilliant, if I do say so myself. Great test run, everybody.'

Annie rolled her eyes. 'No trick-or-treater in their right mind is going to knock on your door, Harley. Besides, you don't even like kids.'

'I do too like kids. But sometimes I think I intimidate them. I thought this might win them over.'

Annie grunted. 'Perfect reasoning. Kids afraid of you? Turn your front yard into a terror trip.'

'Kids love this shit, the scarier the better.' He stroked his full black beard thoughtfully as he eyed the spikes on the top of the fence. 'As a matter of fact, I think we should get some skulls and jam them up there, give the place a more Vlad the Impaler feel.'

Roadrunner nodded. 'Not a bad idea. I know where you can buy some good fake skulls.'

Annie pulled her heels out of the grass and marched to the front door. 'You two frat boys stay out here as long as you want. I'm going back to work.'

Hours later, every light was still on in the third-floor loft, and the three of them were hunched over their computers, working in focused silence.

Annie was having the most fun she'd had since Grace MacBride took off to sail the Caribbean with John Smith. Annie liked John – all of them did – but let's face it. The man had flaws. First of all, he was old; more than twenty years older than Grace and strung tighter than a grand piano treble wire. Worse yet, he was cookie-cutter FBI, even if he was retired. What Grace saw in him was a puzzle. Still, Annie never questioned the choices of the people she loved, and Grace was the best of these. But Annie did miss her.

Last week, life had taken an unexpected upturn when Monkeewrench had landed a juicy contract for their new game to teach children American history through a 3-D CGI program with voice recognition that allowed students to literally walk into a scene and interact with historical avatars. Right now they were working on the node where users would be able to stand on the bank of the Potomac River during George Washington's crossing. It was a big step up from the kids' games they'd started with years ago, but it was nevertheless a return to the education-through-games programs that had made them all wealthy. Besides, Annie loved American history. It had been her minor in college before they'd all dropped out to save Grace from a serial killer.

'Okay.' A tired growl came from across the loft. 'So George Washington asks the kid a question, like what river is this or what's the date, and the kid gets it wrong. What's the penalty? I say shoot the kid's avatar in the head with a musket ball.'

'Don't be a dipshit, Harley,' Roadrunner mumbled. 'You take away points.'

'You're such a buzzkill, Roadrunner. And at the moment, George Washington is bare-ass naked. I need details so I can start rendering the graphics, Annie.'

She looked over at where Harley was punching thick fingers into his keyboard. With all the computers they were running, it was hot in the loft despite all the cooling units they were running to keep the electronics from melting down, so he'd shed his leather jacket and sat there in a muscle T-shirt that showed every stupid tattoo he'd ever gotten. 'I sent you the pictorial,' she said. 'White tights, yellow knickers, blue jacket.'

'Nice.' Harley looked over at Roadrunner, who was hunched over his own computer, his long spine bent like an archer's bow to accommodate a desk far too low for his frame. He was in his customary Lycra biking suit, and today's selection just happened to be yellow and blue with white stripes. 'Huh. Just like Roadrunner. How do you think old Georgie would look in Lycra?'

Roadrunner looked over at Harley. 'What?'

Harley gave him a smug smile. 'Nothing.'

Annie put her chin in her hand and thought about that outfit, wondering what one would look like on her, at least as a Halloween costume. Not nearly as divine as the all-white ensemble she was wearing today, she decided. White was a color she rarely chose to wear, and certainly not after Labor Day, but part of the fun was defying convention, not adhering to it. Besides, she'd scored a pair of white fur high-heeled boots that climbed all the way to her plump knees like some kind of fabulous tundra animal coiling up her legs.

Annie snapped herself out of her fashion reverie and returned her attention to her computer, where she had been puzzling over a particularly complex section of programming before Harley had interrupted her. Normally, it wouldn't have taken her long to work her way through it, but it was late, and she suddenly felt the dull ache of almost a week's worth of exhausting fifteen-hour workdays creeping into her bones. 'This Southern belle is going to start making some bad decisions if I don't get home and sleep for a few hours in my own bed. Are you boys going to work all night?'

Harley leaned back in his chair, stretched, and yawned. 'If you're bailing, I'm bailing. Roadrunner, are you the last man standing?'

Roadrunner spun in his chair and shook his head. 'I

could use a couple hours myself. I'll catch a few on the sofa in a little bit. I'll get you a cab, Annie.'

She gave Roadrunner a gentle pat on his bony shoulder as she took the elevator downstairs to wait for her taxi, which was miraculously already idling in front of Harley's gate. She'd never gotten a cab that fast in her life. The driver got out promptly and opened the back door, which pleased her. They weren't all so polite. 'Good evening,' he said cordially in a thickly accented voice. 'It is a cold night, is it not, miss?'

'It most certainly is,' she said, settling into the backseat.

'I am not accustomed to this cold,' he chuckled. 'I miss the sun and warmth all year.'

Annie met his eyes in the rearview mirror. Like most of the cabdrivers in the city, he was obviously a transplant from someplace where it didn't snow seven months out of the year. 'Where are you from originally?' she asked.

'Somalia, miss.'

11

Claude fed more birch logs into the fire that had mellowed to orange embers in the cabin's hearth. It had been a very fine day, the finest day in his recent memory, spent drinking, laughing, reminiscing, and shooting cans in preparation for tomorrow's big hunt.

Their exertions had taken a toll on everybody, especially Joey, and he hadn't lasted much past sundown before begging off to bed – no surprise, given the boy's sorry condition. Now it was just a couple of old warhorses left standing, on one last mission: to finish what was left of a bottle of fine scotch whiskey before their heads hit the pillows, too.

Claude settled down onto the fieldstone hearth and coaxed the fire with a poker while Chief looked on from a leather lounge chair, his big hands laced over the shelf of his belly.

'You can still shoot, you know that, Chimook?' Chief chuckled, his amusement reverberating like faraway thunder. 'Not half as good as Joey or me, but still pretty damn good for an old cowboy who fucks dogs. I was impressed today.'

'Do the math, Chief – I killed around fifteen more cans than you.'

'You always cheat. Like when we play golf.'

'I don't cheat in golf.'

'Yeah, actually, you do.'

Claude cocked a shaggy, graying brow at his friend. 'You can cheat in golf, but you can't cheat with a gun. Dead is dead, every time, whether it's a can or a man.'

'I suppose you're right about that.' Chief poured the remaining scotch in equal proportion into their watered-down lowballs. 'I think Joey had a good day.'

'Yep. We all did.' Claude lifted his glass for a drink, relishing the oaky heat of new liquor on the back of his throat. 'Way I see it, up here with us, he's not a sick man, he's just a man. That's good for him. No sense letting reality overshadow our time together.'

Chief nodded, his eyes tracking down the hallway that had swallowed up Joe a few hours ago. Claude followed his gaze. 'A sorrowful thing, that. No sound reasoning behind a couple old swamp rats like us who stewed in Agent Orange for two years to outlive such a fine young man.'

'This shouldn't be his road to the High Place. A warrior should die on the battlefield. It's the greatest honor.'

Claude regarded him shrewdly. 'We didn't. And if I recall proper, you saved both our asses that night in Khe Sahn, instead of letting us have our "greatest honor."'

'It wasn't our time. Besides, I didn't save our asses, Mukwa did.'

'Don't you go getting all Indian-mystical on me. You know I don't have any tolerance for that kind of nonsense.'

Chief smiled and pushed himself out of his chair. 'We should think about getting some shut-eye, old man. Bear's on the agenda tomorrow, and that's a thinking man's quarry. We need to be sharp.'

Claude suddenly gave him a puzzled frown. 'You know, Chief, never occurred to me to ask before, but aren't there some sort of rules that say you shouldn't shoot your spirit guide? Seems like it'd be bad luck or something.'

'No. Indians can shoot whatever the hell they want.' They both laughed.

Claude climbed into his bed and felt the dull ache of muscles put to good use – a feeling that didn't irk him one bit. At the age of five, his daddy had deemed him fit to help the ranch hands with the animals, and the chores had only gotten harder with each passing year. He was no stranger to an ache or a pain.

He remembered the one and only time he'd complained about the work. His daddy hadn't said much after hearing his only child's grievances, had just proceeded to drag him to a dusty pickup truck and toss him in the passenger seat. They'd driven for miles and miles that afternoon, his daddy constantly pointing out huge pastures filled with cattle, and endless expanses of steel oil rigs with pumping arms that reminded him of the dinosaurs in his favorite picture book.

Your granddaddy built all this up, boy, from nothin' but hunger, sweat, and a strong back. And I built it up bigger. You want this to be all yours one day, you're gonna have to put some skin in the game, you hear? Anything free ain't worth havin', you remember that.

That entire night, Claude had tossed and turned and fretted in his little race-car-shaped bed, not because he cared one spit about any cows or dumb metal dinosaurs, but because Mrs Carmichael at the general store always gave him a free peppermint stick whenever he visited, and his five-year-old brain couldn't fathom a reason why a free peppermint stick wasn't worth having, even if his daddy had told him as such.

Claude smiled at the ancient memory that had become so warm and comforting after all these years, and reached over to turn off the bedside table light. That's when he noticed the box that hadn't been there earlier, when he'd settled into the room this morning and unpacked.

The box was something very familiar to him, because he had a few of his own – a ceremonial box that held military medals. He sat up in bed and carefully placed it on his lap. He knew what was in there. And he knew where it had come from.

Time passed – Claude wasn't sure how much – before he slowly lifted the cover. Nestled in plush velvet in the bottom of the box was a bronze cross with an eagle in the center, the scroll below the eagle inscribed: FOR VALOR. It was a Distinguished Service Cross, one of the highest honors the military awarded, given to individuals who displayed extraordinary heroism at great risk to their own life – the one Joey had earned trying to save Claude's son, Grover. This was a parting gift, from a brave and honorable man who was distributing a part of his legacy to a place he wanted it to go, while he still had time.

Claude finally picked up the medal and cradled it in his palm. The bronze felt warm to the touch, as if somebody had recently pressed it to their flesh and had held it there.

Claude closed his eyes, leaned back against his pillow, and moved the medal up to rest against his heart.

12

Mukwa visited Chief for only the second time in his life that night – but on this visit, Mukwa didn't tell him about the many roads to the High Place, or lead him to a sniper's nest in a Vietnam jungle. He didn't even ask for clemency during the bear hunt tomorrow. He simply showed him a single loon, floating on a lake in the moonlight. Suddenly, the loon took flight on great wings, disappearing into darkness, the lunar radiance lighting the edges of its feathers. At some point during its flight, it changed into an owl – an omen of death.

Chief lurched up in bed, breathing hard, tangled in sheets that were soaked with his sweat. He turned on the bedside light and sat up for a few minutes, trying to calm his heart and gather his wits.

As much as he loved to taunt Claude with a little Indian mysticism now and again, he didn't really believe in spirit guides the way some of his people did. He knew the messages were purely human instincts the ancients had attributed to a higher power, and the explanation had gotten passed down in lore.

That night in Khe Sahn, the first time Mukwa had come to him, he'd probably subconsciously noted the clicking and chirping of Vietcong snipers communicating with each other as they moved closer to their encampment. He'd picked up on it and, in his dream, had manifested those signals into a message from his spirit guide, because those were his tools of interpretation.

And this time, he knew Mukwa's visit was the same – Joe was dying, and he was the owl. That was obvious. But the loon who'd taken flight in the first part of his dream was a message he didn't quite understand.

Chief disentangled himself from his damp sheets and crept out of his bedroom and into the dark hallway. He could hear Claude snoring like a goddamned chain saw across the hall, but there was no sound coming from Joey's bedroom and the door was partially ajar. He pushed the door open a little wider and peered in – the bed was made, but his suitcase and rifle cases were still there, neatly stacked on the luggage rack at the foot of the bed, like nicer versions of the military footlockers they'd all kept in barracks during their service.

He walked out into the kitchen, but there wasn't coffee brewing and there was no sign of Joe; no sign that he'd ever been here, except for his belongings back in the bedroom. And it was no surprise to Chief that his car was missing from the driveway. He could have taken an early-morning drive around Elbow Lake, sure; but in his heart of hearts, he knew that Joe was gone, for whatever reason. Joe had been the owl, but he'd also been the loon, flying away into the night.

13

In the wee hours of Monday morning, Joe parked in the Riverside hospital ramp, like he always did. The hospital is where everyone would think he would go to die quietly, painlessly, carrying a full load of morphine and ready to accept his end. Only Claude and Chief would understand that he couldn't leave that way.

The pain had been bad during the five-hour drive from the reservation, but now, as he walked down Riverside, it was excruciating. He was oblivious to silhouettes of passing people whose features he couldn't make out as they exited the tall, shabby apartment buildings that were as much a cancer on this urban landscape as the one that was eating his insides, bite by bite. The tiny houses that cuddled up to the behemoth brick buildings on the narrow side street were as run-down as he remembered, dark at this time of night, one of them holding evil within its walls like a scalding crucifix in the hand of a true believer.

He was not aware of holding his side, as if the pain could be pushed inside and somehow negated. He was not aware of the tears streaming down his cheeks as he shuffled along, boots dragging and scraping against concrete sidewalks because his feet were now far too heavy to lift. This was a familiar place, and he felt like he was moving through his own history. It seemed appropriate tonight.

The hospital had been the first marker, where his father had died by his own hand, unable to live with the memories of Vietnam and what he had done there. And yet that wasn't what Joey remembered of that terrible night when he was eight years old and sat with his weeping mother in that dreadful white room with its beeping monitor, ticking off the remaining seconds of his father's life. He didn't know about Vietnam, or what his father had experienced there; he was only eight, after all, and he knew only one thing that had fractured his father's life.

In the Munich Olympics, 1972, the Soviets won gold in basketball. The US team lost by one point, winning silver, and refused the medal because the Soviets had won by the bad call of a bad referee, and the US team refused to accept false accolades for second place when they should have had first. That's who the US team was in those days.

We are not now who we were then.

It was weird, how he kept thinking of that, all these years later. He hadn't even been born when it happened. But he'd watched the newsreels over and over, because his dad had played basketball in college, and kept the films in the basement to play when he needed a beer and alone time to remember who he might have been. Little Joey had crouched on the basement steps while light from the old projector danced across his face and his Superman pajamas, watching what his father watched, taking it in, waiting for the years to pass that would tell him what it really meant.

Funny, he thought, shuffling along the broken sidewalk like the desperately ill man he was. That was one of the memories that had shaped his life. America had refused to accept a false defeat back in Munich, refused to shrug off a wrong without standing up for what was right. Joe vowed he would always do the same. *I am who we were then.*

He had to sit down on the curb in front of the dark little crooked house, because he couldn't breathe very well anymore. And that was silly. You didn't breathe through your pancreas, and that was what was really killing him. Still, he sat there for a moment, trying to suck in air, fighting the pain, his feet planted in the puddles of sand next to the curb left by the last pass of the street sweeper, thinking through the details for the hundredth time, because this had to be done exactly right, whether he could breathe or not.

Lately, he'd been remembering those days in a foreign desert, when his good strong legs had propelled him from sand dune to sand dune to find cover from flying bullets. Now, when his lungs could barely find enough oxygen to keep his heart pumping, the simple act of walking sucked the soul right out of him.

It wasn't like he hadn't done this before. But most of the other times he'd had brothers at his side. The last time, and this time, he was on his own. He was close to wipeout anyway, no reason for other good men to take the risk of keeping up the fight. Trouble was, it didn't seem to matter how many they took down – it was like squashing roaches. You killed one and another hundred swarmed in to take its place. The damn list just kept getting longer and longer.

He'd never really gotten the logic of the war machine. For six years, he'd put his life on the line every goddamned day because his leaders had told him to go overseas and kill the bad guys. Then all of a sudden, when his service was over, those same leaders had said, okay, go home now and blend in, and for God's sake, don't kill the bad guys that are now in your country, in your neighborhoods. We'll take care of that.

But they weren't taking care of that. They couldn't find them all, and when they did find some who seemed to be up to no good, they couldn't do anything about it without jumping through a zillion legal hoops that one day were going to take too long.

He couldn't imagine what the blowback would be when the Feds finally sorted all this out. He'd probably be the first serviceman in history to get a posthumous dishonorable discharge. But none of that bothered him. The people who mattered would understand that all he was doing was the job he'd been trained to do. He just didn't stop when they told him to.

It didn't happen precisely as he'd planned. The men came out of the house when he was still sitting on the curb, his back to them. He saw the light from the doorway shining down the crumbling sidewalk and illuminating the scraggly grass next to him, and all he could think of was oh my God, what if they had come out unarmed? Nothing would work then. Everything would be lost. He'd have to abandon all his grand plans and come back another night, and the big problem there was he wasn't sure he had another night left.

He heard one of them call out to him, and understood just enough of the language to translate 'who the fuck are you and what are you doing here?' which is precisely what he would have asked if he'd had what they had in the house behind them.

He had no real idea what to reply to redeem the situation, and then suddenly he felt like Grover was sitting on his shoulder, whispering in his ear, telling him what to say. He took a deep breath, and without turning around, yelled back in their own language, 'FBI. You're under arrest. Lie facedown, hands behind your head.'

Whoop. Big threat. Beware the dying cancer patient. And thank God for the Internet language program he'd been practicing for weeks, because it worked. Oh, how it worked. He knew that the minute he felt the first slug pierce his back.

Stupid Joe. What if they'd killed you with the first shot? Didn't think of that, did you? Then again, you didn't notice the streetlight when you cased the place over and over, which is what happens when chemo slaughters your brain cells and you never notice in daylight what will be evident in dark. Happily, the idiots were poor shots, and the first slug pierced his right lung and ignored the more important organs.

Lieutenant Joe Hardy was a great shot. Funny, the way cancer and chemo had crippled him. He couldn't take a decent shit, he couldn't fuck or eat spice or do any of the things a man was supposed to do. But he could turn his upper body in an instant and shoot like the eighteen-year-old kid who'd scored nothing but tens on the sniper range.

He killed them both, but not before one of them had fired the fatal shot, blowing apart his heart, the only organ he had left that worked.

This was really good, he thought as his upper body fell

to the crinkly, dried October grass. Perfect, actually. Poor, pathetic, dying man, shot dead trying to stumble his way to the hospital. Jesus Christ that was sad, and the cops were going to tear that house apart now.

14

Emotionally, if not physically, yesterday had been the most exhausting Gino had put in for a long time. Running the investigation on the murder of Aimee Sergeant in that god-awful warehouse lot had ripped him apart. She'd been only a year or so younger than Helen, his own daughter, and he couldn't stop thinking about that.

Different cultures had no differences at all when it came to the death of a child. He'd thought about that girl's parents for most of the day, and it made his heart hurt. That the four children who had been kidnapped with her had been found safe had almost made it worse. Her parents had to be tormented. Why our daughter? Why did she have to die?

Don't take it so personally, Magozzi had said in the park, but that was because he didn't have kids, poor guy. Gino couldn't help taking it personally. This had been a failure of law enforcement. Somebody should have found those girls before Aimee had to die.

Angela, God bless her, knew immediately how to mitigate his tortured thoughts after he'd told her about his day. *She saved the others, Gino. If she hadn't run, if the door-to-door hadn't been initiated to cover every house in Little Mogadishu, they wouldn't have been found.*

Someone should have done the door-to-door earlier.

Gino, you're not thinking clearly right now. No one had any idea they were in Minneapolis. They could have been anywhere.

Wives were extraordinary creatures. At least, his was. She listened; she cut through the crap and showed him another way of looking at things that made it possible to live with himself. Magozzi didn't have a wife, either, and Gino often wondered how he managed the job when he had no one to come home to.

With a mouthful of residual garlic flavor from the shrimp scampi Angela had forced on him, his thoughts blessedly silent after an unprecedented third glass of Chianti, and Angela's warm body sprawled across his chest like a cat in the sun, Gino was in the heaven of his sixth hour of sleep. The shrill ring of the bedside phone was not just an intrusion; it was a sacrilege.

He fumbled for the receiver, put it to his ear, and said something really awful to whoever was on the other end of the line.

'Jeez, Gino, chill out. It's me, a friendly.' Magozzi's voice sounded like Gino felt – wiped out, wrung out, and not happy. 'I just got the call. We have three bodies lying in a front yard in Little Mogadishu.'

Gino propped himself up on one elbow, but he didn't open his eyes. 'Shit. We might as well move there, save ourselves the commute.'

'I'll be there in ten minutes. Put on clothes.'

'I can't go to work. I'm drunk.'

'How can you be drunk? It's six-thirty in the morning.'

'Angela did it. She kept filling my glass. You've got to get yourself a wife.'

'Get dressed, wear long pants. There's frost on the grass.'

It took only twenty minutes to get from Gino's house to the crime scene. He slept for nineteen of those minutes, and only woke up when Magozzi poked him in the arm.

'Rise and shine, sweetheart. We're there.'

Gino snuffled, opened bleary eyes, and tried to focus on his surroundings. 'What time is it?'

'Just after seven.'

'Christ. It's barely light.'

'Just wait. Another week, daylight savings time goes away, and we'll be driving to work in the cold and black.'

'I hate winter. Oh, crap, what's going on here?'

Squads lined the curb in front and the alley in back and blocked north and southbound traffic on the street. Uniforms had already descended like a plague of dapper locusts, stringing tape and protecting the perimeter while they waited for the next chain of command to arrive and give them further orders or dismiss them. A few were making an honest attempt to interview a small cluster of onlookers, mostly older women wearing black headscarves and abayas. The vacant expressions on both sides of the tape confirmed a language barrier much stronger than the plastic ribbon that separated them.

A uniform trotted over when they got out of the car. 'Good morning, Detectives.'

Gino snorted. 'Doesn't look like it from here.'

'Yeah. The first responders are inside, clearing the house. Should be out in a minute. They said the front door was wide open, so they figured the two bodies closest to the house lived here.'

'Okay, thanks.'

Magozzi and Gino moved toward the pair of dead men, sprawled on the lawn close to the front of the house. Their guns were a few inches away from their dead hands.

Magozzi crouched down to get a closer look at the gunshot wounds on each man's torso. 'Messy,' he mumbled. 'Looks like heart shots.'

Gino nodded. 'And it looks like we've got another two dead Middle Eastern types.'

Magozzi slipped on a pair of gloves and patted the two men down. 'Clean, no wallets.'

'Makes sense if they lived here. Something brought them outside, and my guess is our third DB.' Gino turned and pointed to the other corpse on the curb, and they both moved on to the very sick-looking white guy whose gun was still clutched in his hand.

Dead people didn't smile. Magozzi knew that perfectly well. Smile muscles were voluntary, and you had to be alive to make them work. This guy wasn't smiling – that would have been physically impossible – but for some reason, it looked like he had been. It also looked like he had absolutely no reason to smile. Something had been eating his body long before the bullets made those pretty red holes in his back and his chest.

'This guy was halfway to dead before he got here,' he said to Gino. They were both crouched over the remains of an emaciated man, their flashlights shining on the grayish, skeletal face of illness that long preceded the slugs that had actually killed him.

'Riverside Hospital's a couple blocks up,' Gino replied. 'If he had any brain cells left, that's where he was headed.'

'He's off the main thoroughfare. Why would he detour if he was headed to the hospital?'

Gino shrugged. 'Jeez, Leo, look at the poor guy. You and I get lost after a single beer. From the looks of him, it's pretty amazing he could see where he was headed at all, let alone steer his feet. Shit. What do you think? Cancer or druggie? They look kind of alike when they hit the end stages, you know?'

Magozzi had been seven years old when Uncle Marvin came for a visit. It was weird, that he would come without Aunt Mabel, and weirder still that he didn't look one bit like the last time little Leo had seen him at his Ohio farm. He was real skinny, and his pants hung down over the black shoes that had walking creases in the tops and holes in the soles.

What's the matter with Uncle Marvin? He doesn't even want to play dominoes. Remember when he used to play dominoes with me all the time?

He's sick, Leo.

Oh. You mean like a cold or something?

It's a little worse than a cold. Your dad and I are going to take him down to Mayo a few times so he can get better.

What's Mayo?

It's a special hospital. A really good one. And it's real close to us, which is why he's going to stay with us for a while.

Will they fix him so he wants to play dominoes again?

That's what we're hoping. In the meantime, he hurts all over, and he's pretty weak. So if he asks you to help him to the bathroom, or get him a glass of water or something, you'll do that, won't you?

Sure, Mom. Uncle Marvin gave me a ride on the pony whenever I wanted one.

I remember.

Does he still have the pony?

Yes. Aunt Mabel is taking care of him now.

His mom and dad went to pick Aunt Mabel up at the bus station one day, and Leo was feeling pretty good about staying at the house with Uncle Marvin alone, like he was a babysitter or something and really grown up.

That was the first time he'd helped Marvin to the bathroom, and the first time he'd seen a grown man's pee-pee, and it was amazing. 'Jeepers, Uncle Marvin, you've got the biggest ding-a-ling I ever saw.'

Marvin sat down on the toilet then and laughed so hard that tears squirted out of his eyes, and Leo thought that was pretty cool. 'You want me to help you up?'

'No, Leo, goddamnit. Grown men don't need help. Remember that.'

Later he peeked around the kitchen door and saw his uncle trying to cross the room when he dropped the newspaper he'd been carrying. He just stood there watching, because grown men didn't need help, but he felt guilty when he heard Marvin groan as he bent over, fumbling for the paper like it was the brass ring of his life. He couldn't make himself rush over to help, because Uncle Marvin wouldn't have liked that.

Magozzi closed his eyes as he bent over the dead man on the sidewalk, still pissed because his mother had never told him how much pain Marvin had suffered. He'd died that night, pooping in his sheets, and Leo thought for years it was because he hadn't helped him pick up the newspaper.

'Cancer,' he said to Gino.

'Either way, Riverside probably has a record. He's either a patient or a frequent flyer at the ER looking for a hit. Dig for some ID before Crime Scene gets here all possessive.'

Magozzi put on a fresh pair of gloves and found a wallet in the dead man's jacket pocket. 'You got a bag?'

'I do.' Gino looked at the name and picture on the driver's license. 'Joseph Christopher Hardy. Jesus, Leo. The poor guy looks a hundred, but he was only thirty-two.'

'Cancer will do that to you.'

'He doesn't live too far from here if this address is current.' Gino started thumbing through the mass of papers guys always tuck in the bill section of their wallets. 'I got an IN CASE OF EMERGENCY card. Contact is Beth Hardy, and I'm guessing this is her.' He held out a small photo of a pretty woman standing in front of a waterfall. 'There's a doctor's card in here, too. Oncology at Riverside.'

'That'll help.' Magozzi glanced down at the weapon laying loose in the dead hand. 'He brought a gun, Gino. Why the hell would a cancer patient bring a gun to the hospital?'

'Are you kidding? Look around. I'd bring a weapon to have lunch in this neighborhood. And FYI, he's got a permit to carry in here.' He slipped the wallet in the bag and laid it next to the body for Crime Scene to collect. 'So he's on his last legs, gets confused on his way to the hospital, and those two pieces of crap see an easy target and move in.'

Magozzi stood up, pressing his hands to the small of

his back, and looked around at the scene. 'It'd be pretty stupid to mug somebody in front of your own house.' He rubbed at the line between his brows. It felt deeper than it had yesterday. 'Maybe Hardy was making a commotion out here. Calling for help, whatever. It's the middle of the night, the guys inside get spooked, and come out packing. Hardy sees two men coming at him with guns in their hands, he starts shooting, and they shoot back. However it went down, it looks like these three killed each other. Case solved.'

Gino's mouth turned down and his eyebrows went up while he considered. 'I don't know. Five shootings in this neighborhood in two days? This place is on fire all of a sudden. Maybe there's something bigger going down.'

They walked toward the open door of the house just as the first responders came out in a hurry. They looked a little freaked out, which didn't bode well for whatever was in that house, although Magozzi had trouble picturing something worse than the three bodies in the front yard.

One of the officers asked, 'Are you two the detectives?'

Magozzi nodded and showed his shield.

'Then there's something in that house you've gotta see right now.'

Gino narrowed his eyes. 'What are you walking us into, Officer?'

'No shooters, no people, but there are ears out here, you know? Better if you see it for yourselves.'

Magozzi and Gino followed the first responders back into the house, taking in everything they could on the way to the mysterious bad place that had thrown two seasoned beat cops so out of joint.

The interior was nothing but bare walls, and a couple metal folding chairs around a card table that held a laptop and some papers – an eerie ditto of yesterday's crime scene, sans the two dead guys on the floor in the living room.

One of the cops stopped at an open door at the end of the hallway and clicked on his flashlight, illuminating a dark room with boarded-up windows. 'You ever see anything like this, Detectives? I know I haven't, and this is my turf.'

The corona of the flashlight beam made a warm circle around the cold steel of guns and more guns – big, small, and everything in between: heavy artillery, boxes of ammo, and crates of God knew what, all arranged with efficiency and organization. It looked like a weapons repository at a military base.

'Holy shit,' Gino breathed.

'Pretty scary, right? No wonder we can't keep guns off the street. Looks to me like we've got a world-class arms dealer right here in the heart of the city.'

Magozzi pulled out his own flashlight and played it across the room, finally focusing on a rack of RPGs and the stack of crates labeled with explosives warning symbols. 'This isn't just arms we're looking at. This is war stuff. And if this house went up, it would level a city block. We have to get the hell out of here and call in the big boys.'

They all made fast tracks to the exit, but on the way out, Gino grabbed Magozzi's arm and stopped him briefly at the card table, gesturing to a piece of paper. It was a printed calendar page for October, with a bold square of black marker rendered around the thirty-first of the month – Halloween.

15

When Annie returned to Harley's loft Monday morning, resplendent in a shocking pink cashmere sheath, Harley and Roadrunner were already at their workstations. Harley spun in his chair and gave her a once-over. 'You're looking particularly soft and fuzzy this morning.'

Annie curtsied and deposited her tote on the floor by her desk. 'How are you two boys doing?'

Roadrunner smiled up at her. 'Good. We started rendering graphics for the history program. But the phones have been ringing off the hook. Schools all over the country have been calling.'

'Yeah,' Harley grumbled. 'Great for business, bad for work. It's driving us crazy. You want to play secretary today, honey? You could sit on my lap . . .'

'Shut up, Harley,' Annie snipped, pouring herself a mug of coffee at the credenza. There was a tantalizing plate of cookies just sitting there, looking sadly neglected, the poor things. She plucked one up between two pink nails that matched her dress exactly. 'Did anybody get an e-mail from Grace this morning?' she mumbled around a mouthful of chocolate and pecans.

Harley and Roadrunner shook their heads.

'Neither did I. This is the third day in a row I haven't gotten an e-mail from Grace.'

‘Maybe they’re having trouble with the satellite link,’ Roadrunner suggested.

‘Maybe.’ As Annie situated herself at her desk, the phone started ringing. ‘I’ve got it. Monkeewrench, Annie Belinsky speaking.’

The voice on the other end said, ‘Annie, don’t say a word.’

She almost squealed Grace’s name. The e-mails had been great, but hearing her voice after so many months almost made her make a mistake. When Grace said, ‘Don’t say a word,’ you clamped your lips closed and just listened. Annie put her on speaker so Harley and Roadrunner could hear, and waited.

‘You’re going to get an overnight package within the hour. Do exactly what it says.’

Annie nodded as if Grace could see it. ‘Yes’ was all she said, then the connection was broken.

She and Harley and Roadrunner looked at one another for a moment, then Harley kicked his chair out from under him. ‘I’ll go downstairs and open the gate.’

‘What do you think it is?’ Roadrunner asked quietly after Harley had left.

Annie didn’t raise her eyes. ‘Nothing good.’

When Harley came back upstairs with a FedEx envelope, Annie snatched it out of his hand and ripped it open. There were flash drives, two enlarged photocopies of Florida driver’s licenses, a picture of John Smith, and a note in Grace’s handwriting.

Licenses belong to two men who boarded our boat last night at sea and tried to kill John. I had to shoot them. They had John’s photo with them; he's a target. Flashes are a mirror of his hard drive. Find out who and why. I'm on my way home. John's off the grid.

The three of them stood in stunned silence, reading and rereading the note, as if the contents would change if they just kept looking at it.

'Jesus.' Harley was the first of them to say anything. 'This is completely freaking me out on so many levels, I don't even know where to start.'

Roadrunner was pale. Annie thought he looked like a quaking aspen that a stiff breeze could topple. 'Poor Grace,' he finally murmured. 'She had to kill two people.'

Annie nodded sympathetically because she knew exactly how it felt to kill somebody. She'd learned how hard it was at the age of seventeen, and Grace was dealing with all of that now. But the experience had given Annie a resilience and a cold pragmatism that neither Roadrunner nor Harley seemed to possess, because they were just standing there dieseling in idle like two slack-jawed idiots.

She grabbed the flash drives and shoved them into Harley's hands. 'You upload John's hard drive into the Beast – that's your baby.'

The Beast was a linked processing cluster of computers that performed like a supercomputer, and among the many tasks it could handle was finding, sorting, comparing, and collating massive amounts of information. The only trouble was, it was occupied at the moment. 'Annie, that thing is in the middle of rendering graphics for the American history thing right now, and it's using just about all the computing power we have. We have to shut it down and back it up before we even start to enter new data and repurpose it to search.'

'Well, what are you waiting for? Roadrunner, fire up our other search programs and start hacking John's FBI files. See if there's any underbrush hiding the wolves. I'll plug in the Florida IDs and follow the trail. I want to see where those two wannabe assassins have been, who they know, and, with any kind of luck, who put them on to John.'

Roadrunner bobbed his head.

Harley scratched his beard, thinking. 'Hey, Roadrunner. You know that new search platform you've been tweaking?'

'Yeah?'

'That thing is a turbo logarithmic monster. Think it's ready for a test drive?'

He smiled. 'Now's as good a time as any. I'll run home and get it. Can you guys handle the Beast until I get back?'

Harley crossed his massive arms across his equally massive chest. 'We made the Beast together, you skinny little shit. I can ride it like a cowboy. You want a lift back to your place?'

Roadrunner shook his head. 'I could use the fresh air.'

Annie touched him on the shoulder. 'Are you sure, honey? It's cold out there.'

He gave her a shy smile. 'Perfect biking weather.'

She clucked her tongue. 'Sloe-plum mad, you exercise people. I'll never get it.'

Every time Roadrunner mounted his bike and began to ride, he broke free from the dark, terrifying chrysalis that had suffocated him since childhood. On his bike, he could fly, and the faster he pedaled, the more distance he put between himself and the ugly shadows of his past – like the man with the hammer, for instance.

As his legs pumped furiously, he felt himself transforming into a different person, the person he wished he could be all the time, strong and fearless and powerful, capable of doing what needed to be done, no matter how hard it was. Maybe he could get there one day, just like Grace had finally done on John Smith's boat.

Faster, faster, faster, he chanted to himself. *I'm Lance Armstrong. Just a few more miles until the yellow shirt* . . .

Streetlights flashed by like strobes as he whipped down Summit Avenue, oblivious to traffic, oblivious to the blaring horns as he blazed through intersections, oblivious to everything except for the burn in his thighs, the booming of his heart, and the cold air searing his face.

He cut off into a quiet residential area that would save him a quarter mile, ripping so hard into the turn, his knee nearly scraped the pavement, but he never flinched, never wobbled; he just pumped faster and harder than Lance Armstrong ever had.

After the fifth mile, he got the secondary adrenaline rush he waited for whenever he rode hard, when the purity of his focus coalesced into a magical unity of man and machine. He wasn't Roadrunner anymore, he was an amalgamation of blood and bone and titanium – a superhero of his own design, and way better than anything from a comic book.

So strong was his focus, he'd never even noticed the taxi cab that had been tailing him since he'd left Harley's, creeping off the curb to follow him. And had he been paying any attention at all, he would have noticed that his tail had managed to stay with him until he'd finally reached his driveway in a very quiet neighborhood on Nicollet Island.

He left the garage door open while he wiped down his bike with a chamois, framing himself in broad daylight. On the street, the taxi passed his house, inched down to the end of the block, then turned around and moved slowly up to the curb in front of a house across the street. And that's when Roadrunner finally noticed it and completely dismissed it. There were always cabs in his neighborhood, idling at curbs for a pickup, just like there were in every neighborhood in every city. And he knew his neighbors across the street were both flight attendants and traveled a lot. There was nothing unusual about a cab waiting for a pickup on a chilly autumn day.

16

In any other part of the city, you start stringing yellow police tape and the neighbors come out of the woodwork, camera phones held high to catch the action. But not in Little Mogadishu. Maybe the residents here were used to seeing three dead bodies in a front yard, or maybe they had a little more respect than your average, camera-toting suburbanite. At any rate, by the time Gino and Magozzi and the first responders came out of the house, the street was virtually deserted. The women wearing abayas had skittered back to their hidey-holes and blinds were drawn over every window.

Gino looked around, puzzled. 'Where did everybody go?'

One of the officers made a face. 'They're back in their houses with their doors locked, and you better believe they won't open them again until we're out of here. We got lucky catching those few gals in the black shrouds on the street.'

'Abayas,' Magozzi said.

'Huh?'

'That's what you call their outfits.'

'Oh. Whatever. This is a real tight, closed community. Nobody here trusts the cops. You got to remember, a lot of these people came from countries where anybody in a uniform could chop their head off just for looking at them.'

A blue sedan snugged up to the curb and a tall man in a well-cut suit stepped out, looked around, then headed toward them. He looked FBI, but the suit sure didn't. No off-the-rack rumples for this guy. He also had an impressive bristle of blond hair and a tanned face with some age on it, but not much. He couldn't have been more than thirty.

The man stopped a few feet away and cocked his head. 'Detectives?'

Magozzi nodded. 'Yes. Leo Magozzi and my partner, Gino Rolseth.'

He offered a hand. 'Special Agent Dahl. I head the Bureau's anti-terror task force here. Thank you for the prompt call. I assume you called Hazmat.'

'They're en route. So's the Emergency Response Team.'

'Good. I'm not going to be able to do a walk-through until they clear the scene, but you've been in there, so tell me exactly what kind of ordnance you saw in that back room.'

Gino's tone wasn't exactly hostile, but it was close. 'What we saw was a buttload of weapons and explosives and RPGs and what I want to know is how they got here without you people knowing about it. I thought the Feds were supposed to be on the lookout for losers like that.' He jerked a thumb at the two bodies closest to the house.

Dahl met Gino's eyes head-on, which was pretty impressive, like facing down a bulldog. 'For your information, Detective, we've had these two on our radar for almost a month, ever since we received an anonymous tip on this address via an e-mail we couldn't trace.'

'Well, your radar sucks.'

Dahl sighed and glanced at Magozzi. 'Is he always like this?'

'Pretty much. What did the tip say?'

'All it said was: "Terror chatter on computer with al-Qaeda and al-Shabaab operatives," and then the address. So we put the house on twenty-four/seven surveillance for three weeks. That's about our limit for unsubstantiated tips. These two were not on the national watch list. They were students at the university on legitimate visas. They went to campus every morning, came back every night. Nothing remotely untoward, nothing to justify a subpoena. So we terminated twenty-four/seven and put them on our local watch list. We still had eyes on them, but not around the clock.'

Gino folded his lips together and shook his head. 'Well, when your eyes weren't on them, these guys stockpiled an armory and I'm guessing they weren't getting RPGs through the US mail. There had to be some big trucks going in and out and you guys missed it. Nice going.'

Dahl straightened his shoulders and took such a deep breath that his nostrils compressed. 'Listen, Detective, we have about fifty houses in this neighborhood alone on our local watch list. We've been watching some of them for five years, so we're spread a little thin. Besides, they could have accumulated whatever is in that room long before we got the tip.'

Gino tried to backtrack without backing down. 'Okay, I'll give you that,' he grumbled.

Dahl glanced over at the house. 'Is there a computer in there?'

Magozzi nodded. 'A computer and a lot of paperwork.

Your translators are going to be working around the clock. But look at the bright side – our homicides are solved and they gave you free entry, so you don't need a subpoena. But there's something else in there that caught our eye. Yesterday, we covered the homicides of the two Somali men who had the four Native American girls locked up in their house.'

Dahl nodded. 'I saw the coverage. That was a nice catch.'

'It was pure luck. If those two hadn't been killed, we never would have found the girls. But in that house we also noticed a calendar with October thirty-first circled. We saw the same thing inside this house. And my first creepy thought was, gee, four Somalis, all dirtbags, with the same date front and center? What if something's going down on Halloween?'

'I'll look into it. Can you send me copies of your reports?'

Gino snorted. 'No problem. We happen to believe in intra-agency cooperation.'

Dahl's mouth twitched in a faint smile. 'So do I. I've never been a big fan of turf wars between agencies.'

Wow, Magozzi thought. An up-front Fed who wasn't marking territory. Maybe this was a whole new breed of agent he was too old to know about until now.

Within fifteen minutes the number of vehicles on the street had tripled. Hazmat was there; so was Homeland Security, the Bureau of Criminal Apprehension, the ERT boys, and maybe the Future Farmers of America, for all Magozzi knew. Young men and women in Medical Examiner windbreakers worked the bodies with Crime Scene techs, oblivious to the chaos around them.

Jimmy Grimm was there, trying to direct the inexperienced in the proper management of a homicide scene, but if the team he had at Aimee's murder site was the B team, these baby faces had to be even deeper into the alphabet. Every department was getting spread too thin these days. Jimmy looked seriously frustrated; the youngsters under him kept glancing worriedly at the Hazmat truck.

Hazmat went in first – dangerous material on-site was the one and only condition that put evidence at a homicide scene in second place. Magozzi felt a little sorry for the Hazmat boys. Mostly they handled suspicious packages and vehicles. It wasn't often they had to walk past fresh kills on their way to work. Magozzi hoped they were all practiced at holding down their cookies. Throwing up in one of those sealed helmets would be a bitch.

Magozzi's, Gino's, and Dahl's heads swiveled at the same time. They'd all been on potential hazard sites enough times to know that when a guy jumped out of the Hazmat command truck and started running full bore toward the cops controlling the scene, something bad was coming down.

'You know him?' Dahl asked.

Magozzi nodded. 'You bet. That's Barney Wollmeyer, one of the best we've got. What he says, we do.'

Wollmeyer stopped in front of Magozzi, kept his headphones on, but tipped his microphone away from his mouth. 'The boys inside say evacuate four city blocks ASAP. They're not moving any of the stuff in there until it's clear. They found detonators connected to some real bad chemicals. No way to know if they're activated.'

Magozzi was running toward the sergeant on scene before Wollmeyer stopped talking. 'Clear 'em out, Sergeant. Four city blocks in no time.'

The sergeant's brow furrowed. 'What's in that house?'

'Explosives, just for starters.'

'You're shitting me.'

'I'm not.'

'We're going to need a hell of a lot more translators to clear four city blocks.'

Magozzi blew out a nervous breath. 'They work on call. It'll take a while to get them here. In the meantime, clear these houses. I don't care how you do it. Hazmat is scared.'

While Magozzi was talking to the sergeant, Gino made a beeline for Jimmy Grimm. 'Load these bodies up, Jimmy. Get them out of here before you don't have any bodies left to transport.'

'We're not finished with the in situ.'

'Fuck the in situ. We're evacuating. There's some bad shit in that house.'

As everyone scrambled to clear the bodies from the scene, Magozzi and Gino rejoined Agent Dahl at the curb. He was watching the sudden activity as people loaded the dead into body bags and hand-carried them to the van. No time for gurneys; no time for anything.

Gino glanced down at the pathetic remains of Joe Hardy being shoved unceremoniously into a bag by panicked techs, then looked away.

Evacuations were usually fast and very orderly – you tell any Minnesotan there's a natural gas leak or a creep with a gun in the neighborhood, they walked right out of their houses with kids in tow, pets under their arms, and did exactly what they were told. This one wasn't much different after the sergeant figured out how to communicate without a translator. He and the troops immediately started running from house to house, waving their arms and shouting 'BOOM!,' frantically gesturing the evacuees to follow the pied piper cop trotting toward Franklin Avenue five blocks away.

Magozzi watched a parade of women – some of them in Western garb, some in traditional Muslim clothing, all moving quickly but calmly to follow the officer leading them to safety. They hurried their children along or carried them, like any mothers of any culture, in spite of any mistrust they may have had of authority, and something about that made Magozzi sad.

He listened to the cacophonous chatter of those who probably understood a bit of English explaining the emergency to those who didn't, and wondered what they were thinking. Were the strangers in uniforms leading them to safety or into danger? It must have been an agonizing doubt, until one of the men in blue scooped up a tired child next to a tired mother and held him close as he trotted forward.

In that moment, Magozzi loved his city, his brothers on the force, and his country. That was the story here, he thought as he watched the media film the fleeing caravan.

But that wasn't the video that made YouTube and Facebook and most of the media almost instantaneously. The video that went viral showed four women in abayas running helter-skelter down the street screaming while a cop tried to chase them down and point them in the right direction.

After the human traffic in the street had thinned, all the official vehicles burned a little rubber leaving the four-block zone. Only the Hazmat van was left.

Magozzi weaved the Cadillac around the hastily erected road barriers and headed for the freeway. They passed the big, lumbering Hazmat containment truck coming in as they went out. 'Hazmat is going to be in there for hours, probably all night.' He glanced over at Gino. 'You know what that means.'

Gino pulled the seat belt away from his belly and just hung on to it to keep his hands still. 'Yeah. I know. Now, after everything else that's gone down today, we have to tell some poor woman her husband is dead.'

17

Beth Hardy was in her kitchen, weeping over a burned chicken, which was absolutely ridiculous. She'd lived through Joe's three tours in Iraq and Afghanistan and then she'd lived through the diagnosis of pancreatic cancer and his death sentence and not once had she cried. She'd sucked it up, kept on a happy face, and never once given in to the emotions that were eating her from the inside out. And now a stupid burned chicken had reduced her to tears. It felt like she would never be able to stop crying. But of course she would.

She jumped when she heard car doors slamming. Oh God. For all the years Joe was overseas, the sound of a car pulling up to the front of the house terrified her. It was so unreasonable – friends, family, the mailman – everyone came in cars – but that didn't stop the fear. She'd been waiting for the bad car, waiting for two Marines in full dress to come up her walk and tell her Joe was dead. Even though he wasn't overseas anymore, old fears, like old habits, died hard. She took a breath to calm herself, wiped away her tears, and walked to the front door.

The Hardy residence was a judiciously tended, two-story stucco in the southwestern part of the city, just off Minnehaha Creek. Magozzi pulled the Cadillac up to the curb. Driveways were for family and friends and people who were invited and welcome, and he and Gino certainly didn't fit into any of those categories.

Magozzi looked over the lawn cropped close for winter, the neatly trimmed shrubs, flower beds still blooming despite the lateness of the season. Somebody went to a lot of trouble to keep up the place, to keep it looking fine and loved, and it sure as hell wasn't the poor emaciated guy they'd found on that scruffy, untended Little Mogadishu curb. No way he would have had the strength.

'No leaves on this lawn, Leo.'

'Yeah.'

'Somebody in this house was watching their world fall apart, and they still raked the lawn.'

'Gino, you're killing me.'

'Sorry. I hate notifications.'

Magozzi straightened his own tie. 'You ready?'

'No.'

'Let's go.'

They walked slowly up the straight, carefully edged walk to a porch with a white railing. Potted flowers, some purple stuff, corn shocks, and pumpkins adorned both sides of the front steps. 'Nice place,' Gino murmured. 'Really nice.'

Lately he'd been obsessed with landscaping and seasonal decorations. Where that had come from, Magozzi had no clue. Probably from watching the same evil home and garden channel that marginalized people who didn't rake.

'It reminds me of my grandma's house,' Magozzi said. 'She had stacks of journals where she kept records on how she decorated for this or that holiday, so she never did the same thing twice.'

'No kidding? Hell, my grandma threw a pumpkin on the porch for Halloween and a plastic Santa in the yard for Christmas and called it a day. Both of them usually stuck around until spring.'

They'd reached the front door by then and put on their game faces, the nervous distraction of family memories on hold.

The lock clicked immediately and the door swung open. She wasn't as young as she was in the wallet photo, and not nearly as fresh-faced. She had short blond hair and blue eyes still puffy from crying, or maybe lack of sleep. She looked puzzled and slightly alarmed to see two strangers in suits on her front stoop.

Gino and Magozzi showed her their shields. 'Good morning, ma'am. I'm Detective Magozzi, and this is Detective Rolseth. Are you Mrs Joseph Hardy?'

She frowned, deep lines suddenly etching ancient worry into a face that otherwise seemed quite youthful, at least in repose. 'Yes, I'm Beth Hardy.'

'Could we have a word with you?'

'Of course.' Her response was pleasant but guarded as she opened the door and gestured them inside. 'How can I help you?'

'We're so sorry, Mrs Hardy, but we're not here with good news. There was a shooting in Minneapolis last night with three fatalities. We believe your husband was one of the victims.'

You never knew how survivors were going to react when you delivered this kind of news. Magozzi thought he'd seen the full spectrum of emotions over the years, but Beth Hardy didn't express any of them. No horror, no grief, no hysteria; she just looked confused. 'That's impossible. There's been a mistake. Joe isn't even in the city. He's up north on a hunting trip with his friends.'

'I'm sorry, but he was carrying his wallet.'

She shook her head strongly. 'No. I'm sorry for whoever it was, and he might have had Joe's wallet, but it wasn't Joe. I told you, he's up north. He called me when he got there, and again before he went to bed. I talked to Joe, I talked to his friends. They even put the phone on speaker so I could hear the loons crying on the lake.'

'The driver's license photo matched the victim, Mrs Hardy.'

'Well, it wasn't Joe. I'll call him right now and prove it.' She grabbed a phone from the foyer table and punched in a number, listened for a moment, then put it down. 'Voice mail. I'll try his friends.' She punched in another set of numbers and put the phone on speaker.

After a few rings, a Texas drawl filled the room. 'Beth, darlin', is that you?'

'Yes, it's me. Put Joe on, will you, Claude?'

'Well, I'd be tickled to do that just as soon as he gets back.'

'Back from where? Where is he?'

'Lord knows. Woke up and he'd already lit out. We figured he went to pick us up some breakfast before the hunt. Should be back any time now. How about I have him give you a ring back?'

'Claude, the Minneapolis police are here. There was a shooting last night and one of the victims had Joe's wallet. They think it's him.'

'Well, that's pure-ass impossible. We tucked Joey in not

too long after he called you, then Chief and I stayed up 'til the wee hours, drinkin' a little, jawin' a little . . .' He stopped in midsentence and silence filled the foyer. Beth Hardy stood there, expressionless, as if someone had just pushed the pause button on her life.

'Beth?' The drawl came back through the speaker, gentle now. 'Beth, Joe had his wallet with him last night. Pulled it out to show us that picture he took of you at Minnehaha Falls. Lord in heaven.'

Beth just closed her eyes.

No matter how many rooms you had in your house, there was always the one that was truly lived in. For the Hardy family, it was a cozy sitting room with well-used leather furniture, a big-screen TV, and lots of personal stuff – family photos, trophies, little knickknacks picked up here and there that were meaningful to the home dwellers and no one else. It was a place of comfort, of family, of solace, and every survivor of a crime took the cops to the room that made them feel safest.

Magozzi noticed a framed photo of a robust man in his Marine dress uniform, a chest full of medals winking at the camera lens. There was no mistaking the man's identity, despite the sixty- or seventy-pound weight loss that had occurred since this shot had been taken – this was a photo of Joe Hardy in full health. There were other photos of Joe with two older men – one tall and lanky, the other much broader, with a long black braid shot through with gray and striking features that alluded to Native American blood. In all the photos, the trio was standing over one dead animal or another, holding big guns and wearing bigger smiles. Joe's hunting buddies.

'Please, sit down, Detectives.' Beth gestured to the sofa while she sank into an opposite facing club chair. The end table beside it was adorned with nothing more than a Kleenex box concealed in a bamboo tissue holder, a poignant and telling detail. When life circumstances made you cry a lot – and cancer tended to have that effect on one's lachrymal glands – you integrated useful survival tools into the decor.

Even though Beth Hardy was the perfect portrait of a military wife – brave, dry-eyed, and probably in shock to learn that her husband had been killed by a bullet instead of cancer – she still pulled out several tissues and crumpled them in her hands, worrying them like prayer beads in her lap. The Kimberly-Clark rosary – Magozzi and Gino had seen it countless times. 'Tell me what happened, Detectives, because I'm very confused right now.'

Magozzi leaned forward in his seat. 'We were called to a crime scene early this morning, at six-forty-two Camden Drive. We found your husband and two other men outside. All of them had guns. It's our assumption that they killed each other, but ballistics will have to officially confirm that.'

She nodded slowly. 'Joe always carried a gun. He was being treated for pancreatic cancer at Riverside and the neighborhood made him nervous.'

Gino nodded a sympathetic acknowledgment. 'Does that address on Camden mean anything to you or did Joe ever mention it?'

'No. I only know it's close to the hospital. I grew up in that neighborhood, and so did Joe.' She turned to look out the window. 'I don't know why he was down there. It doesn't make sense.'

'Can you think of any circumstances where your husband might have come back to Minneapolis unexpectedly? Perhaps to visit his doctor?'

She shook her head adamantly. 'Not without calling me. And not without telling his friends. And if he'd been that sick, he would have gone to a hospital close to Elbow Lake.' Beth Hardy looked down at her lap, at the shredded tissue making sad, stringy confetti on her thighs. 'But if he had come down for treatment, he wouldn't have parked on Camden. He always parked in the hospital lot.'

Gino and Magozzi shared a pained glance. 'We found his car in the hospital lot, Mrs Hardy,' Magozzi said. 'And we asked ourselves that same question. We thought that maybe he'd become disoriented because of his condition and got lost. Stumbled into a bad situation at a bad time of night. If you know the area, you know there's a lot of gang activity there now, a lot of shady characters, and . . . well . . . a man walking into somebody's yard at that hour of the night, maybe asking for help, might cause problems.' Magozzi hesitated and then jumped in. 'Especially that particular yard.'

'Why that particular yard?'

'You haven't seen the news today?'

She shook her head.

'The house where we found your husband was filled with weapons and explosives. Which might explain why the two men inside considered anyone approaching the house a threat.'

Beth looked over at the photograph of Joe in his dress blues. 'Where is he?' she whispered.

Gino and Magozzi shared a miserable glance. It was one thing to hear somebody you loved had died; it was another thing altogether to imagine them in a morgue cooler getting prodded and violated by a stranger. 'He's with the Medical Examiner,' Magozzi finally said.

'When will he be . . . released?'

'I can promise you we'll do everything we can to make sure it's as soon as possible.'

Beth nodded woodenly. 'Thank you for that.'

18

Juan Flores sat in the dark, hot living room of his Culver City, California rental, listening to the violent smacks of palm fronds against the side of the bungalow, as if they were clamoring for indoor shelter from the ferocious Santa Ana winds that were shredding them.

The storied winds had blown in earlier in the day, engulfing Los Angeles in bone-dry, superheated desert air, along with the potential for disaster. It was late in the year, and wildfires were already starting to pop up in the canyons and along the backbones of the Santa Monica and San Bernadino Mountains, feeding on the summer-scorched scrub, fueled by the wind. Malibu was already bracing for an onslaught, because they were always in the danger zone – the posh western terminus for eager fires racing from inland to sea as if they wanted to extinguish themselves, and do it in a good zip code while they were at it.

Most Angelenos shuttered themselves up when the hot winds came, waiting out the fierce temperatures, dusty air, and sometimes even ash blown in from a seared hillside somewhere upwind. Those who had the luxury of doing such a thing in the comfort of their air-conditioned offices, homes, and apartments prayed that the city's fragile, overtaxed power grid could meet the energy demands that were keeping them cool. If they had extra prayers to spread around, they'd use them on additionally imploring God to stop the fires. But not before He made damn sure Pacific Gas and Electric had their shit together so a brownout wouldn't interrupt their climate control.

Big pussies, Juan thought, entertaining a brief fantasy of seeing all those Italian-suit-wearing, German-car-driving whiners hoofing it through the Iraqi desert with sixty-pound packs on their backs like he'd done for the past two years of his life. They didn't know shit about what real heat was. And they didn't know shit about what real sacrifice was, which was a hell of a lot more than living without central air for an hour.

The lights flickered for the sixth time in the past fifteen minutes, a sure precursor to an inevitable brownout. But he was prepared, with a gun, a beer, and a flashlight. A man didn't need much more than that to survive. Now all he had to do was wait.

It was half past midnight when the cell phone on the end table next to him finally started buzzing, an unfamiliar area code lighting up the display in the twilight of the room. The number would be fake, he knew. These days, if you knew what you were doing, you could program any phone to display as an incoming call from the McDonald's in Pushkin Square if you wanted to.

This particular phone had been silent for a while, but he'd been notified yesterday to expect this call tonight, a call to duty, and he was ready for it. 'Been waiting to hear from you, man,' he answered.

'Should I take that as an affirmative?'

Juan looked up as the single light overhead in the kitchen flickered, then finally died. 'You should take that as a

"Hell, yes."' He crooked the phone between his ear and shoulder, clicked on the flashlight, and followed its faint photon trail to the front window to peer through the slats in the dusty vinyl shade. The neighborhood was dark, and the view he had of the city farther out looked black, too. LA, or at least a big part of it, was off the grid. PG&E had finally given up the ghost. 'You have a location for me?'

The man rattled off an address about two miles east of his Culver City bungalow, and Juan burned it into his memory, then recited it back. He didn't want to write anything down, but he didn't want to make a mistake either. 'Perfect timing. We just went into brownout here, and it looks like the target is in the zone. I've got everything going for me tonight.'

There was a slight hesitation on the other end of the line. 'You need to know something. Our source tracked three different computers and three different cell phone signals coming out of the house. Multiple user names and ISPs, set up with separate dummy accounts.'

'So there's three of them.'

'Or more.'

'No problem. I've got this covered. Check the LA police report bulletin tomorrow morning, and that'll be your mission complete from me.'

The faceless, nameless caller he'd been speaking with for a couple months was silent for a long time, and Juan thought he heard the clatter of a keyboard in the background. 'Godspeed,' he finally said. 'Be safe.'

'Semper fi.'

'Semper fi.'

Juan hung up and pulled a duffel bag out from underneath his sofa. He didn't need the flashlight to find it; he knew where it was at all times, down to the millimeter. It looked like a workout bag, and nobody in LA ever questioned a fit man carrying a workout bag late at night, especially if they were wearing gym clothes, which he was. It was the perfect cover. Nobody would ever guess what was really inside his bag. It was go time.

It took less than an hour for Juan to jog to his site with his duffel, get in position under the cover of an untended oleander hedge, and recon his targets. The shades on the east side of the house weren't drawn, which gave him a clean line of sight into the kitchen. Through his night vision goggles he saw the glowing green figures of five men, all sitting around a table. Perfect. This was going to be easier than target practice.

When the first bullet hit its mark, the remaining four men froze at the table, startled by the shot, but unaware of the hole in their companion's forehead. Damn, Juan was loving this power outage.

Two, three, four . . . dropping like flies . . . oh Jesus. Shit. Where was the fifth one?

19

By Tuesday morning, the Little Mogadishu shootings had become the most searched news story on the Web – the video of the screaming ladies running from the cop was media crack and network and cable were running it non-stop. To make matters worse, someone had leaked a little too much about the contents of the weapons cache and the IDs of the victims. Great fodder for conspiracy theorists, who had apparently decided overnight that Minneapolis was home to an unknown supercell of global terrorists who were regrouping in the naive heartland.

The city was taking center stage on the terrorist front. Again. Made the city look bad; made law enforcement in the city look worse.

Gino and Magozzi had ranted about it over the phone last night after they'd both watched Chief Malcherson and Special Agent in Charge Paul Shafer deliver their non-answers to a few questions from reporters still mobbing the crime scene.

No, we can't confirm the types of weapons found in the house, nor can we confirm that there were bomb-making materials and schematics on-site. No, the shooting victims have not been positively identified as Somali students. The investigation is ongoing. There will be no comment on those issues at this time.

Well, Christ. How stupid was that? Photos and biographies of the two victims were all over the Internet, although God knew how anyone had gotten hold of them, and there was MPD and the FBI both saying that they couldn't confirm that the emperor had no clothes. Pissed Magozzi off.

And what pissed him off more was that the explosives house had pushed the murder of a fifteen-year-old Native girl and the rescue of the other four girls that had been kidnapped with her right off the media radar. The story had been top of the news, right where it should have been, until two dirtbags sitting on a buttload of explosives met their maker early. The bad guys were dead and the Native American girls were a media ghost of breaking news past.

He turned off the TV in disgust, rinsed out his cereal bowl, and left the house. The air was crisp this morning, and dew had shellacked everything with a layer of wet, from the grass to the cars parked out on his street. There was the slightest hint of burning wood in the air, mingling with the vegetal smell of wet leaves, and something mysteriously fruity behind it all, which brought Magozzi right back to his first day of kindergarten.

Their neighbor Earl had let him pick a fragrant, ripe apple from his front yard tree to bring to his teacher, and his father had walked with him the two blocks to the school, carrying his lunch box for him. The apple had scored him big-time points with the teacher, and she'd eaten it during snack time. Nowadays, a teacher wouldn't dare eat anything a student brought in for fear it would be laced with rat poison. He was officially old.

Johnny McLaren was the only one in the office when Magozzi and Gino arrived, his elbows propped on his desk, his fingers raking upward through his red hair, making him look like Bozo the Clown. He'd caught the domestic shooting that had left five dead.

'You have your case sewn up, Johnny?' Magozzi asked.

Johnny raised his head and showed bloodshot eyes and a two-day stubble. 'It'll be in the courts for months. Normally, the asshole who kills his ex-girlfriend and half her family has the decency to shoot himself in the head afterward. Not this guy. He just stands there over the mess he made, holding the gun until the cops arrived. Now he'll get a nice long trial, thirty or forty appeals, and then probably do a few years until some sappy parole board decides he's been rehabilitated and deserves a second chance outside. Christ.' He made a futile effort to smooth down his hair. 'And just think, I'm the lucky one. You guys really walked into a shit storm in Little Mogadishu yesterday. I caught some of the coverage. Rolseth, your ass ate up the screen.'

'Screw you, McLaren.'

'It was good stuff, especially the cop carrying that kid.'

'The guys on scene did a good job,' Magozzi said.

'Yeah, well that's not what al-Jazeera is saying.'

'You watch al-Jazeera?' Magozzi asked.

'Yeah. My Arabic needs work. Anyhow, they're running a loop of those four women running and screaming while the cop tried to turn them around. INFIDEL AMERICAN POLICE HUNT DOWN AND KILL OUR WOMEN was the caption.'

'Super,' Gino muttered, sorting through the pile of incoming mail on his desk that had accumulated since yesterday. He took his time with the report from Ballistics and said, 'Crap. The rifling on the slugs the ME pulled out of the kidnappers doesn't match any gun on the registry. No suspects, no gun. We're going to have to wait for that particular shooter to pop someone else, or this is going into Unsolveds.'

'But,' Magozzi said, holding aloft a piece of paper from his own desk, 'the knife in the sink had Aimee Sergeant's blood on it, and the prints match one of the dead Somalis'.'

Chief Malcherson had a tendency to fill up the room when he walked in, not just because he was tall, but because the man had a presence. As always, he looked like a well-dressed mistake who had been errantly dropped into an alien environment that was defined by worn acoustical panels, no-frills office furniture, and the off-the-rack suits and ties of his underlings.

All three detectives said good morning to the Chief at the same time.

Malcherson nodded a greeting to all of them, then focused on Magozzi and Gino. 'I hear you gentlemen think there may be a connection between the two men who kidnapped the girls and the homicides at the explosives house.'

'Where did you hear that, sir?' Gino asked.

'Special Agent in Charge Shafer said his man at the evacuation yesterday told him about the calendars you saw in both houses. That was nice attention to detail, Detectives.'

'It may not mean anything. Let's hope it doesn't,' Magozzi said.

'Agent Shafer also asked me to let you know that agents questioned the girls at the hospital. Each one of them positively identified the murdered Somali men who were holding them as the men who also took them from the reservation. He said to thank you for helping them solve their kidnapping case.'

Gino smiled with one side of his mouth. 'And I'm sure Shafer will give MPD full credit in his next press conference.'

Malcherson looked at Gino like he was an obnoxious relative who showed up once a year on Thanksgiving and told off-color jokes at the dinner table. 'Keep me apprised of your progress on the four homicides.'

McLaren waited until the door closed behind Malcherson before getting out of his chair and slipping on a sad-sack sports coat. 'I hate to leave you guys all alone, but I've got a hearing over at the courthouse.'

'DUI?' Gino asked pleasantly.

'Nah, that puke bag who killed five members of the same family filed a police brutality charge against me because his cuffs were too tight.'

'Did his hands fall off?'

'No.'

'You're golden, then. See you later.'

Gino dropped into his chair like a rock, then started shuffling papers.

Magozzi followed suit, fiddling with the settings on his new office chair, which he hadn't quite figured out yet. Amazing how chairs could be more complicated than computer operating systems.

20

Ten minutes after McLaren left, the direct Homicide line lit up, and Magozzi stared down at the clunky old phone that probably dated back a decade. Technology moved faster now, and ten years by today's standards was more like a century. But it still worked, and budgets were too tight to squander money on unnecessary new phone systems. The added bonus of the department's frugality was that he knew how to run it and he could actually see the buttons, unlike the microscopic ones on his new smartphone. By his prediction, it wouldn't be long before the entire world got streamlined down to the size of a peanut and humans wouldn't fit in it anymore.

'Great,' Gino opined from his adjoining desk. 'Another murder.'

Magozzi read the caller ID tag on the display console. 'It's not Dispatch, and it's not a transfer from the switchboard. Direct dial, outside line.' He picked up and answered. 'Minneapolis Homicide, Detective Magozzi speaking.'

'Detective Steve Kramer here, Detroit Homicide. I know you have your hands full this morning, but do you have a couple minutes?' The man's voice was stressed, terse, and crunchy, like he was getting over a case of laryngitis, or maybe a late night out.

Magozzi paused for a moment. Detroit Homicide? That was weird, and he wondered if a crank call had slipped through somehow. It happened sometimes, especially after a splashy case that went national – but then he heard what sounded like a million phones ringing in the background and a lot of competing voices, shouting out things only cops would. The call was legit, and business was obviously booming in Detroit. 'You've got all the time you need, Detective Kramer. Let me conference in my partner, Gino Rolseth.' He gestured for Gino to pick up the phone, then quickly scrawled a brief, explanatory note so he'd know who he was about to talk to.

Gino's pale eyebrows rose and punctuated his forehead with little question marks as he joined in on the conversation. 'Good morning, Detective Kramer. Gino Rolseth here.'

'Great, glad I caught you both. I'll keep this short, but I wanted to touch base with you on your terror case that's burning up the news right now. This might be a desperate homicide cop's last stab at solving his own cold case, but I think I might have some kind of a weird dovetail here in Detroit.'

Magozzi and Gino shared a hopeful glance. 'What kind of dovetail?' Magozzi asked.

Kramer blew out a breath. 'Basically, a murdered terrorist – an Egyptian national with a lot of bomb-making crap stashed in his kitchen cupboards, along with some al-Qaeda cheerleading manuals, that according to the Feds. No suspects. Obviously, I don't know all the details of your case, just what I heard on the news this morning, but does that pretty much sum up your situation there?'

'Yeah,' Magozzi said, his brain quickly firing out of early a.m. sludge mode. 'Except we have *two* murdered terrorists, which we are not allowed to call terrorists yet, they were Somali, not Egyptian, and they were sitting on a pile of guns and explosives.'

'Terror's an equal-opportunity job,' Kramer said, his voice laced with cynicism. 'You can be from anywhere and want to blow up shit.'

'Good point. When did your case go down?'

'About a month and a half ago. I know it's early in the game for you two, but any viable suspects straight out of the gate?'

'No. And the Feds have all the evidence now. All we have are the bodies and the guns, and we've only got them because they were in the front yard. If there were any tells in the house, we're not going to see them until the Feds decide to read us in.'

'Yeah, I know about that, trust me, but it's not necessarily a bad thing. The computers they confiscated at our scene here in Detroit churned up a whole mess of stuff, and it led to some more arrests in Detroit and Dearborn. And Massachusetts. Listen, I'm pretty close to retirement and I'd love to go out with the perfect closing record I'm sitting on now, but in this one case, I don't care if I go out with an unsolved. In my mind, the only good terrorist is a dead one, and somebody took care of it. But I sure as hell would like to find out what kind of perp uses a garrote to kill people.'

'He was *garroted*?' Gino asked incredulously. 'You mean, like piano wire stuff?'

'Yeah, I probably forgot to mention that. But the ME confirmed cause of death. See what I mean about a weird dovetail? Similar scenes, but different MOs. Nothing to hang our hats on. If something pops on your end, give me a call, will you?'

'Sure thing, Detective . . .' Gino started to say, but Magozzi interrupted.

'I know this is kind of a weird question, Detective Kramer, but we found a calendar at our scene with Halloween circled. You see anything like that at yours?'

Kramer was silent for a few moments. 'Yeah, I did. Another weird dovetail. Is it going anywhere?'

'The Feds on our end are looking into it. You might want to give a heads-up to your field office.'

Magozzi signed off and glanced up at Gino. 'So what do you think?'

Gino looked down at his desk calendar. October twenty-fifth. 'I think I'll call Agent Dahl.'

While Gino was talking to Dahl, Magozzi played with the lumbar-support button on his chair, and immediately felt the stitch in his back disappear. Amazing.

Gino hung up. 'Dahl says hi and to give you a big, fat kiss for sharing info. He also said to turn on the television.'

'Why?'

Gino shrugged and walked over to turn on the tiny television on the file cabinet and the sound and a female news anchor's voice filled up the room.

'. . . five men gathered around a kitchen table were targeted and assassinated by a single gunman in the Culver City neighborhood of Los Angeles last night, who was himself the victim of return fire. But the story doesn't end there. Within an hour of the reported shootings, Hazmat crews were on-site and a neighborhood evacuation was under way, implying that there was something brewing in that house besides coffee.' The screen cut to a night shot of police cars, Hazmat trucks, and fleeing neighbors that looked a lot like the scene in Minneapolis yesterday.

Magozzi pulled out his national police directory and punched in a number. 'I'm going to call Culver City. I figure our only shot at information is from the local first responders. Every other agency is going to be shut down tight.'

'Good thought.'

Magozzi went through the song and dance of getting connected to the right department and the right man, then hooked the receiver in his shoulder as he scribbled notes. When the conversation ended abruptly, he threw his notepad on his desk.

'That was a short call.'

'They are seriously freaked out there. The first responder I talked to was scared to death someone was going to walk in on him. The Feds are crawling all over his office.'

'So what'd you get?'

Magozzi said, 'Basically, their scene was pretty much a duplicate of ours – and Detroit's for that matter. A houseful of explosives, and a whole lot of radical Islamist crap lying around. The guys inside were Arab types, the cop said, but by his own admission he can't tell a Somali from a Samurai. The shooter bought it, so they got an immediate ID on him. One Juan Flores, ex-Marine, did a couple tours in Iraq, came home and landed a job as a diesel mechanic with some big trucking outfit. No criminal record.'

Gino leaned forward, pressing his belly on the edge of his desk. 'What did he say when you asked him about a calendar?'

'They've got one, too.'

21

A woman who reminded Magozzi of Grace MacBride was sitting on his front porch when he pulled into his driveway Tuesday night. Then again, almost every woman reminded him of Grace, no matter how thin the resemblance.

This one had dark hair like Grace, but it was really, really short, and she was wearing sandals and a sundress. Tanned, bare legs, bare arms, no boots, nowhere to conceal a gun. Not Grace. Not that exposed. Besides, this woman was holding a purse. As far as he knew, Grace didn't even own a purse, and this one was weird – cheap vinyl with fish appliqués all over it. Definitely not her style. But there was something about her rigid posture, something about her demeanor and the intensity that emanated from her, that made him think twice about her identity.

Move, feet. Maybe Grace, maybe not, but you're never going to find out standing here in the driveway looking like a dork.

Halfway to the porch he could see her, he could *feel* her, and suddenly his legs felt funny, like those multijointed wooden puppets that bobble and collapse at the whim of whoever was pulling the strings. He reached for the railing to steady himself as he climbed the three wooden steps. 'Grace.'

Magozzi hardly knew what to do with all the body parts and emotions fighting for prominence. Oddly, the hardest thing to deal with was her hair. The bare legs and arms and her tanned toes in sandals screamed change, but the short hair frightened him in some way his Italian genes may have understood but his logic missed. So he stood there on the porch, looking down at the crappy chaise, paralyzed.

And then a truly frightening thing happened. She stood up, hesitated for the smallest of seconds, then moved into him, wrapping her arms around his neck, burying her head with that short, scary hair into his shoulder.

'Hello, Magozzi.'

It hadn't been an easy three months for Magozzi. He hadn't been sorting through his feelings or anything stupid like that, just dealing with them when they showed up.

Feeling sorry for himself was useless, humiliating. That had lasted for about five seconds after Grace told him that night she needed to get away, from him, from everything.

I need a change, Magozzi. I have to change.

Why? You're perfect.

No. I'm not. I'm scared all the time.

And you think getting away is going to change that?

Maybe.

To where?

John's going to take me sailing for a few months.

Bingo. The rage had exploded in his stomach and climbed up to his face, making it red and hot. So he'd turned away from her and headed for the door, just like that.

Wait, Magozzi. Let me explain.

Yeah, right. Thanks very much but no thanks. When a

woman says sayonara, I'm going to go off with another man for a few months, you didn't hang around for explanations, looking weird and out of place. You just turned on your heel and split.

The rage had faded in a hurry. It was just plain unproductive. The only emotion that kept cropping up through the months was bitterness. He was hanging on to that like an old woman clutching her pocketbook.

But he was better. He'd dated a couple women whose company he really enjoyed, and a few more who'd bored him silly. So, step by step he was putting his life back together again. And just when he felt like he was making some progress, here comes Grace, popping back into his world without his permission, messing with his head.

He kept his hands at his sides so he wouldn't touch her, but feeling her arms around his neck, her breath on his skin, felt like coming home. Shit. He took a quick step backward. The first words he said were utterly frivolous and completely important. 'Where's Charlie?'

'I dropped him off at Harley's before I came here. Can we go inside? I'm freezing.'

Magozzi eyed her scanty wardrobe, wondering what in the hell she had been thinking. Hot fall days here were one thing, but the night temperatures always plummeted. 'Of course you're freezing. You're dressed like you're still in Florida.'

'I've been driving nonstop for two and a half days. I didn't have time to change. I haven't even been home yet. Let me in or kick me out, but do it soon, because I don't have much left in me right now, and I know you've got a lot on your plate this week.'

Magozzi conceded the point by tipping his head.

'Harley brought me up to date on what's been going on. The murders, the kidnapped girls . . .'

'Is this going somewhere, Grace?'

She took a breath. 'I just want you to know I understand what you're dealing with.'

Magozzi turned away from her and keyed open the door. Grace felt some fracture between them, as if she didn't have the privilege of discussing his cases with him anymore. There was too much on the periphery, nibbling at the way they related. He was clearly exhausted, and so was she. But he was also tormented by her leaving, and probably by what kind of relationship she had with John, even though he wouldn't ask her outright. It felt like an open hand against her chest, holding her at a distance.

'I need a favor, Magozzi. I know you're busy. It's a few phone calls, if you could see your way clear to doing that.'

Magozzi didn't hesitate. It didn't matter much, he thought, when people you cared about hurt you; when they asked for help, you had to be there. 'What do you need?'

'Thank you,' she said. 'Three nights ago, we were anchored ten miles off the Keys when two men boarded our boat and tried to kill John. By the time I got abovedecks, they were starting to slash his throat. I had to shoot them.'

It was so matter-of-fact, so out there, that Magozzi had trouble taking it in. He just stood there, his hands hanging from his wrists, looking stupefied. 'You killed them?'

'I did.'

'Jesus, Grace.'

'They were killing him, Magozzi. I didn't have a choice.'

Magozzi took a breath, rubbed his forefinger over his upper lip. He needed a shave. 'Let's go inside.'

Funny how doing familiar, automatic things could give you breathing space. Magozzi walked in, wiped his feet, and hung his holster on the coatrack under his jacket. *Grace killed two men.* He walked to the kitchen. He got wineglasses out of the cupboard and the remains of a cheap bottle of Chardonnay out of the refrigerator. *Grace killed two men.* Damnit, it didn't matter how busy he kept his hands; that single, shocking phrase kept running a loop in his head. He filled the glasses and sat down at the table where he and Grace had shared so many meals.

She took a sip of the wine and wrinkled her nose. 'Thanks.'

'It's not Harley's wine.'

'It's fine.' She looked sad and scared all at the same time and Magozzi didn't know how to make that look go away. What did you say to someone who'd just confessed to murder? He knew what he'd say on the job, but this wasn't an interrogation room, and Grace wasn't any suspect off the street. But it was murder and investigating homicides was what he did for a living.

'Magozzi?'

His eyes jerked back to her face. He'd been silent too long. 'Sorry. You've had a few days to take this in. I'm just starting.'

'I know.'

Be the detective. 'You said you were ten miles out. So they had a boat.'

'A dinghy.'

'Pirates?'

'That's what we thought at first, until we found a picture of John in one of their pockets.'

Magozzi leaned back in his chair, stunned. 'Smith was a target?'

Grace nodded.

'I need to talk to him right now. Where is he?'

'I don't know. He's off the grid. We threw our computers and cells overboard, took the boat right back to the marina, and went our separate ways. He doesn't want me anywhere near him until he finds out who ordered the hit.'

'Come on, Grace. John's the only one with the answers. Pirates are one thing, but most people don't have a price on their heads without some idea of who wants them dead. What did he tell you?'

Grace shook her head. 'Nothing that makes sense. The men who tried to kill him were Saudis here on student visas, but he's never worked counterterrorism for the Bureau, no old cases rearing their heads. He has been monitoring the jihadist websites just to keep his hand in, and when he finds something suspicious, he passes the word on to law enforcement.'

Magozzi shrugged. 'There must be thousands of agents who do that every day.'

'Exactly. So why would John be singled out for death? That's what we have to find out, because if they're looking for John, eventually they're going to look for people who knew him. That means me and Monkeewrench.' She looked directly at him. 'Our association with John was all over the news when we worked together on the Internet killers. We'll do what we can with computer searches – I made a copy of John's hard drive, and Monkeewrench is running it through our software now. But we need a little pull with the local police and the Feds. They're not going to share information with strangers over the phone, but you can use your badge to see if anyone's been making inquiries about John in DC or Florida.'

Magozzi pulled his notebook from his pocket and started writing. 'We can do that. What about the marina where John keeps his boat?'

Grace lifted her purse from the floor, pulled out her Sig from its new home, and then a list that had been tucked beneath it. She pushed the paper across the table. 'Those are contacts and their numbers. Don Kardon is the marina owner. I told him you'd be calling. The rest are Florida and DC cops and the Feds he worked with.'

'I'll get right on it. What did the Florida cops say?'

Grace blinked. 'What do you mean?'

'About the two dead men, the crime scene on the boat?'

Grace's gaze didn't waver. 'I pushed the bodies overboard. We didn't report it.'

Magozzi couldn't take his eyes off her. 'Seriously?'

She exhaled sharply. 'They came to kill John. If whoever was behind it heard on the news that he wasn't dead, he wouldn't have had time to disappear. Listen, you're a cop. I know how that hits you. It's all we could do. Think about it.'

'I will.'

She pushed a sheaf of papers across the table. 'Those are copies of what we found in the killers' wallets. Monkeewrench is checking their backgrounds now.'

Magozzi focused on the student visas, his brow troubled.

'Is something wrong?'

'I don't know. I'll check it out.'

'Thank you. I've got to get back to the office.'

'I'll call you as soon as I get anything.'

She scribbled a number on a piece of paper. 'I picked up a prepaid cell. Use this number if you want to reach me. Don't call the Monkeewrench office, don't call any number except this one. We don't know who might be listening.'

'This doesn't sound good, Grace.'

'It doesn't feel good, either.' She hesitated at the front door, looking down at her hand on the knob. 'John and I never slept together, Magozzi. If it matters.'

He took a breath. 'It matters.'

He stood in the foyer for a long time after she'd left, not thinking, not feeling. He didn't know where this was going. He didn't know what he could do. But he didn't believe in coincidence – no cop did – and the contents of those wallets were making the hairs on the back of his neck stand up. He reached for the phone. 'Gino? Come on over. Yeah, right now.'

22

After Gino arrived, Magozzi talked for ten straight minutes. The transformation in Gino's expression as he listened was fascinating to watch. It was like his face was ruffling a deck of emotions so fast, they all blurred together. 'Is that it?' he asked when Magozzi stopped talking.

'That's it.'

'I just want to make sure I've got this straight. Grace shot two guys in cold blood . . .'

'Defending John. Justifiable.'

'Yeah, whatever. Then she dumps the bodies overboard, cuts their dinghy loose, and never reports the crime. I see about twenty felonies here, Leo, and if we don't report it, we're accessories after the fact, am I right?'

Magozzi gave him a great poker face. 'Technically, it's hearsay. And personally, I don't believe a word of it. Do you?'

Gino stuck his lips out. 'No, I most certainly do not. Bullshit, is what it is.'

'That's what I was thinking.'

'So all Grace wants us to do is use our spiffy cop creds to call around and see if any suspicious characters with big knives have been hanging around asking for John.'

'I think she wanted us to be a little more discreet than that.'

'Okay, I'll pull out my own little book of bullshit, but before we hit the phones, I'm compelled to make an observation.'

'Shoot.'

'We got two homicide scenes right here in River City which involve terror types; another in Detroit, another in Los Angeles. At the same time, two Saudi nationals try to assassinate a retired Fed in Florida. I know I'm reaching here, but I don't like the parallels.'

'I hear you.'

'Just so we're on the same page, where do we start?'

Magozzi pushed a sheet of paper across the table. 'Here are some phone numbers. DC and Key West PDs, FBI contacts at his home office, et cetera. I figured we could split up the list and get you home before bedtime.'

'What about the marina where John keeps his boat?'

'Grace talked to the owner this morning, but so far, no action down there. I'll call him anyhow.'

Magozzi took his cell and his half of the list to the living room while Gino stayed in the kitchen to work. After an unproductive half hour, he called the marina.

'Coral Beach Marina,' a raspy voice answered.

'Is Don Kardon available?'

The voice on the other end hesitated for a moment. 'Who wants to know?'

'Detective Leo Magozzi from . . .'

'Oh. Yeah. I talked to Grace again this morning and she said you might be calling. I've been watching the boat just like she asked, but nobody's been snooping around. That's about all I can tell you. Really pissed me off, though, that some yahoo would call John and threaten him. He's a hell of a nice guy.'

Magozzi closed his eyes. So that's what she'd told him.

'So nothing suspicious? No strangers hanging around the marina, asking around about him?'

For some reason, Don Kardon thought that was amusing. 'A lot of people come down here to disappear, and when strangers start poking around, we get real paranoid. And trust me, I got a sharp bad-guy radar because I used to be one. Did ten at the San Quentin Hilton. If somebody sketchy comes around asking about Smith . . .' Kardon's voice trailed off for a second. 'You know, there was something that seemed a little off. I got a call earlier today from a guy who's trying to buy Smith's boat. Said he'd been in negotiations with him for a while, and suddenly he dropped off the face of the earth.'

Ex-felons were generally good at reading faces and voices, so Magozzi asked, 'What did he sound like?'

'He sounded like a pissed-off beach bum who was hoping to set sail by Christmas.'

'Did he leave a phone number?'

Kardon grunted. 'Come to think of it, no. And I didn't ask.'

'Do you have the number on your caller ID?'

'I suppose, but I have to hang up to get it. Give me your number and I'll call you back.'

While he waited, Gino strolled into the living room. 'You get anything, Leo?'

'Maybe. Waiting for a callback. How about you?'

'I tried John's condo manager in DC, but no answer.

I left a message. DC cops are going to send a courtesy patrol to pay Smith's condo a visit when they can spare a guy, see if there's any sign of monkey business. Same with Key West. They're going to keep an eye on his boat. Won't hear from any of them until tomorrow, probably.'

'How about the FBI?'

Gino got a troubled look on his face. 'Weirdest thing. For all the years Smith worked there, nobody knew him.'

'What do you mean?'

'I mean, he worked alone, didn't have any friends in the Bureau. Never went to a single Christmas party, for God's sake. Nobody even knew he had a boat. The only thing I got out of it is that Smith never had a life. Kind of sad.'

Magozzi worked that through in his head. 'He's in trouble and he didn't go back to the nest. Interesting.'

Gino shrugged. 'If he went there for help, they wouldn't tell us; they'd just slap him in some safe house and pretend they never heard from him.'

Magozzi's phone rang. 'Hang on, Gino, this is the marina . . . Hello?'

'Don Kardon, here. I got your number, Detective.' He read it off, and Magozzi thanked him.

Gino was looking at him curiously. 'You got a number?'

'Some guy called the marina, said he'd been in negotiations with Smith to buy his boat.'

'So you think the price was a little too high and this guy sent out a hit squad, or what?'

Magozzi rolled his eyes. 'You want to call the number and see who's on the other end of the line or should I?'

'Oh, please, let me. I'm feeling a little shortchanged on the interrogation front lately.'

Magozzi handed him the sheet of paper where he'd scrawled down the number Don Kardon had given him. 'Knock yourself out.'

As Gino was retreating back to his ad hoc office in the kitchen, Magozzi called Grace. 'Where are you?'

'Just pulling into Harley's.'

'Listen, I just got off the phone with Don Kardon. Some guy called him earlier today looking for Smith . . .'

'Did Don get a number?'

'Yeah, Gino's checking it out now.'

'Give it to me.'

Magozzi read off the number. 'So, this guy who called Kardon said he was in negotiations with Smith to buy his boat. Was it on the market?'

Grace responded instantly, and with certainty. 'Absolutely not. John would never sell that boat. Ever.'

'So the bad guys are still looking for him.'

She didn't respond for a while. 'I guess they are.'

After Magozzi signed off, he tossed his cell phone on the table next to him and dragged his hands down his face, as if he could wipe away his frustration.

When Gino came back into the room, he found his partner with his head in his hands. He folded his arms across his chest and rocked back on his heels. 'I'm guessing you're not asleep, so what's up?'

Magozzi shook his head and mentally dusted himself off. 'I just talked to Grace, and she said there's no way Smith would ever sell his boat. Somebody's still looking for him.'

'Yeah, I figured that out myself. No answer, no outgoing message at the number you gave me, so I did a little legwork. The call to the marina came from a throwaway cell. It only made that one call, no activity since. I've got a red flag on the number, but my guess is it's already in a trash can somewhere.'

Magozzi looked up, wondering if his eyes looked as bloodshot as they felt. 'Dead end?'

Gino nodded. 'Dead end.'

23

Harley Davidson's mansion was aglow with light, as if the grand old structure had gussied itself up in celebration of Grace MacBride's safe return from her solo road trip. She'd stopped briefly at the mansion to drop off Charlie, then immediately left to see Magozzi. None of them were happy about letting her go so soon, but it was hard to dampen their relief at having her home again. For the first time since Grace had left for Florida, the mood and dynamics in the house seemed blessedly normal.

Oh, sure, there'd been a few dark wrinkles, like someone trying to kill John, and Grace killing two men, but by God, Grace was home and safe, and together the four of them could solve any problem, make everything right again. But, oh my, it was taking a long time.

They'd been working almost nonstop since the package from Grace had arrived yesterday afternoon. It had taken most of last night to reprogram the Beast to search the Web for any common matches between John Smith and the two students who'd tried to kill him. Now the damn thing had been running all day, and not a single match had been found. Trouble was, the Web had too much information flooding it to sort through, unless your parameters were really tight. And then there was the dreaded possibility that no match existed. The Beast was still humming, still searching, but they were all on edge waiting for it to stop and display NO MATCHES FOUND on the screen.

Annie and Roadrunner were reading the last of John's FBI files and cases they'd hacked into, and Harley was tackling John's mirror drive, starting with a ton of e-mails that were all business-oriented and really boring. He worked the mouse with his left hand and stroked Charlie's head with his right. The dog had been a lively distraction for the first half hour, his stubby, chewed-off tail wagging furiously as he made his way from chair to chair, licking the daylights out of their hands and faces, but Harley was his ultimate destination. He sat next to his chair and plopped his head in Harley's lap, and there he stayed.

Harley gave the dog a last vigorous ear scratching, then pushed away from his desk, rubbing his eyes. 'I have to break. I'm going blind and I'm starving to death. How long has Grace been gone?'

'Two hours and four minutes,' Roadrunner said. 'Do you think we should call Magozzi?'

Suddenly, Charlie lifted his head, then scrambled across the polished maple floor on his way to the stairs.

'Don't bother,' Harley said, chuckling at the dog's hasty exit. 'I think she's here.'

They found her in the kitchen with Charlie at her feet, staring into Harley's refrigerator. 'Harley, there's nothing in here but sausage.'

'Not true. I have deli cuts in the meat drawer and a gallon of matzoh ball soup from Cecil's Deli in the freezer.'

'Perfect.' She slipped onto a stool at the prep counter. 'Wait on me. I'm exhausted.'

'And yet you don't look it. That tan is hot. Annie, slice that loaf of Italian bread, will you?'

Grace put her elbows on the counter and closed her eyes for just a moment, letting the warm comfort of being home wash over her. Annie put an arm around her. 'Are you sleeping, sugar?'

'Just resting my eyes. It's been a long three days. Did you find anything yet?'

Harley put the soup in the microwave and set the timer for five minutes. 'Not a damn thing. We plugged in John's mirror info and all the data from the wallets you gave us into the Beast. If those three ever crossed cyberspace paths, we haven't found it yet. I'm doing an eyes-on of John's mirror drive, but it's slow work.'

Annie nibbled on a piece of deli ham. 'Did Magozzi have any ideas?'

Grace lifted her shoulders. The gesture seemed an enormous effort. 'He and Gino are already making calls to law enforcement in Florida and DC. The bad news is, Don Kardon – he's the marina owner – got a call from a stranger with some lame story about being in negotiations to buy his boat, and that never happened.'

Annie's brows lifted. It was one of those expressions she rarely used, ever since she'd noticed that first tiny wrinkle in her forehead.

'So, someone is still trying to track him down. I surely hope that boy's a good hider.'

'He is. But we're right out there. If they want John badly enough, they're going to start looking for people he's connected to. That's us, so keep a sharp eye.'

'For what?' asked Roadrunner.

'Things, cars, people that don't belong.'

Harley set a steaming bowl of soup in front of her and Grace leaned over it and breathed deeply, as if she could absorb the nourishment without the effort of actually eating. 'We've got it all covered, Grace. Eat first, then get some sleep.'

After she'd eaten, Annie followed her up to the guest bedroom Grace used when they worked nights and tucked her in. 'I need a shower,' Grace said as the comforter settled over her.

'You can shower in the morning.'

'Will you feed Charlie?'

'Of course we will. Sleep.'

24

Don Kardon was sitting on an overturned bait bucket on the dock in front of the dark marina office, sipping a beer and listening to the plastic crackle of palm fronds as they swayed in the warm, night breeze. He smelled the faint hint of jasmine and salt mingling in the air, felt the easy motion of water as it ruffled beneath him like a liquid lullaby. Farther out in the harbor, a wiggly blur of lights from the docked boats stretched across the water, as if they were yearning for the adventure of the dark Atlantic beyond.

He chuckled to himself. Most people probably didn't figure ex-cons for poetical types, pondering jasmine and the play of lights on water, but they'd be wrong. A lifetime of ugliness put you in the pen, and the ugliness sure as hell didn't stop there, it only got worse. But if you were smart and lucky and got out alive, you started seeing things in a real different light. Kardon was no beauty. Never had been, and he sometimes wondered if his life would have taken a different tack if he'd been able to get a date in high school. That's surely all it would have taken, all he ever wanted, really: one person in this world who actually wanted to be with him, or at least liked him a little bit. Funny thing. He was looking fifty in the eye and never once knew what it was like to wake up with a woman next to him he hadn't paid, or a kid bouncing on his chest who thought his dad put up the sun every morning.

He wasn't complaining – no victim, he – just imagining what it might have been like. Not that life was bad now. He had a lot of money from the marina, a decent slice of the American Dream, and a few friends he could count on. Maybe that was enough.

He caught a flicker of movement in the corner of his eye, and his wandering thoughts stopped dead. It could have been a dog on one of the marina docks or a possum searching for scraps. It could have been nothing. Or it could be something. After ten years inside, Kardon's instincts always went with something. Ignoring that feeling that things weren't quite right could get you killed in the yard of a prison, or in your own front yard on the outside. The footsteps behind you on a dark deserted street? Run like hell. Screw making that person feel bad about himself. Screw appearing paranoid or weak. Listen to that little warning voice inside you. That's what you learned in the pen, and wasn't it amazing that the murder rate was lower in prisons than it was in an equal population on the outside? That's what Kardon told a lot of seminars he spoke at to fulfill the community service part of his probation.

Some of the people listened, and probably they were the ones who were still walking around. Listen to the voice.

But Kardon hadn't heard that voice since he'd moved to the Keys, and the sorry truth was it scared the hell out of him.

He felt a sharp crick in his neck and realized he'd been

frozen in place for a long time, his head cocked at an unusual angle, his eyes glued to that place where he'd seen movement.

He saw shadowy silhouettes of boats, the pink and green neon sign of the bar across the little harbor, and not much else. Maybe his instincts were rusty. Maybe he was scaring himself like a stupid kid watching a horror movie. Or maybe not. He caught his breath in his throat and let his eyes pierce the dark and remembered the night John and Grace had gone out to sea and come hightailing back under power in the middle of the night, both of them a little rattled. They didn't tell him anything, and he didn't ask, but he knew damn well something had happened out there.

Keep an eye out, will you, Don? If anyone comes around looking for me, play dumb, stay out of their way, then call Grace and let her know.

Suddenly, there was a light where one hadn't existed a second ago. Normally, that wouldn't bother him. Most of the marina lights went out at full dark so those patrons who slept on their boats wouldn't be disturbed, and many of them used Maglites to find their way home after a night of clubbing. But now there were two beams from two Maglites, and they were coursing along the side of John Smith's boat.

This was not good. Don knew it in his heart, which was now pounding furiously and half in his throat as his basest survival instincts took over automatically; another thing he knew plenty about. These were not drunk or drugged-up kids poking around for a joy ride to steal. There was some purpose here.

Fight or flight?

It was a split-second decision: both. You had to assess your enemy before you could engage or evacuate. There were at least two of them, most likely armed. If he confronted them now at a hundred feet away, he'd give up his current position, and then the advantage was theirs. They probably wouldn't want to shoot, because they were here for something else, maybe something from the boat, or even records from his office, so cops on the premises might be their greatest fear. That meant cops on the premises was the best possible solution for him personally, and a great irony, Don thought, as a man who'd spent half his life evading them.

So he withdrew very slowly and carefully into the shadows, backing into the dark marina office in a reverse crab walk. He grabbed the phone from his desk, pushed away his office chair, and crawled under the cubbyhole. He groped in the dark and felt the reassuring steel of the sawed-off shotgun he had fastened on the front panel for emergencies, but decided to go the lawful route for now. It was illegal for felons to own guns, and God knew what crimes had been committed by this one he'd bought off the street. Probably heinous ones, where he might not have an alibi, which would send him back to the pen for life, maybe. He couldn't go there now, although he did take it off the rack in case his near future required some firepower as a last resort.

He punched the number nine into the phone, but before he could complete his 9-1-1 emergency call, a hand landed on his shoulder and pulled him out from under the desk.

Shit. There were at least three of them.

'What the fuck!' Don screamed, knowing his options were running out fast, hoping somebody would hear him and call the cops. He felt a crunch in his jaw as his head slammed down onto his desk blotter. He tasted blood in his mouth a second later and heard more footsteps, moving closer. This was not going to end well, because he heard the screech of duct tape being ripped from a roll, and no way Don Kardon was going on that ride.

He grabbed the hands of the man who was on him, twisted him around, and jammed his knee into his nuts with a satisfying crunch, then flipped him over the desk. 'Motherfucker!' he screamed again, as loud as he could, then jumped back into the cubbyhole, grabbed the shotgun, and started firing with impunity as he felt slugs hitting his body in really critical places that he knew would kill him. He thought of night-blooming jasmine and how good it smelled, then he thought of the American Dream. His would die tonight, but not without a goddamned fight.

25

Harley and sleep had never been strangers. He could nod off just about anywhere, any time – on a plane, in a car, on the sofa in front of the TV. Even when he was in high-octane mode, pursuing his work or another of his passions, he could turn his intensity off like a faucet when he needed to rest. But tonight sleep had been elusive. He'd tossed and turned in his big bed, catching tiny bursts of half sleep here and there until he'd finally given up the fight near dawn.

He took the stairs up to the office so the whir of the elevator didn't wake the others, started a pot of coffee, then sank into his desk chair and woke up his monitor so he could check on the computers.

After staring at the screen for a few seconds, he shifted his gaze sideways and rubbed his sleep-blurred eyes to make sure he wasn't seeing things. All their computers were connected to the Beast, and how Harley loved that machine. He was its primary architect and he could tell it to do anything: how to distribute tasks, how its autonomous nodes should communicate, either by message or shared memory.

Normally an alarm would sound when the Beast made a connection, but at night the alarm went silent and lights blinked on whatever computer showed activity. Tonight that was Harley's, and the jury-rigged numeric keyboard was flashing all its numbers at once. Not one connection, not two, but several.

He walked over to the Beast on the back wall, pushed print, and a long sheet rolled out of the machine. It was a list of websites – dozens of them. He called up a few of them and just sat there, staring at them, breathing hard, before he went to wake up Roadrunner.

'This better be good,' the thin man mumbled as he stood looking over Harley's shoulder. He was tying a striped robe around a pair of sagging Jockey shorts, a gesture Harley deeply appreciated. You looked at Roadrunner's ribs too long, you wanted to rub him with spices and slap him on the grill.

'None of it's good. It's all bad. Check this out.' He cued up one of the websites and leaned sideways to give Roadrunner a good look at the screen. Roadrunner was instantly, completely awake. He leaned closer to the monitor, gaping at John Smith's headshot staring back at him from the screen. All the writing on the page was in Arabic except for a few English words printed below John's face in large block letters. JOHN SMITH, FBI, LOCATION UNKNOWN – JIHAD.

'Jesus, Harley. What the hell is this?'

Harley's voice was grim. 'It's a jihadist website. Every time some freaked-out radical imam decides someone should die, they put a death warrant out on the Web that goes viral, like they did with that Dutch filmmaker, remember? This is the new strategy, thanks to our friend the Internet. No need for massive organization, no need for long-term planning – just throw out the jihad and let the lone wolf freelancers hunt him down.'

Roadrunner look stricken. 'A jihad?'

Harley nodded. 'Worldwide. There are a couple dozen more of these sites with John front and center. Turns out the two Saudis who tried to kill John published a couple of radical papers on these sites under their own names. John visited the same sites, and his photo popped up on all of them two weeks ago. That's the connection the Beast finally picked up. John's name and theirs on the same sites. Apparently our boy did something to really piss an imam off.'

Roadrunner tugged his robe closer, suddenly cold. His face was chalk white. 'Holy shit. How do you piss off terrorists?'

'That's what we've got to find out.'

26

The first thing that hit you when you walked into City Hall in the morning was the smell of coffee. Gino stopped just inside the door and took a few deep breaths with his eyes closed. Magozzi frowned at him. 'What the hell are you doing?'

Gino took another breath and opened his eyes. 'Inhaling caffeine. I'm thinking it might be the only good experience I have today. Besides, I have just detected the very specific odor of one of those Starbucks white mocha things with extra espresso shots. Who the hell in this building has a salary that can afford that?'

'A better question is, how do you know about girlie Starbucks drinks? We're men. We're cops. We drink our coffee black.'

'Amen to that, but I've got a teenager in my house, and she brings that swill home all the time. On her dime, not mine, by the way. You know how girls used to wear perfume? I swear to God, the new perfume is what kind of coffee drink you have on your breath.'

Magozzi scrunched up his nose as he pondered coffee as a pheromone. His only youthful scent memories were all those great, sugary discount store scents his high school dates used to bathe themselves in. Social progress never took the path you'd imagined in your own youth.

The second thing about City Hall was that the place

was always buzzing. This morning, it was more than just buzzing; it was like one of those monster wasps' nests that suddenly appear beneath your garage eaves overnight. But the wasps swirling around the building this morning were mostly the white Anglo-Saxon types.

There were cops, reporters, cameramen and -women, brass from every department, and a lot of administrative suits you rarely saw, including the mayor and the head of MPD public relations. All of them were maintaining a brisk pace and harried expressions. The media furor after all the murders and the evacuation in Little Mogadishu showed no signs of letting up, and every politician in the state wanted to comment, just to get face time on television.

'Gonna be another tough morning,' Gino observed. 'Let's get the hell into our cubicles and stay there. Maybe we can solve some crime today.'

'Sounds good to me.' And that, in a nutshell, was normally the best thing about working Homicide – you were always heading toward a single, sharply defined goal: catch the killer. The Feds were handling the terrorist and kidnapping angles; all Gino and Magozzi had to do was find out who killed the terrorists and the kidnappers. Nothing muddled about that.

They made a pit stop at Tommy Espinoza's office on the way to their own. He was the MPD's resident IT geek – a third Swedish, a third Hispanic, and a third processing chip – and he handled all the computer forensics for the department. Occasionally, he would call Monkeewrench in for a consult, but after working with them for a couple years and benefiting from their tutelage, he was a technological force to be reckoned with in his own right.

He rarely left his office, and when he did, it was usually to poach free junk food from the vending machines, which he did by inserting a mysterious little card into the slot where the dollar bills were supposed to go.

He looked up when Magozzi and Gino knocked on the frame of his open door. 'Come on in, guys.' He tossed them each a candy bar from his desktop stash, which he kept in a faded plastic Halloween pumpkin. 'I'm guessing you could both use a sugar rush right about now. Man, you guys are getting slammed.'

Gino tore into his Almond Joy. 'We've had better weeks.'

'Did you get anything from the kidnappers' computer yet?' Magozzi asked.

Tommy nodded. 'Everything's in Arabic, and the translator is still working on it.'

'Thanks, Tommy. Keep us posted.'

When Magozzi and Gino got to the entry of Homicide, there was another new receptionist standing behind the glass window, looking them up and down like they were a couple of gun-toting reprobates trying to break in and blow the department to bits.

Gino blew out a sigh and put an elbow on the ledge. 'Detectives Rolseth and Magozzi,' he told her. 'We belong here. We're the good guys.'

They'd had a slew of these temps in ever since Gloria had gone on leave to take a shot at law school. God, he missed her. Sassy and wicked-smart, she'd been a fixture in Homicide for as long as he could remember. He missed her savvy about office routine and her utter lack of anything resembling civility. The long string of temps had been mostly young girls who looked prepubescent, interning to get a star on their résumés that would put them on the fast track to the academy.

This one was different. She had short gray hair and wore a black dress with a white collar that crept up her neck to her chin, making her look a little like a dropout from the convent. She gave Gino one of those level, straight-on gazes that always made him nervous when a woman delivered it. 'I'm going to need to see your identification.'

Exasperated, Gino opened his badge case and slapped it against the glass. 'Ten years in this department, no one's ever asked for my ID.'

'Then this should be a new and thrilling experience for you. Unfortunately, you don't look very much like this photo. Have you put on a lot of weight recently?'

Gino glared at her. 'Have you had a death wish recently?'

She gave him a smile that made her look a lot less like a nun. 'I'm a friend of Gloria's. She told me you respond well to verbal abuse.'

'Well, she was wrong, and you, my friend, have the potential to become a real pain in the ass.'

She looked at his ID once more, noting the name. 'I had a dog named Gino once. We had to put him down.'

As she buzzed them through, Magozzi looked at Gino. 'I think you won her over.'

By the time they got to their desks, Magozzi's cell was ringing. He looked at the display, then cocked a curious brow at Gino. 'Key West PD. Maybe they've got something for us on Smith.'

Magozzi listened for a few minutes, thanked whoever was on the other end, then pushed in the new number for Grace's throwaway cell.

'What's up, Leo?'

Magozzi held up one finger. 'I have to call Grace. Listen in . . .'

Harley picked up on the first ring. 'Hey, Magozzi.'

'Put Grace on, Harley.'

'She's in the shower. Is this something I can handle?'

'Do you know who Don Kardon is, Harley?'

'Sure. John and Grace's friend from the marina.'

'Well, we just got a callback from Key West. Kardon was murdered last night.'

Harley's voice was normally big and boisterous, but now it sounded like it had been squeezed down into a whisper. 'Oh, shit. How?'

'He took a lot of bullets. The cop who called me said there were three attackers. Kardon fought back and did some serious damage before they finally killed him. The perps left behind a lot of their own blood.'

Harley was silent for a moment. 'Any chance this was a robbery, maybe something from his past come back to bite him? Grace said he did some time.'

Magozzi rubbed his eyes. 'I don't think so. Whoever it was tossed John's boat. Every drawer upended, every closet trashed. They were looking for something and they didn't care who knew it. Key West put out a sweep on every hospital and clinic in the state, but nothing popped. They're kind of at a dead end down there. For all they know, the killers could have come in by boat and left the same way.'

Gino was listening intently to the conversation, rubbing his upper lip, remembering a scanty mustache he'd had a million years ago when men still wore baggy flowered shirts they never tucked in.

Harley let out a long sigh. 'This isn't good, Magozzi. Someone else – maybe a lot of someones – is still trying to hunt down John.'

Magozzi closed his eyes, then frowned. 'What do you mean "a lot of someones"?'

'Write down these Web addresses and call them up. We just found out there's a jihad out on John and it's all over the Net.'

Gino's mouth fell open and stayed that way the whole time he scribbled down the addresses Harley dictated.

Harley continued. 'We're burning up the computers, trying to find out how the hell John got on a jihad list, but it's going to take time, and I'm not so sure finding the reason would do any good. You know how this works. Some radical imam puts a jihad out on the Web, and every homegrown crazy decides to make a name for himself by taking out the target.'

'Can you shut down the sites?'

'Roadrunner's working on it.'

'You're blowing us away, Harley. A jihad on John? Where the hell do you go with that? We've still got all our feelers out with the law enforcement Grace wanted us to contact, but Kardon's murder was the only thing that came of that.'

Harley grunted. 'Makes sense. The marina was the natural place for them to look. I guess the best we can do is hope that they don't look any farther than that.'

Magozzi felt a prickle on the back of his neck. 'What do you mean?'

'Hell, I don't know. How serious is this jihad thing? Do these freelancers hunt you down like a dog, or do they just go after targets that happen to be in their general neck of the woods? Now, when the mob was doing big business, those guys dug deep and never gave up the chase when they wanted to off someone. Those are the kind of people that would tear your background apart and find everyone who ever knew you and poke pins into their eyes until they talked.'

'Nice visual, Harley.'

'Yeah, I'm just bouncing stuff off the wall, going for the dark side.'

'Let us know if there's anything more we can do to help.'

'Thanks, buddy, but this is going to be mostly computer operations. Besides, you've done enough going through law enforcement for us, especially when you've got your hands full. Gotta tell you, every time I check the news, I see your pretty face. Take care out there, fellas. Sounds like it's murder season.'

Magozzi had no clue how long he and Gino sat shoulder to shoulder in front of his computer, jumping from site to site, staring at John Smith's face in utter disbelief. Gino finally pushed back from the desk, shaking his head. 'This has got to be a joke. A bad joke. I mean, what the fuck? How do you get a goddamned jihad put on your head? Was he drawing cartoons of Muhammad, or what?'

Magozzi moved his head back and forth slowly, feeling

like he'd just stepped into a Salvador Dalí scape. 'He had to have been into something more than just monitoring radical websites. And we better hope like hell that Monkeewrench can figure it out.'

Gino was frowning so hard, his forehead looked corrugated. 'There's something real jiggy going on, Leo. And I have a bad feeling that we're in the middle of it and we don't even know it.' He looked down at his desk calendar and ripped off yesterday's page. 'It's October twenty-sixth, Leo. Five days to Halloween.'

27

Grace stood under the shower for a very long time, trying to comprehend a jihad on John, wondering if he'd figured it out on his own by now, and praying that he was all right. It seemed so preposterous, and yet it was reality, and the frustration of not being able to connect the dots was almost paralyzing.

She sighed, cranked off the water, and dressed in the familiar black armor of her past. After months in skimpy clothes, they felt heavy and oppressive, and the knee-high riding boots were stiff and unyielding. But she'd get used to them again.

The loft smelled like coffee and cinnamon – somebody had set out a big plate of caramel rolls. Charlie was asleep on the chair beside her desk, and Annie, Roadrunner, and Harley were all so focused on their monitors, it took them all a few moments to realize she was standing in the doorway. 'Did anything pop while I was in the shower?'

They all looked up, their distress playing across their faces as bold as neon, and she felt a ball of dread clench her stomach. 'What's wrong?'

'Honey, Magozzi just called,' Annie said softly. 'Don Kardon was killed last night. I'm so sorry.'

Grace looked at them for a long time. She'd only known the man for three months, and it wasn't like they'd become fast friends, but they had developed a mutual respect.

Don Kardon was a loner with a dark past, which was something Grace knew all about; and they'd instantly recognized themselves in each other. And now he was gone.

She excused herself quietly and her friends knew better than to follow. Grace always grieved alone.

For as long as Roadrunner could remember, he'd always seen things a lot differently than other people. At the age of five, he'd picked up a smashed radio from a ditch, looked at the guts, and saw instantly how it could be fixed. The wires and circuit boards weren't broken components to him, they were a unified, three-dimensional universe that talked to him through pictures in his mind. And that universe was much better than the one he'd been living in at the time – he'd finally found an escape from his reality right around the time he'd started kindergarten.

By the time he was ten, he was working at an electronics repair shop on the sly for pennies on the dollar, repairing everything from fancy toasters to computers, and eventually learning the labyrinthine processing of anything with a board or a chip. His gift had been forged by a freak of genetics, but his tightly honed skills had helped him parlay that into a genius for programming which had never failed him – until now.

He was staring at John Smith's hard drive, which was a Byzantine mess of programming that had him baffled. And frustrated. It was the first time in his life he'd looked into a machine and hadn't instinctively known how to fix it. 'This is a disaster,' he muttered to himself.

On the other side of the room, Annie glanced up from

the sheaf of papers she was poring through. 'Something bothering you, sugar?'

Roadrunner threw up his hands in temporary defeat. 'Smith's computer. He tweaked the programming into knots and it's not making any sense.'

'It's not like you to run into a wall. What's wrong?'

'I don't know. Maybe I've been at this too long, but it looks like he was messing with the Monkeewrench software programming language. But I can't find the command lines for it.'

That got Harley's attention. He got up from his own desk and clomped over to Roadrunner's station. Annie, never one to miss a party, got up and joined them, clickity-clacking across the floor on ruby red stilettos that were horrifyingly out of season, but were the last new pair she had in her closet at Harley's.

'How did he mess with it?' Harley asked, squinting down at the screen.

Roadrunner hammered in a few commands on his keyboard and jabbed a finger at the monitor. 'Check this out, this is the weird thing. I'm only reading a partial signature of our programming in his drive, but it's so corrupt, I can't tell what he was trying to do with it.'

Harley grunted. 'Man, I hate amateurs.'

28

Magozzi woke up Thursday morning to the raucous voices of the irreverent hosts of a morning talk show coming from his clock radio. He hated the station, but used it as his alarm, because there was no way you could sleep through the puerile noise of two loudmouths spouting off-color jokes at that hour. He fumbled for the off button and noticed the digital readout: 6:00 A.M. OCTOBER 27TH.

Shit. Four days to Halloween. Four days to either a terrorist attack or a terrorist prom, or maybe four days to nothing. He liked the last option and, for the time being, forced the first option to the back of his mind.

He dragged himself out of bed and went to the nearest window – it was a little OCD thing that seeped into your psyche when you lived in Minnesota, especially this time of year. Autumn was dicey – you could wake up to unseasonable heat or unseasonable cold – actually, the meteorologists labeled all conditions unseasonable, as if they had no right to be there at that particular time. Still, you had to know how to dress.

He pulled apart the slats of the bargain window blinds he'd picked up at some home improvement store, and looked out onto his yard. The sun was shining, but the sky was that scary dark blue that looked like a theater curtain hiding winter behind it. A few days ago it had been blistering hot; this morning there was an icy glaze coating his unraked leaves. That was one of the things he hated about Minnesota – there were no segues between seasons.

He turned on the TV and listened to the weather girl with the really big head tell him the day would be pleasant and warm unless the cold front en route from Canada moved down faster than expected, in which case, he could anticipate freezing his balls off. Life shouldn't be this uncertain.

He was having his first cup of caffeine out on the porch, watching his breath make frosty air bubbles, when Gino pulled into the drive. He'd barely buckled his seat belt before Gino started to rant.

'This is just bullshit, Leo, you know that? I had to scrape my windshield this morning. Nobody told me Armageddon on Ice was coming to a theater near me, and I've got a four-year-old bawling into his board shorts right now because he wanted to be a surfer dude for Halloween.'

'The Accident wants to be a surfer dude? How is that even on his radar?'

Gino grunted. 'Nice, calm shows with pretty locations and big waves are Valium to kids. I never figured he'd actually pick up on the content, and now he's obsessed with the *Endless Summer* documentary.'

'Well, at least there's no violence,' Magozzi offered.

'Yeah, there is that. The downside is he might become inspired to live in our basement until he's fifty. We're getting ballistics on the Hardy scene this morning, right?'

'That was the promise.'

'Good. Then we can seal that case, file our report, and go on a cruise.'

'You hate boats.'

'Yeah, but I like open bars, and I'm going to need one to get the taste of this week out of my mouth.'

Compared to yesterday's melee, City Hall was damn near deserted. All the media vultures had apparently flown off to find the next tragedy. And where cameras went, the pandering politicians followed. The relative quiet was nice, but a little creepy at the same time, like they were the last survivors after the pandemic.

Unfortunately, the temporary receptionist was behind the glass in the Homicide farm, standing guard like a Doberman. She gave Magozzi a tiny smile, then glared at Gino. 'May I see some identification, please?'

Gino made a face. 'Was that supposed to be a joke?'

'Yes.' She buzzed them in.

McLaren was cleaning off his desk, a truly disturbing event since it had never happened before. He had a little color in his face, which meant he'd either caught up on his sleep or had gone on a bender.

Gino saw a missed patch of red whiskers on his left cheek and voted for the latter. He held a wastebasket up to the edge of his desk and swept a stack of clutter into it. 'No one killed anybody so far this morning. Chief Malcherson said I could help you two out until something new comes in. You got anything for me?'

Magozzi gathered his copies of the case files and put them on the newly clean spot on McLaren's desk. 'Here. We've got nothing on who murdered the two kidnappers at the house where the girls were found. Maybe you can see something in the reports we missed.'

'And the three bodies at the explosives house?'

'We'll probably be able to close that one when the ballistics report comes in. They said they'd call today.' Magozzi went to his desk. Gino sat opposite him at his own desk and started abusing a Snickers bar. He flipped it end to end, cracking the chocolate coating and smooshing the caramel. There was no greater demonstration of his distress than assault on a food product. 'You're destroying a candy bar. That's not like you.'

'Yeah, I know. I actually made the mistake of reading the paper this morning. They had a big feature on Joe Hardy that put me in the dumps. The guy serves three tours for his country, comes back with more medals than you can shake a stick at, fights cancer for over a year, and gets shot to pieces by a couple terrorists in his own city. It just isn't fair.'

Magozzi didn't know what to say. Fortunately, his direct office line buzzed, saving him from further, depressing conversation about good men dying. 'Detective Magozzi,' he answered.

'Hey, Magozzi, this is Dave from Ballistics.'

Magozzi pushed the speaker button. 'Go ahead, Dave. Gino and McLaren are listening in.'

'Hi, McLaren. Hey, Gino, how'd you do with the garage sale last weekend?'

Gino seemed happy for the distraction. 'Pretty great. How's that beanbag chair I fleeced you for working out?'

Dave snorted. 'Best fifty cents I ever spent. Most comfortable chair in the house. Of course, the wife banished it to the basement, but that's okay by me – I've got my flat screen down there.'

Magozzi cocked a brow. He hadn't figured Dave for a savvy shopper. 'Got anything for us on the Hardy case?'

An unexpectedly morose sigh came over the speaker loud and clear. 'More than you bargained for, probably.'

Gino frowned his puzzlement at the phone. 'What's going on?'

'Well, I've got all kinds of weird for you, but good news first – your case is solved – your three vics killed each other. Joe Hardy's gun took out the two Somalis, and Hardy took his bullets from theirs. Picture-perfect match all around.'

'Hallelujah,' Gino said. 'Just like we figured.'

'But what you probably didn't figure on was Joe Hardy, or at least his gun, has been busy.'

Magozzi and Gino shared a glance. 'What do you mean?'

'When I finally got around to logging the guns and the tool-mark results into all the ballistics registries, I got a NIBIN hit.'

NIBIN stood for National Integrated Ballistic Identification Network – a stroke of sheer genius that cataloged ballistics information from crimes all across the country for cross-matching. Monkeewrench hadn't developed the original software, but they contributed updates and improvements pro bono on a regular basis, Magozzi knew.

'On *Hardy's* gun?' Gino asked incredulously.

'Yeah. Same gun killed those two at the house where you found the kidnapped girls.'

McLaren looked up from his reading, finally interested. 'What?'

'I told you I had all kinds of weird for you.'

Gino shook his head in denial. 'No way. There's gotta be a mistake.'

'Look, I didn't want to believe it either. Hell, I've been reading the paper and watching the news just like everybody else, and I know about Joe Hardy and his story. The guy was a bona fide hero.' Dave paused and sighed. 'Sorry to be the bearer of bad tidings.'

'Well, this just bites,' Gino mumbled once they'd signed off. 'And I have to tell you, ballistics matches or not, there's something seriously wrong with this scenario. Joe Hardy was a soldier, but he wasn't a cold-blooded killer. It's one thing to do a nasty job in a theater of war, but he was back at home. Decommissioned. *Dying of cancer.* And taking care of everybody around him. There are more angles to this, there has to be.'

Magozzi leaned back in his chair and found a cobweb on the ceiling to ponder. 'When you come right down to it, we don't really know who Joe Hardy was.'

Johnny spun his chair to face them, a folder open on his lap. He was wearing a yellow-and-green-plaid jacket that looked like a leprechaun had exploded. 'Well, we know he was a Class A sharpshooter in Special Ops and that most of his service record is redacted. I haven't seen this much black on a page since Billy Douglas spilled a bottle of India ink on my Santa Claus drawing in the third grade. The military doesn't block this shit out because the soldier was sitting down staring at his belly button. I'm guessing our Joe Hardy was one badass.'

Gino scowled. 'Joe Hardy was a hero.'

'That's what heroes are in wartime, my man. Badasses.'

29

It took Gino almost a full minute to tunnel through his brain and find a way to negate McLaren's image of Joe Hardy as some kind of badass. He used the time wisely, tearing into the wrapper of his mangled Snickers bar and taking a ferocious bite, channeling his distress by enthusiastic mastication.

'Okay. I think I've got a new theory,' he said, spraying pieces of broken chocolate onto his desk blotter with abandon. 'The gun and the bullets match, that I believe. But like Dave said, Joe's *gun* was busy, and without any witnesses, there's no way to prove he was actually the shooter at the kidnappers' house. I mean, seriously, the guy was a dead man walking. I just can't believe he'd suddenly go out on a whack fest to fill up all the spare time he must have had between all his chemo appointments.'

Magozzi grunted. 'You mean like the mysterious one-armed man in *The Fugitive*?'

'Yeah, nobody believed in the one-armed man, but in the end, there was one.'

'It was a movie, Gino.'

'So. Doesn't mean it couldn't happen.'

McLaren put his elbow on his desk and his chin in his hand. He loved watching these two guys bat it back and forth. It was like having a front-row seat at Wimbledon.

'That gun has been registered in Joe's name for six

years,' Magozzi said. 'Never reported stolen. You think Beth did it, or what?'

'Of course not.'

'So then what? He loaned out his gun to a friend for target practice, and the friend turns out to be a homicidal maniac?'

Gino screwed up his mouth sourly. 'We can't rule out a second shooter.'

'Look at the timeline, Gino. It's tight. The first two murders happened late Sunday morning according to the ME. Joe went up to Elbow Lake that afternoon. Could the imaginary homicidal friend who theoretically had Joe's gun on loan return it to him before he made the drive up north? Sure. Kill two people, let the gun cool off, give it a good cleaning, and return it by lunchtime. But is it likely?'

Gino put his head in his hands. 'No. Jesus. Okay. Let's just say Joe was the shooter. What the hell was his motive?'

Magozzi gnawed at his lower lip, an annoying habit that he'd long ago come to associate with clear thinking. 'Joe Hardy did three tours in a couple seriously nasty wars. He saw horrible things, lost men in horrible ways. That would mess with anybody's mind, so let's just say it messed with his. He comes home, finds out he's dying of cancer, and gets angry. Plus, he's doing his chemo in a neighborhood filled with people who look like the bad guys. The war followed him home and something snaps, simple as that.'

Since the candy bar was gone, Gino busied himself by dismantling a perfectly innocent pen. 'Doesn't track. We've been fighting in the Middle East for what, a hundred million years? A lot of vets come home totally messed up, and who can blame them? Every now and then, and I'm talking rare here, you hear on the news that one of them totally loses it and maybe you've got a domestic, maybe you've got a bar fight, but mostly those poor saps who can't deal end up offing themselves. They don't get trigger-happy with people who look like their old enemies, and they sure as hell don't calculate hits like contract killers. You're jumping right on the crazy train, throwing Joe under the bus, and we don't even know if he had that gun the whole time.'

Magozzi grabbed three aspirin from the bottle in his desk drawer and washed them down with cold coffee. 'You're right. We've got to talk to Beth again.'

'Oh, super. You want to go now? "Oh, hey, Beth, wow, your mascara held up really well through all this mourning. I know Joe's only been cold for a couple days, but we think he was a psycho killer. We'd be so stoked if you could alibi him, so we can all feel better about ourselves."' Gino sagged a little in his chair and chucked pieces of pen into his desk drawer.

Magozzi leaned back and studied Gino. This was messing with him big-time. Gino had found a hero in Joe Hardy and was reluctant to let go, maybe because he so desperately wanted to believe heroes existed. The superhero comic book influence. Amazing how pulp fiction was totally relevant most of the time. It just left out the little detail about heroes being flawed like everybody else. 'Call her, Gino. Your track record's a hell of a lot better than mine when it comes to communicating with women. Put it on speaker. I'll jump in if I need to.'

Beth answered on the third ring and they heard the faint hum of background noise – either the TV or a distant roomful of mourners, it was hard to tell which. 'Mrs Hardy. This is Detectives Rolseth and Magozzi calling. We're really sorry to bother you, but something has come up in our investigation of your husband's murder that simply can't wait.'

'It's all right, Detectives. I appreciate your attention to the case.'

'Are there people with you?'

'Yes. Family, friends, there are a lot of people here.'

'That's good to know. We won't keep you. All we really need to ask is if you have any knowledge about the location of Joe's sidearm over the few days before his death. Particularly on the day he headed up north to hunt with his friends.'

Beth hesitated. She was no fool. She knew there was something behind the question. 'Joe never let that gun out of his sight. He carried whenever he went out, even to the hospital. He took it out of the gun safe Sunday morning before he went to chemo, and when he came home, he packed it in his duffel before he left for Elbow Lake.'

Gino raised his brows at Magozzi. 'Joe had chemo on Sunday?'

'Well, not exactly. He went to his appointment, but he never actually had the treatment.' There was a long, sad pause. 'It wasn't working. The doctor said there was no point.'

'I'm sorry, Mrs Hardy. So Joe didn't loan his gun to anyone?'

'Of course not. Joe would never do that.'

Magozzi and Gino shared a gloomy look as the truth about Joe Hardy sank in – he was the shooter at both houses. The second may have been self-defense, but the first was premeditated.

A hint of trepidation crept into Beth's tone. 'Why are you asking about Joe's gun?'

Gino held up his hands and volleyed the conversation to Magozzi. He didn't want to go any further with this.

'Detective Magozzi here, Mrs Hardy. We just needed to confirm the location of that weapon for our investigation.'

Over the speaker, Magozzi and Gino heard a different woman's voice in the background. 'Beth? Are you all right? Sit down, dear.'

'I'm fine, Mother. I'll just be a minute. Detectives?'

Magozzi said, 'We're still here, Mrs Hardy. We'll let you go now.'

'No. You're trying to protect me from something. I don't know what. Joe always did that, too. But this is the way it is. You watch someone you love go off to war three times, you're a lot stronger than anyone gives you credit for. What's this all about, Detectives?'

'For now, we're just tying up loose ends so we can close the case. And as soon as we do, we'll be sure to call you.' Magozzi's mind was racing now, tripping over mental hurdles as he considered how much further to push. 'Uh . . . there is one last thing, ma'am, if you don't mind?'

'Go ahead.'

'Can you tell us if Joe had any problems with PTSD when he came back from his tours? Or a particular mistrust or dislike for men of Middle Eastern descent?'

Gino's shoulders rolled forward in a cringe as he pinched his eyes shut.

'Hardly,' Beth answered without hesitation.

'So Joe didn't harbor any blanket resentment?'

Beth breathed a soft sigh that was impossible to interpret. 'Joe hated criminals, Detective, whatever their nationality. And he always knew the difference.'

'I think you just tied up all your loose ends, guys,' McLaren said after they hung up.

Gino had his head in his hands. 'Yeah. Closed cases, happy ending all around. Now all we have to do is figure out how to tell Beth her dead hero husband went off the rails and started murdering people.'

'Maybe he had a reason.'

Gino looked up hopefully. 'Like what?'

McLaren shrugged. 'Well, it wasn't like he was going door to door, plugging everybody. Take the first house where you found the girls. Those guys kidnapped five girls and murdered one of them. And God knows what those assholes in the second house were planning to do with all those explosives. Those guys were terrorists. And the kidnapped girls were in the first house. Maybe somebody was feeding Hardy information on bad guys in the 'hood – you know, like a neighborhood watch kind of thing – and he decided to take care of business himself instead of passing on the information to law enforcement. He was dying anyhow. Two more hero trips on the way out isn't such a bad way to go if you're a soldier.'

Magozzi thought that was a pretty ridiculous theory, unless you thought about it too long, and then it started to make a weird kind of sense.

30

Tommy called a few minutes after Gino and Magozzi had talked to Beth Hardy. 'Get down here right now, Magozzi.'

Magozzi hung up the phone with a puzzled expression.

'Who was that?' Gino asked.

'Tommy. He hung up on me.'

'You're kidding? That little shit. What did he want?'

'He said to get down there right now. Roll the phones over to switchboard and come along, McLaren. You're part of this now.'

Tommy was pacing when they got down to his office, worrying the sleeves of his sweater into fuzzy pills. He talked really fast, and his voice kept climbing the scale until he remembered to breathe. 'We're not finished yet, the translator just took a break, but we'll probably have to kill him anyway, can't have just anybody walking around with information like this, but there's some really bad shit on that computer you pulled out of the house where you found the Native American girls, and you've gotta see it now, and then we gotta call the Feds and maybe the Army.' His shoulders slumped and he collapsed in his chair.

'Jeez, Tommy, take a chill.' Gino actually looked worried. 'You're going to stroke out.'

Tommy jumped out of his chair and started pacing again, but now he was actually wringing his hands. 'No chilling, no time, look at the screen. Oh, shit, you can't read Arabic, I forgot. So listen, this is the deal, there's nothing happy on that computer except for somebody's Tunisian grandma's recipe for brik, whatever that is, and a response saying add more cumin, which our translator thought was a great idea, since he's Tunisian . . .'

'Tommy.' Magozzi took him by his shoulders and pushed him back down into his chair, then squatted to look into his eyes, which was weird, because men from Minnesota didn't normally look at each other. 'Deep breaths, slow and easy. There. Better?'

Tommy nodded.

'Good. Now tell us what you found on that computer.'

'You know what a flash mob is?'

McLaren nodded. 'Sure. Teenagers break into stores en masse and steal stuff. It didn't start out that way. Just a bunch of weirdos agreeing to meet up and dance or otherwise make asses out of themselves in some public place at a particular time . . .'

'Shut up, Johnny.' Tommy took a breath. 'Sorry. I didn't mean that. This is a terrorist flash mob spread out all over the goddamned country. They've already got their stuff ready to go. Explosives, chemicals, weapons – I mean this is *exactly* like a flash mob. There's no leader, no organizational planning, somebody just posts, "Gee, I've got an idea, let's everybody get together at noon on such and such a date and do Michael Jackson's 'Thriller' in the middle of Times Square," except these creeps are planning a kill-the-infidels day.'

'Jesus,' Gino whispered, and Tommy just kept talking.

'We found tons of posts from all over the country and we've just scratched the surface. God knows how many are out there, or how many are actually going to do it, but these are not kids playing games. These are seriously radicalized dudes, some of them bragging about summer fun at terror camps in the Middle East, and there are a bunch of imams doing some online cheerleading from American-loving places like Yemen, Saudi Arabia, Somalia. You get the drift.'

Magozzi felt all his blood rush from his head to his feet. There was business as usual, where the people you were fighting made sense. And then, there was the incomprehensible violence of people who had been programmed to hate. 'Did you find a timeline for this thing?'

Tommy dragged his hands down his face, puddling a bunch of skin on his chin line. 'Four days from now. October thirty-first.'

Gino and Magozzi both closed their eyes.

Tommy grabbed a sheet of paper and passed it to Magozzi. 'Here's a list of the cities we've pulled off the posts so far. We'll keep at it until the Feds get here and confiscate this computer.'

'You burned copies of the hard drive, right?'

'Oh, yeah.'

Gino and McLaren closed in on either side of Magozzi as they all read the horrifyingly long list of American cities.

'Damn,' McLaren breathed. 'Minneapolis is on that list.'

'Can you trace these posts to exact locations so we can give the Feds something to work with on the fly?' Magozzi asked Tommy, trying to keep himself calm even though the floor beneath him felt like quicksand.

Tommy threw up his hands in frustration. 'Hell, no, not

from where I'm sitting. I don't have the computing power. Now, Monkeewrench, for instance – they might be able to get the job done, if someone were to send them the information they needed . . .' He shrugged. 'And who knows? Maybe somebody already did.'

Magozzi smiled. 'Good work, Tommy. We'll let you get back to it.'

Magozzi called Agent Dahl on the way back to Homicide, told him enough to scare him to death without broadcasting any details over the cell network, because he kept hearing Grace's words from the other night. *We don't know who might be listening.* Given the tone of the man's voice, he would probably already be en route. Poor bastard – he wouldn't be sleeping much for the next four days. Then again, none of them would.

Back at the cube farm, Gino practically fell into his chair. 'LA, Detroit, Minneapolis. They were all on that list, Leo, and every one of those cities has dead terrorists chilling down in a morgue cooler.'

Magozzi nodded. 'Somebody's hunting these guys down before we do.'

Gino looked at him, spreading his hands. 'Not just somebody. Joe Hardy got four of them. The dead shooter in LA got five more. He was a vet, too, Leo, remember?'

Magozzi sighed. 'I remember.'

31

Gino and Magozzi were sitting on a bench in the front lobby of City Hall, waiting for Dahl and Company to arrive. Gino was staring out the front window, mesmerized by something on the concrete steps.

'What are you looking at?'

'I like the way those bits of quartz in the cement flash back the sunlight.'

'Bullshit.'

'Okay, I'm just giving my eyes a place to rest while my brain tries to sort through all this crap. Vets killing terrorists before they can do damage . . .'

'We don't know for sure that's what's happening.'

'Yeah, but say it is. Am I happy about this? Because if that's what they're doing, technically, they're murderers. I'm not supposed to like murderers. On the other hand, they might be preventing terror attacks on the homeland. So what's our role here? Hunt down vets and lock them up so the terrorists can blow up our cities? I'm having a serious existential conflict, Leo.' Gino spun around on the bench until his back was to the door.

'What are you doing?'

'I'm going blind from the sun. Why did you bring us down here anyway? Dahl can trek up to the office without an escort. I feel like I'm picking up a date at the door.'

Magozzi shrugged. 'Change of scenery. Besides, I love

the way the light from the front windows glistens on your hair.'

'Screw you.'

Magozzi nodded toward a gray sedan that had just pulled up to City Hall's front curb, disgorging Dahl and two other men wearing FBI windbreakers.

Magozzi had learned to respect Agent Dahl for the way he had handled the joint jurisdiction with MPD at the explosives house and the subsequent evacuation of the neighborhood. He'd shared information, he'd respected the police department's handling of the situation, and had been damn near friendly. But he didn't look all that friendly today. He had tight little lines around his mouth and two bright spots of color riding high on his cheeks.

'That was a pretty ambiguous phone call, Detective Magozzi. Come to City Hall ASAP? Hundreds of lives are at stake?'

'Lately, I've become a little paranoid about assuming cell phone conversations are private.'

'That's a sensible precaution. You can't be certain who's listening in.'

'A friend of mine told me that very thing not so long ago.'

'Well, listen to your friend. The cell networks are wide open. I can sit in my living room and monitor every call in and out of your cell on my computer.'

'That's really creepy,' Gino said.

'That's the new world.'

Magozzi glanced at the two men Dahl had brought with him. 'You might want to have your friends wait for you down here.'

Dahl's brows lifted. 'They're agents, Magozzi.'

'Same clearance as you?'

'Not quite.'

'Take a look at what we've got for you, then you can decide if you want to read them in.'

Dahl tipped his head toward the bench by the door. 'Take a load off, gentlemen.'

Gino and Magozzi started walking down the wide hallway faster than usual, briefing Dahl on the way. 'We pulled a computer from the house where we found the kidnapped Native American girls and it turned up some pretty scary stuff. Stuff you need to see right now. Our computer forensics guy will give you the rundown, but afterward, meet us in Homicide. We uncovered a wrinkle that puts a whole new spin on things.'

Half an hour later, Dahl walked into Homicide, bullied his way past the new temp, and headed for Gino's and Magozzi's facing desks. Now he looked scary FBI, but also scared, which was not in the demeanor rule book. His expression was even more tense than it had been when they'd met him downstairs, which was saying something. His anxiety level had obviously amped up to a level so toxic, you could almost see it rising off his skin. What you could definitely see was his pulse pounding in a vein on his forehead.

'Tommy briefed you?' Gino offered him a spare chair next to his terminally disarrayed credenza.

Dahl sank into it like he never wanted to get out. 'In great and miserable detail. So far we have some terrorist chatter from the computer we took out of the explosives house, but nothing like this.' He closed his eyes. 'Goddamnit, we missed it. Multiple times. The two Somalis at the kidnappers' house weren't on the watch list. And neither were the victims in Detroit and Los Angeles.'

Magozzi lifted a brow. He didn't think he'd ever heard a Fed swear before. 'So how the hell did these people slip through the cracks?'

Dahl gave him a grim look. 'At any given time, there are four hundred thousand people on our international watch list . . .'

'Four hundred thousand?' Gino asked incredulously.

'Yes. But those are operatives who have already been linked to terrorism or terrorist organizations. The lone wolves are the biggest, newest threat, and they aren't connected to any organization, or even each other, which is why we can't find them. We're riding a razor, Detectives. Always.'

Magozzi felt his stomach churn. That little insight was not what he'd wanted to hear. The visual wasn't all that great, either.

Dahl rubbed his brow and breathed a weary sigh. 'So what's this new wrinkle, Detectives? And please tell me it's going to put a prettier spin on things, because as of right now, the Bureau has four days to avert a possible national disaster and the clock is ticking.'

'Okay, here's the deal,' Magozzi said. 'Joe Hardy didn't just kill the two Somalis who killed him; he also murdered the two in the kidnapping house. We don't know who the shooter was in Detroit, but we know the shooter in LA was a vet, just like Joe Hardy. The coincidence bothered us.'

'Where are you going with this, Detective?'

Magozzi cleared his throat. 'What if veterans all over the country are targeting and eliminating terrorists the FBI doesn't have a bead on yet.'

Dahl raised his head and stared at them for a long time before he spoke. 'If that's true, then they're getting their information from somewhere. I need Joe Hardy's computer. Right now.'

Gino winced. 'Jeez, Dahl, his widow is making funeral plans, and you want to show up at her door with Storm Troopers and a warrant?'

'Not particularly. You two want to run interference?'

Gino held up one finger and reached for his phone. 'Wait one.'

Dahl was fidgeting in his chair, counting lost seconds, when Gino hung up with Beth.

'What did you tell her?' Magozzi asked.

'Same old lame line about tying up loose ends.'

'Did she buy it?'

'Hell, no, but she'll give us the computer. Trouble is, it's up at Elbow Lake Reservation in his duffel bag. She said she'd tell his friends to give it to us if we promised to tell her later what this is all about.'

Dahl jumped to his feet. 'Are you two still on the inter-agency cooperation train?'

'For this, you bet,' Magozzi told him.

'So where is Elbow Lake?'

'About five hours north.'

Dahl shook his head. 'That's too long.'

'That's where it is.'

Dahl started walking out in a hurry. 'Stay by your phone. I'll get back to you within half an hour.'

32

Twenty minutes after Agent Dahl left the Homicide office, he called them back as promised. Magozzi listened, scribbled notes, then hung up and looked at Gino. 'We're going to Elbow Lake. Dahl cleared our time with Chief Malcherson.'

'Great. This is double time. Five hours up, five hours back . . .'

'We're flying. The Feds booked us on a charter at two this afternoon out of Holman Field in St Paul.'

Gino lowered his head and started massaging his temples vigorously, redirecting his forehead skin to places it had probably never been before. 'Come on, Leo. You know I don't fly, especially in the kind of crop dusters that would service a nowhere place like Elbow Lake. Besides, you know what kind of stuff flies out of Holman? The shit people build in their garages out of Popsicle sticks and Gorilla Glue. I have a tramp art lamp in my house built better than some of those things.'

'This is a charter, Gino. A private plane service. They fly up there all the time to service the big snowmobile plant and the window factory.'

'By private plane, do you mean the Citation X type or do you mean the kind with flimsy little props made out of balsa wood that crash down into cornfields and kill rock stars? Because I refuse to board anything that doesn't have turbines. At least two of them. Period.'

'There's nothing wrong with props. In fact, the good thing about props is that if you stall out in midair, you can restart the engines. A jet stalls out in midair, you're pretty much toast.'

Gino's face turned gray. 'Jesus Christ, is that supposed to make me feel better?'

'Makes me feel better. Besides, statistically, flying is much safer than . . .'

'Yeah, yeah, yeah, safer than driving, and I fucking hate it when people roll out that stupid comparison. Statistically speaking, you actually have a chance of surviving a car wreck. *Statistically speaking,* if you're in a plane wreck, you get vaporized and some coroner ends up identifying you by your teeth. If those don't get vaporized, too.'

Magozzi sighed impatiently. 'Look, Gino, I know you got a problem with planes, but we have to take the flight. The Feds need that computer, and it won't hurt us to talk to Joe's friends face-to-face. Maybe they knew what he was into and where he was getting his information. There's a lot at stake here.'

Gino looked down at his hands, probably envisioning them being vaporized. 'Shit,' he finally mumbled.

Magozzi took it as a good sign that Gino wasn't protesting anymore. Maybe he'd gone into shock. 'It's going to be fine, Gino. You think the Feds would entrust that computer to a sketchy charter service? No way.'

Gino closed his eyes. 'I have to call Angela. Remind her where the will is.'

Magozzi parked in the guest lot of Holman Field and

he and Gino walked into the terminal, which was little more than one room with a counter, a couple computers, some seating, and a vending machine.

A lean, middle-aged guy with a salt-and-pepper buzz cut was behind the counter, tapping away at his keyboard. He was wearing a pilot's uniform, which seemed to be a slight consolation for Gino.

'Afternoon,' he said as he greeted them. 'You must be the two detectives.'

'That's right.'

'Lieutenant Colonel Fuhrman, USAF retired, at your service. I'll be your pilot today.'

Gino relaxed a little. 'Air Force, huh? Did you fly?'

'Yes, sir. Fifteen years. Flew twenty-seven sorties in the first two desert operations. Killed a lot of camels.' He chuckled.

'So what kind of craft are we talking about for our trip?'

'Today, we rustled up a nice Beech for you.'

'Rustled up?' Gino asked, his voice suddenly small. 'That sounds like you picked it up at a thrift store.'

Fuhrman laughed. 'Nervous one, are you? Don't worry, Detective. Small planes scare most everybody. Thing is, they're low-tech and easy to fly. I'll get you there and back in one piece, guaranteed.' He checked his watch. 'We should be good to go in thirty. I just need you two to step on the scale.'

Gino looked alarmed. 'Why?'

'So we can distribute the cabin load properly. We don't want to be doing any barrel rolls today,' he said with a little smile.

Gino jumped on the scale. He'd probably already lost five pounds in sweat during the drive to the airfield.

'Okay, Detectives, you can follow me out to the strip. I'll do my preflight check and we can take to the friendly skies. Weather shouldn't be too much of a problem, but I'd prepare myself for some bumps along the way – there's a tiny little system moving in from the west.'

'Oh my God,' Gino breathed as they walked out to the tarmac. 'Shouldn't be too much of a problem? What the hell is that supposed to mean?'

Magozzi pointed to the plane, which was a lot smaller than he thought it would be, but it looked pretty decent. No twist ties holding on the wings or anything. 'Look at that. See? No Popsicle sticks. Genuine metal. And check out those props. That's a beefy plane, Gino.'

Fuhrman turned around. 'It's a solid craft, Detective.'

'How old is it?'

'Twenty years old.'

'That sounds old.'

'It is. But these things last forever. One of these babies hasn't gone down in almost four years.'

Gino stopped dead. 'Leo, I can't do this. I cannot do this. I'm walking up to Elbow Lake, unless we find a better plane.'

'Trust me, this is the best game in town to suit your purposes,' Fuhrman said. 'In fact, you two got lucky today with this little honey,' he said, slapping the wing fondly. 'I usually fly this route in a fork-tailed doctor killer.'

Magozzi had seen his partner work through a myriad of stressors over the years, and his reaction had always been pretty consistent – he ranted until he ran out of steam, then knuckled under and worked it through. This was the first time he'd ever seen Gino completely paralyzed.

He gave Fuhrman a nasty look for his effort, which seemed to take the wind out of his sadistic, smart-ass sails a little bit. The pilot disappeared into the plane and came down with two tiny airline bottles and held them out to Gino.

'Cheap vodka. Down these babies and you'll have the time of your life. Welcome to the world of private air travel.'

Gino unscrewed the cap and drained one bottle. 'Five of these, and I might be okay,' he said, wincing.

'Five more of those, and you won't be able to get up those steps,' Magozzi said, snatching the other bottle out of Gino's hand. 'Come on, before you bail for real. You ever think about getting a prescription for tranquilizers when you fly?'

'I don't fly. I don't plan to ever again. It would be a waste of pharmaceuticals.'

The interior of the plane was about the size of a test tube, and there were only six seats laid out in a weird configuration, where some faced each other and some faced the backs of the other seats. Everything seemed miniaturized compared to a normal plane, right down to the tiny round windows that offered a hazy glance at the terra firma beneath them. Gino was panting and sighing a lot – a sure indication of extreme anxiety.

'See, this isn't so bad, is it?' Magozzi asked, feeling a little anxious himself.

'Oh, it's just peachy, Leo,' he hissed, tugging at the floral shower curtain hanging between the main fuselage and the cockpit.

'This is a goddamned shower curtain! And it's out in plain view! If you go to a restaurant and there are cockroaches crawling on the tables, do you eat the shit that comes out of the kitchen? No. So what do you think we'd find if we looked under the hood of this thing? Maybe they shop at Bed Bath and Beyond for spare engine parts, too!'

Magozzi lowered his head and pinched the bridge of his nose. This was going to be a long flight. He shoved the second vodka bottle into Gino's hand. 'Come on. Let's go sit down.'

33

Grace was standing in front of the Beast, watching as it spit out a stream of printouts, thinking that for all the miracles technology offered, there were just certain tasks that had to be done eyes-on. The Beast could sort, collate, and identify patterns on a massive scale, but it couldn't take raw data and analyze the importance of its content. And it couldn't tell her why a seemingly innocent activity like hacking and monitoring certain websites could earn you a jihad. That kind of analysis required gray matter.

She pressed a hand to the small of her back while she waited, trying to work out the aches and pains. After the past three months in sandals, she'd forgotten how uncomfortable riding boots were, and how their flat, unsupported soles threw your posture totally out of whack. They were designed to rest in stirrups, not walk you around.

When the printer finally finished, she grabbed a sheaf of paper, tossed it on her desk, then distributed the rest to Harley and Annie. 'These are John's e-mails from the last three months. Sort out all the ones he sent to law enforcement and read them line by line. He was monitoring terrorist sites and passing information on. There has to be something there.' She glanced over at Roadrunner, who was in a deeper hunch than usual in front of his computer, every single vertebra outlined in Lycra. 'How are you doing, Roadrunner?'

He looked up, his eyelids heavy from lack of sleep and hours of screen time, but his mouth was actually toying with a faint smile. 'Great. My latest caffeine buzz is finally kicking in, and I just sent Tommy Espinoza location traces for all the chat room posts he was so hot about . . .' His voice trailed off and he focused bloodshot eyes on Grace. 'And he was *really* hot about them, and really secretive. Have you talked to Magozzi to get the scoop?'

Grace shook her head. 'I haven't talked to him since last night. But if Tommy is shook up, obviously something big is happening at MPD. Magozzi will call when he has a minute.'

Roadrunner bobbed his head. 'Right, he will. But I've got something else, guys – I just found a pretty impressive chunk of malware on John's computer. Somebody piggybacked on our butchered software. There were some eyes in his computer, and he didn't even know it.'

Harley grunted and ran his fingers through his black beard, which was looking shaggier by the day. 'Stupid. I still don't get why he even bothered to modify our program if he was just data mining.'

Annie, the only one of them who'd managed to survive the long workdays splendidly coiffed, smoothed out the colorful feathers that adorned her skirt and did a quick read of an e-mail on top of her stack. 'Here's one of them. Listen to this – an e-mail sent to the FBI and police department in Jackson, Mississippi: *1624 Magnolia Street. Al-Qaeda domestic operatives. Possible weapons cache.*'

Harley slapped his leather-clad knee with a fist. 'Well, holy shit on a shingle. That clever son of a bitch wasn't just data mining – he was tracing traffic off the jihadist websites and homing in on their locations with our worm. And letting people who could do something about it know.'

Roadrunner frowned. 'That still doesn't explain the kind of trouble he's in, does it?'

Grace shook her head. 'I don't know. Maybe.'

'Well, look at it this way, honey. Maybe these bad guys were getting busted left and right because of John's information, and they decided it was time to stop him.'

Harley's fingers clattered on his keyboard. 'Well, I just did a quick search on that address, and the men who lived on Magnolia Street didn't get busted. They got shot dead. Some gang thing, according to the news reports.'

Grace sighed and pushed up out of her chair. 'Find the other e-mails and do a search on all of them. I'll go cook some dinner.'

Harley beamed at her. 'Go for it.'

34

Grace was doing what she always did when her good brain was too cluttered with a jumble of conflicting thoughts. There was solace in the kitchen, comfort in the very predictable behavior of foods that never varied in their response. Cook the onions and garlic and celery and carrots in a wading pool of good olive oil and bacon fat until they caramelized, growing sugar like a crop in a skillet field. They were browning now, releasing a sweet aroma, doing exactly what they were supposed to do, unlike most humans.

She resisted the strong impulse to disturb those nuggets of flavor, so she just breathed in the fragrance and felt her body relax.

No one set foot in Harley's kitchen when Grace was cooking. They all knew better. Only John Smith had dared to enter this world, and only after he'd been invited. Of all the months at sea, all the experiences she had shared with him, the most vivid remained that day when John had cooked with her in this very kitchen for the first time; a silent, happily willing partner who found the same blessed peace in food preparation that she did.

She looked over at the cutting board where her Sig Sauer lay loaded and ready, thinking how odd it was to make magic with humble vegetables while a gun lay waiting. Annie, Roadrunner, and Harley were all upstairs, respecting her privacy certainly, but mostly anticipating her food. Normally she appreciated that, but tonight the kitchen was lonely.

She actually smiled when Roadrunner poked his head tentatively around the corner. His Lycra suit was black today, and for some reason that bothered her. His crippled, rawboned hands hung out of the snug sleeves, no place to go, nothing to do.

'Hi, Roadrunner. Half an hour to supper.'

He gave her a shy smile. 'Smells great.'

'Bacon,' she said, jerking the skillet and sending the vegetables aloft to fall perfectly back into the pan where they belonged. 'Your socks would smell good sautéed in this.'

'Grace?'

'Yes?'

'So far we found three more e-mails to law enforcement and ran the addresses through a search. All of the people who lived at those addresses are dead. One of them is the Minneapolis address of the house with all the explosives where Magozzi and Gino were working. The three dead men in the front yard. I tried calling Magozzi's cell; no answer. Detective McLaren told me they're in a plane, on their way up north working another case. They'll be out of touch for another few hours.'

Grace just stood there, oil dripping off the wooden spoon and onto the stove. 'John's e-mails were getting terrorists killed?' she whispered.

'It looks that way. We haven't gone through the whole stack, but it's starting to look that way, which explains the jihad.'

'Oh my God.'

'There's something else, Grace. I just took a call over the transom. Some FBI agent looking for John's notes on the case we worked with him.'

She looked down at the skillet and moved it off the heat. 'But that case was solved. Why would the Feds want his notes?'

'I don't know.'

'Did you check him out?'

'Yes. Hung up, called DC headquarters. His ID number and name checked out. They said he wasn't in the office, but that he worked from home like a lot of the agents. Seemed legit.'

Grace wiped her hands on her apron and looked at him. Roadrunner had icy blue eyes that most people glossed over nervously, the color seemed so cold. But Grace had always seen a warm heart behind those cool eyes. 'So it seemed legit, but you don't think so.'

He moved his bony shoulders. 'Paranoia, probably. It all seemed right, but it didn't feel right.'

'What did you tell him?'

'I told them the people that worked with Smith weren't working here anymore.'

Grace looked down at the vegetables, coddled, perfect, knowing inside they would never make their way into the dish she'd planned. 'Is the Range Rover still in the garage?'

'Yes.'

'Load the weapons in the back.'

Roadrunner's body parts moved randomly. 'All of them?'

Grace looked at him, connecting. 'Yes.'

Her cell phone rang the moment Roadrunner left the room. A voice on the other end said, 'Grace?'

She caught her breath and whispered, 'John. You're all over the Web. There's a jihad on you.'

'I know.'

'And we just had a call. Someone looking for you. He said he was a Fed from DC.'

'I know that, too. I had a tap on your line, and that call wasn't from DC, it was from Minneapolis. They're here. Get out, Grace. All of you. Right now. Meet me at hole in one. Do you understand?'

'Yes.'

'Don't pack, don't think, just go.'

Grace punched a button on the intercom for Annie up in the office and spoke quickly, tersely. 'Get down here fast. Bring Charlie. We're leaving.'

For the first five minutes Grace drove very fast, squealing around corners, blowing past stop signs, carving a very intentional zigzag route through the neighborhood while Annie, Harley, and Roadrunner watched for a tail. When they gave the all-clear she slowed down.

Evasive driving, class. The cops learn it in the academy, but it isn't rocket science. Never go in a straight line. Stay off the freeways, stick to the secondary roads. Backtrack when you can, make unexpected turns, park and turn off your lights, wait to see if anyone follows. And above all, blend into the traffic. A speeding car is a target, so stop for all the lights, don't exceed the speed limit, and you are like every other car on the road. You are inconspicuous. Invisible.

Grace had learned that lesson well and followed it carefully as she made her convoluted way through the city.

35

The whine and grind of the engines jolted Magozzi awake. Apparently, he'd dozed off the second he'd buckled himself in. Gino was snugged into the seat facing his.

'You snore,' Gino informed him, his eyes focused on Fuhrman at the front of the plane as he made his final announcements, as if there were a planeload of passengers instead of just two.

'Are we there yet?'

'No. We're taking off any minute. The gerbils are finally warmed up.'

Fuhrman walked down the aisle and stopped beside Gino. 'Detective, I'm going to have to ask you to move to a seat on the other side of the aircraft.'

'You're kidding.'

'Nope. You and your partner can't be this close together. You remember what I said about barrel rolls, right?'

Gino's face lost all color as he stood up. 'You're a funny guy, you know that?'

Fuhrman wisely kept a clamp on his smile. 'Okay, we're ready to go. Fasten your seat belts and enjoy the flight.' He disappeared into the cockpit and closed the shower curtain behind him.

Gino sat down, buckled in, and braced his hands against the seat in front of him. He tried to take some deep breaths, because somebody had told him once that it was supposed to be calming. That somebody was a moron, because all it did was make you hyperventilate, which he soon discovered. 'The engines sound funny,' he puffed without looking at Magozzi, thinking that using up some spare air on words might help.

'Relax, Gino. We're going to be fine. You want a puke bag?'

'No. Absolutely not. I hate to puke. I refuse to puke . . .'

The plane lurched forward and started speeding down the runway. Gino clutched his armrests and squeezed his eyes shut. 'Oh my God.' And then suddenly they were aloft, bouncing up, up, up. A few minutes later, there was a thunk as the landing gear either went up into the belly or fell off, he wasn't sure which. He figured he'd find out soon enough.

'There,' Magozzi said from across the narrow aisle. 'That wasn't so bad, was it?'

Gino opened his eyes slowly, careful to avoid catching a glimpse of the land receding through the crappy little windows. 'It ain't over, buddy.'

The loudspeaker suddenly crackled and Fuhrman came on. 'We're just about at cruising altitude now, folks, but I'd stay in my seats if I were you. We're going to be hitting a few bumps in a bit. That little storm rolling in from the west seems to be getting a lot bigger in a hurry.'

Gino risked tipping over the stupid plane by turning to scowl at Magozzi. 'Told you.' He cracked open the second vodka bottle.

36

Go to the dark. Look for the darkest corner in the darkest part of any alley, any closet, any piece of the world you're living in, and go there.

It was a survival skill Grace MacBride had never been formally schooled in, unlike the evasive driving tactics. This was pure animal instinct that most people lost in a childhood populated with caring people. But she'd never been that lucky, so the instinct had survived in her and had served her well. She responded to instinct long before thought could catch up, which was why she turned off the Rover's headlights when she was blocks away from the country club.

The moon was big and bright, glancing off skittish clouds, and that, along with the regularly stationed street-lamps, made the headlights entirely unnecessary. When she pulled into the private entrance, the recessed lights on either side of the smooth asphalt were an unerring guide to the large, empty parking lot.

'Damn, the moon is brighter than Yankee Stadium on game night,' Harley whispered from the backseat. 'We're not exactly blending in here.' Charlie sat between him and Roadrunner, and both men had an arm around the dog, like a couple of kids clutching a stuffed animal for comfort.

They'd all been whispering since leaving Harley's,

except for that scary moment when Grace had almost hit a city bus and Annie had yelled out a warning. Normally she would have encouraged hitting one of the metallic behemoths. Damn things stopped traffic, took up the whole road, and the self-entitled, arrogant drivers thought they owned the streets. But tonight wasn't the night to pick a fight with some overpaid city employee.

Annie scooched down in the shotgun seat as they cruised slowly to the edge of the parking lot closest to the eighteenth hole, where John Smith had lived through his first real police action with Gino and Magozzi last summer. She reached down to unclip her seat belt, which was wreaking dreadful havoc with her feathered skirt, but Grace apparently wasn't parking. Instead, she gunned the accelerator and drove hell-bent for leather over the concrete curb that divided the lot from the course proper, and sped over the carefully cropped, meticulously tended fairways, leaving deep ruts behind as she headed toward the eighteenth green.

'Lordy, girl, what are you doing?' Annie gasped. 'This is major destruction of property.'

Grace ignored her and finally came to a stop when she could see the moonlight reflecting off the red and white flag in the center of the last green. She turned off the key to stop the muted rumble of the SUV's big engine, but kept her hand on it, ready.

'What are we doing?' Annie whispered.

'Waiting.' Grace looked out the side windows, into all the mirrors, through the windshield, but still never saw him coming.

Harley went airborne when the face suddenly appeared

at his window, seat belt cutting into his gut. But he had his .357 out and pointed at the man outside his window before his butt came back down on the leather. 'Jesus,' he muttered, his finger quivering on the trigger. The guy looked old, with a gray ponytail, a stubble of gray whiskers, and ratty clothes, surely some homeless druggie. Then the man smiled because there were four guns pointed right at him. That was good.

'Oh my God.' Harley released a tight breath, recognizing the rarely seen smile, if not the man. 'It's John.'

Grace caught her breath and the muzzle of her Sig lowered as John piled into the seat behind Grace, pushing Harley into the middle next to Roadrunner, and forcing Charlie into the cargo bay behind the backseat, which was fine with the dog since it gave his tongue a straight shot at the back of John's neck. He whined a happy but subdued greeting as John reached back to fondle his ears.

There were no salutations, no small talk, but John did lean forward to put his hand on Grace's shoulder, just for a second.

'You sure you weren't followed?' he asked her.

'Positive.' Grace was already rolling the Rover toward the entrance road, lights still off. 'Where to, John?'

'Just out of the city for now. Straight, flat roads where we can see a long way behind us.'

'Man, you've got some talking to do, amigo,' Harley said.

'Later. After we're out of the city and certain that we're not being followed.'

When Grace eased back out onto the quiet residential street, none of them saw anything suspicious, just parked cars in front of sleepy houses with no garages. Grace drove at the speed limit as all of them watched for a tail that might pull away from the curb to follow. Nothing. Eventually she made a turn to circuit Pattern Lake and started an evasive course that would eventually lead to the I-94 freeway. Northwest was the fastest road out of the city; flat and straight.

Behind Grace, John leaned back in his seat, took the first deep breath he'd taken in a while, and smiled just a little. He was back with the only friends he'd ever known and trusted, and this was the place where he wanted to live forever.

There was a vestigial survival instinct at work here. For a full half hour, none of the Monkeewrench partners said a word. They were tense with watchfulness, looking out the front, back, and side windows. Grace kept checking her mirrors, eyes on every vehicle that passed her. Occasionally she caught a glimpse of John, his head back, eyes closed, apparently sleeping. His face was smooth and at peace, like a child who implicitly trusts the people he is with to keep him safe. It made her wonder what he'd been through this past week.

Part of her wanted to wait for him to tell her what to do. *Drop the mains'l, Grace, but slowly now, then we can come about without being dumped by the crosswinds.* It was easy to take direction because she hadn't known a thing about sailing, and those were the first moments she'd felt the blessed relief of completely trusting in someone else to do the right thing. The feeling of abdicating responsibility for her own well-being had been stunning. John was probably feeling the same thing now, closing his eyes because he trusted in the eyes of others.

But it was different now. She was on her roads in her territory and she knew exactly what to do without asking anyone. She left the freeway and stopped at the top of a long exit ramp, watching her rearview mirror. 'There's a Minnesota map in the glove compartment, Annie. Find a side road heading north.'

'I told you to get GPS in this thing.'

'Not for all the money in the world.'

'Can I turn on the map light?'

'No. There's a mini flash in the console.'

After much quiet grumbling and paper rustling, Annie said, 'One mile right, left on County 27 for a few miles – you have a destination in mind here? I can get you to Canada, North Dakota . . .'

'We need a pay phone,' John said from the backseat. 'No gas stations, no place with lights.'

'Good luck with that,' Harley grumbled. 'I haven't seen a pay phone in a decade. The cells killed them.' Under most circumstances, Harley Davidson was a massive, imposing figure. Crunched into the middle of the backseat like the bad kid, big, booted feet straddling the transmission hump, he seemed a little diminished.

'Look for wayside signs,' Grace said. 'The farther north we get, the better chance we'll find a pay phone. They still don't trust cells in farm country.'

Roadrunner released a sigh of relief. He never had a whole lot to say, but found the noise of his partners' chatter somehow comforting. It had been too quiet for too long in this car, and the silence had been disturbing. 'Who are we going to call?' he asked timidly.

'I need to call Magozzi,' Grace said. 'If he tries to call me and gets no answer, he's going to panic.'

'That's who I need to call,' John said. 'He and Gino are handling the murders in Little Mogadishu. That's going to break this thing wide open.'

Annie looked back without shifting a single feather on her skirt. 'We already broke this thing wide open, darling. Turns out you've been getting a lot of terrorists killed.'

John nodded. 'So it would seem. I just don't know how. How much else do you know so far from what you got off the copy of my hard drive?'

Harley folded his massive arms across his chest. 'We know you were tracking terrorists off extremist websites and anonymously sharing your information with the law. Using our illegal worm, I might add, which you totally butchered when you tried to reprogram it. It busted up our firewalls and left your computer wide open. What's that all about?'

John cringed. 'I reprogrammed it to read Arabic and then used it to hack the private e-mails of the people who were signing on to the jihadist sites. That mined out a long list of suspects that the Bureau was missing – lone wolves, a lot of domestic solo operators. Not one of them was on the national or international watch lists, and that scared me.'

'But obviously you're not killing any of these people, so who is?' Harley asked.

'The only thing I can figure is that someone who got a couple of my anonymous tips decided to start taking out bad guys without dancing through the system.'

'Wait a minute, John,' Annie interrupted. 'Are you saying some people in law enforcement are taking your tips and going on a killing spree?'

'It's possible.'

Grace had been listening to everything, even though she'd been focused on plotting a sensible course for them with Annie's map of Minnesota and the GPS that resided in her brain. Highway 27 it was, for at least twelve miles. They'd make a new decision after that, if they hadn't found a pay phone by then.

She finally looked up into the rearview mirror and saw all three backseat occupants staring at nothing, their faces pinched like deflated balloons as they considered the possibility that someone in law enforcement had read John's warning e-mails and organized a nationwide network to kill terror suspects. At the moment, Grace didn't care who it was. Right now, job one was finding a safe place.

She pushed down on the accelerator, cranked the wheel, and powered the Rover down the tiny, winding road that was County 27.

37

In a tiny house on the backstreets of Little Mogadishu, a tall, dark man clicked off the burner cell he had activated only this morning. He had boxes of them stacked in a corner of the kitchen. He used them for only one day, then disposed of them in the nearby river.

'Who was it?' a heavyset man asked from the stove. It was shameful for a man to prepare food, but the woman who normally performed this task had been barred from the house for the past week. At this critical time, a third pair of eyes, no matter how trusted, could not be permitted to witness their activities.

'The Monkeewrench partners have left the city.'

'The phone call to their office?'

'Perhaps. Someone was listening. How many men do we have ready?'

'At least twenty immediately. More within the hour.'

'Contact them. Use a clean phone, then dispose of it.'

'Where should I send them?'

'Northwest on I-94 to begin. Further directions to come.'

'We don't know their final destination?'

'It doesn't matter. They stopped once and picked up John Smith.'

The heavyset man smiled.

38

Apparently little planes could fly, but they couldn't land for shit.

'Sorry for the bumps, Detectives.' Fuhrman's voice came over the tinny speaker. 'Bad crosswinds today, and we had to one-wheel it a couple times.'

Gino closed his eyes and pictured the plane skidding along on one wheel, then tipping over, the wing snapping off, the fuselage cartwheeling, and then the explosion. 'Thank God,' he whispered down at his lap, then thought maybe he should hold off on the gratitude. Just because they hadn't crashed and burned this time didn't mean it couldn't happen on the way home.

Gino knew he had legs. He could see them filling out his pants, but they didn't want to stand up, and he didn't blame them. They'd had a long, scary plane ride, a really stressful time, and they deserved a chance to just lay there for a while and recover.

'Up and at 'em, buddy.'

Gino glared at Magozzi. 'My legs are asleep.'

'Then you should stand up, get the blood moving.'

Gino muttered a very bad word, grabbed the seat back in front of him, which nearly broke in half, and pulled himself up. His legs did that pins-and-needles thing as he shuffled into the dinky aisle. 'Go ahead, but go fast. I could collapse at any moment.'

Magozzi raised his brows in one of those expressions he always wore when Gino went off on some rant of exaggeration.

Gino thought if he could only balance on his cramped legs, he might punch his partner in the nose. 'Don't give me that look, you bastard. And you know what, Mr Smart Alec? There are more potholes in the sky than there are on a Minnesota road in spring. I think I cracked my tooth on that last bump when my head hit the ceiling.'

'You were very brave.' Magozzi punched him in the arm, then headed for the door of the pretend plane and shook hands with the rotten pilot.

Bracing his hands on the few seats in front of him, Gino made his way forward. The pilot smiled at him. 'Thank you for flying with us, sir.'

'Fuck you.'

'Happy to oblige, sir. I look forward to seeing you on your return flight. I'll show you what this baby can really do.'

Gino looked down at the teeny-weeny steps that led to blessed, stable land, so close and yet so far away. He figured he'd stumble and fall and crack his head open on the concrete and die a horrible death. He looked around for his faithful partner, who was nowhere to be seen.

There wasn't an actual terminal – just a steel building with a single glass door. Magozzi was inside, collecting their luggage, chatting up some Indian-looking dude behind the counter. Gino walked up to stand beside him and nodded toward the door. 'Those are the two in that hunting picture in Joe Hardy's house, right?'

Magozzi turned his head and saw two older men

walking toward them. One was tall, rangy, and had bright blue eyes that age hadn't dulled. His companion was a little shorter, and much broader, with a long black braid shot with gray.

'Detectives.' The taller man grabbed their hands and shook them hard. 'I'm Claude Gerlock, and I'm very pleased to meet you.' The man breathed out Texas and alcohol. 'This jack pine savage here is Chief of Tribal Police Bellanger, but it's been so long since anyone's called him anything but Chief, he can't remember his own name.' He wrapped an arm around the Chief's shoulders.

'Nice to meet you, Detectives,' Chief said. 'Beth told us you wanted Joey's computer.'

Magozzi nodded. 'That's right. Did you bring it with you?'

'We figured we'd take you back to the cabin and give you a meal since your return flight doesn't leave for a few hours.'

'We'd like to buy you dinner if you'd let us. We're on Hennepin County's dime tonight, and we really appreciate your help with the computer.'

Chief chuckled low in his throat. 'Son, there isn't an open restaurant for about twenty miles, and we're just a hop from the cabin. We've got great food, really great whiskey, and we'd be grateful for the chance to learn what happened to our Joey. Besides, it's the least we can do. Beth told us you've been really kind to her. Claude's ride is just outside.'

The night air this far north had a fierce chill to it when they walked outside to the parking lot, and Magozzi buttoned up his overcoat, wishing he'd brought some gloves.

They all piled into a high-end SUV, Claude behind the wheel, with Chief as his copilot while Gino and Magozzi took the backseat. Once they'd left the lighted parking lot of the airport and got on a skinny black ribbon of road that wound through thick pine forest, absolute blackness swallowed them. Even the halogen headlights of the truck seemed pathetically ineffective against such pervasive dark. Magozzi stared straight ahead at the twin paths of light they followed, trying to ignore the rising uneasiness of claustrophobia.

Gino, on the other hand, seemed enchanted by it all. 'Man, I've never seen a night this dark before in my life. And look at those stars, Leo. Unbelievable. It's like somebody threw a bag of powdered sugar up there.'

Chief seemed to like that, because he let out a low chuckle. 'No ambient light from any city up here to wreck things.'

'Well, you've got it good if you see stars like that every night. Are we on the reservation yet?'

'You were on the reservation the minute you stepped off that plane.'

Gino mulled that over for a moment. 'You have your own airport?'

'Sure. Doesn't every Indian reservation?' Claude and the Chief shared a chuckle.

'So you're rich?'

'Nope. We just do our piece and get by like everybody else. But it wasn't always like that up here.'

'Hell, no, it wasn't,' Claude agreed. 'First time I came up here in '74, it was wild as hell, just like all the movies and documentaries you ever saw about reservations. Gut-rot drunks with guns, rusted cars on blocks in front of rustier trailers on blocks with no plumbing.' He took a turn onto an even skinnier strip of road, this one almost as bumpy as their plane ride. Magozzi dared a look into the ever-thickening forest and thought he caught a glimpse of some glowing yellow eyes. 'So it's different now?' he asked, hoping the answer would be yes, because he was looking forward to a hot meal at some point.

'Way different,' Chief said. 'We still have our struggles, no question about that. The wounds of history run deep, and you still see the fallout on reservations all over this country, including this one. But Elbow Lake's done well, and for that I'm thankful.'

'What changed it?' Gino asked, his face still pressed against the window as he gazed up at the amazing clutter of stars.

'Billy Eight-Toes,' Chief explained. 'That young brave came home to the reservation two toes short after sloshing through the hot jungles and swamps of 'Nam, and suddenly life up here seemed like paradise compared to what he'd seen, even though it wasn't. And it just so happened that a few hundred acres of pretty spruce forest on the northern edge of the rez went up on the block for back taxes the week he came home. When was that, Claude?'

'In '75. And the state had no interest in a little bitty few hundred acres of wilderness that backed up to a bunch of crazy Indians with a lot of guns and bathtub gin. But Billy hadn't seen it that way. If it was paradise to him, he figured it might be paradise to a lot of other folks and weekend warriors, it just needed tidying up a little bit. So he started thinking on a hunting camp, because the game was plentiful. Still is.'

Chief nodded, smiling at his memories. 'So Billy and his brothers built the lodge, plus a bunch of cabins with native timber. Then the crafty son of a bitch started advertising, in the back of a few sportsman magazines, a hunting camp with genuine Indian guides. Outsiders weren't one bit put off by the proximity of the reservation. Billy thought some of them came up just for the sheer adventure of it, as if a settlement of impoverished Indians added an element of danger to their all-boy vacations. Billy didn't care much what they thought as long as their money was green and they kept telling their friends about the place.'

'Sounds like a smart guy,' Magozzi said, keeping a lookout for more spooky eyes.

'It was pure genius,' Claude said. 'Within a few years the lodge and cabins were full up most of the year with hunters, snowmobilers, and fishermen, and Billy employed over half the reservation's population. The money was flowing, but the change to the reservation was slow as a one-legged armadillo in coming, I can tell you that.'

'Yes, sir,' Chief agreed. 'You take a dead-broke, beaten-down people and give them income for real work instead of giving them handouts, they do funny things with money. If you live in a paper bag, a cardboard box is spittin' rich. It took almost two generations to change the mind-set.'

'Is Billy Eight-Toes still around?' Gino asked.

'No. Poor old Billy never quite got the war out of his head – hell, nobody does – and he drank himself half to death one night and wrapped his new truck around a tree.'

'That's sad.'

Chief shrugged as Claude made another turn, this one onto a dirt road so narrow, tree branches brushed both sides of the SUV. 'Sad outcome for Billy, but he did a lot for his people. Left a legacy . . .'

'Uh . . .' Magozzi interrupted, tapping his finger on the window. 'Uh . . .'

Chief turned around in his seat. 'What is it, Detective?'

Magozzi continued to point out the window, but he couldn't find his voice.

Chief's eyes followed the direction of Magozzi's finger and he smiled. 'I'll be damned, stop the truck, Claude. We've got ourselves a mukwa, making a special appearance for our friends.'

'I see him.' Claude stopped the truck and turned off all but the fog lights.

'Holy shit!' Gino whispered, staring at a monstrous form emerging from the woods right toward them.

'That is one big son of a bitch,' the Chief said quietly. 'You got your bear gun in the back, Chimook?'

'Damn my soul to hell, I don't. Figured it might spook the detectives.'

Magozzi and Gino stared silently out the window, their mouths hanging open as a huge bear lumbered up close to the side of the skinny road and started sniffing around, his big, black nose quivering, wary eyes never leaving the truck. Or maybe they were hungry eyes. Or homicidal eyes.

'That . . . that's really close,' Gino stammered.

'It's a beaut, though, isn't it?' Claude asked, admiration in his voice. 'Look at the coat on him. One fine animal.'

Well, Magozzi couldn't help but agree – the bear was beautiful, impressive, majestic even – and then the goddamned thing stood up on its hind legs until it was about forty feet tall and made some really nasty sound he could only interpret as 'Get the fuck out of my woods' in bearspeak.

'Oh Jesus,' Gino said, recoiling in his seat. 'It's gonna kill us. I lived through the flight, and now I'm going to get eaten by a bear . . .'

'He won't eat you,' Claude said confidently. 'You saved his life tonight, kept me from running over him. He owes you one.' Then he put the truck back into gear and started rolling slowly away.

Gino and Magozzi were both straddling a fine line between terror and thrilled fascination as they watched the bear in the glow of the taillights. He dropped down, walked into the middle of the road, and stood up again in final warning.

'That's a special thing, seeing a bear up close like that,' the Chief said. 'Hope you two enjoyed it.'

'Oh, yeah,' Gino said, catching his breath. 'Real special. Does that happen often?'

'Not too often. They're mostly shy, and won't do you any harm unless you're in the way of something they want, or if you're threatening them. At least most of the time.'

'Most of the time?'

'Well, you get a rogue every once in a while. No different from humans, except bears are a hell of a lot more predictable.'

'Amen,' Claude said. 'But now you know, these woods

are full of all kinds of things you don't want to get surprised by, so if you get a hankering for a hike, make sure you're prepared. Those little peashooters you two are carrying ain't gonna do the job.'

39

The cabin wasn't at all what Gino and Magozzi had been expecting. There was nothing rustic about the place, save for the extremely dangerous wildlife that was lurking in the woods, waiting to dismember unsuspecting tourists. To Magozzi, it looked like a pricey ski chalet, uprooted from Aspen or Telluride and plopped down in the middle of northern Minnesota nowhere. Not that he'd ever been to either of those places, but he'd seen pictures in those glossy celeb rags they always had in the dentist's waiting room.

Claude and Chief led them to an impressive great room with lots of fieldstone, glass, and polished wood, decorated with an array of stuffed animal heads that stared down at them with accusatory glass eyes. Magozzi had never been a big fan of stuffed anything, unless it was a Thanksgiving turkey, but taxidermy aside, he could see himself spending time here. 'Beautiful place.'

'It's a little slice of paradise, no question,' Claude agreed, stepping behind a granite-topped bar and lining up four lowball tumblers. 'You gentlemen in the mood for a little fuel?'

Gino and Magozzi looked at each other, then Gino nodded. 'That would be nice, thank you.'

Claude smiled his approval. 'We'll toast to Joey. He'd be pleased to know you both shared a drink in his honor.

That boy loved his whiskey. At least when he could still countenance it . . .' His voice suddenly sizzled away like a drop of water on a hot skillet.

'Bring your drinks into the dining room,' Chief said, breaking in to fill the silence. 'We've got chili, every meat you can think of for sandwiches, and a bunch of man salads Noya whipped up.'

'What's a man salad?' Gino asked.

'Just the *p*'s. Pasta or potatoes, no green stuff.'

'Good deal. Who's Noya?'

'She's my wife.'

'Why isn't she here?'

'Oh, she never comes to the cabin if she can help it. Too much testosterone, she says.'

They sat at the table long enough for Gino to make considerable craters in every platter, then went to the living room to sit by the fire. Gino frowned at the sporadic ping of icy pellets on the windows, already worrying about their ten o'clock return flight.

Chief settled himself in a leather recliner and cradled his full stomach in his hands. 'Now, why don't you tell us why you're really up here. Planes aren't cheap, and a last-minute trip to get Joey's computer tells me there's something more to this.'

'There is something more,' Magozzi finally said.

Chief nodded. 'Appreciate you being straight with us.'

'This doesn't leave this room. This goes beyond Homicide and we're stepping on Federal toes right now, talking out of school.'

Claude shook his glass and smiled a little, stirring a couple ice cubes that were bathing in a whole lot of whiskey.

'Chief and I were both Special Ops in 'Nam. "Cleaners," they called us. We know how to keep our pie holes clamped, so talk when you're ready to.'

Gino stepped in and told them Joe hadn't just killed the two men who'd killed him; he'd also killed another two Somalis in cold blood a day earlier.

Both men's jaws sagged open, and the disbelief on their faces was genuine; it was the kind of absolute shock that couldn't be put on like a mask.

'First thing, Joey wouldn't do that,' Claude finally said quietly. 'Second thing, he couldn't do that. He was so weak, he could hardly walk from his car to the front door of the cabin.'

Gino didn't like where this was going – he liked these guys. He respected the sacrifices they'd made to serve their country, but this was what happened in a homicide investigation. You had to put your personal feelings aside sometimes and push a possible witness past the point you wanted to go. 'He took a silencer to the first house. He went there to kill. Those men were his targets. And it seems to follow that the men he killed the night he died were targets, too, especially since all four of them turned out to be major terror players, tied up with a very nasty plot that's set to hit cities all across the country four days from now – a plot the Feds didn't know about until we pulled evidence from our homicides.'

Claude and Chief had been relaxed in their chairs, but now they were both sitting, almost at attention, like two proud men taking a physical beating they couldn't do anything to stop. 'You're sure?' Claude whispered.

'As sure as it gets.'

Chief looked like a tree that was about to topple. He braced his hand on the chair arms to steady himself.

Claude looked at his friend, then refilled all their glasses with a shaky hand. 'What can we do to help?'

Magozzi looked down into his glass. 'If Joe had information that somebody was planning a terrorist attack, was he the kind of man who would act on that information? Would he be capable of murder?'

Chief looked at him. 'To save his country? Damn right he would. That's what he was trained to do.'

'But he never told you what he was planning?'

Chief actually smiled at that. 'That's a pretty loaded question from one cop to another, Detective. And the answer is no. No way that boy should have been out on the mean streets alone playing hero, goddamnit. We would have stopped him.' He looked worriedly at the windows. The sound of ice pellets hitting the glass had intensified, and now the wind was howling. 'That doesn't sound good.'

Gino got up immediately and went to the window. The deck was already glazed with ice. 'It doesn't look good, either.'

Claude called the airport, listened for a long time, then replaced the receiver. 'Sorry, fellas. Looks like you're going to be stuck here for the night, at least. This little storm took a sharp turn north, and nothing's flying out tonight.'

40

After Claude and the Chief had stumbled off to their respective bedrooms, Magozzi called Agent Dahl to tell him they wouldn't be back tonight, asked him to pass the word to Chief Malcherson, then he and Gino refilled their glasses and plopped into down-filled chairs by the fireplace.

'What did he say?'

'He wasn't happy.'

'Well, neither am I. Man, I feel like crap about tonight, Leo,' Gino sighed, listlessly swirling the ice cubes in his lowball. 'I mean, Claude and Chief come to pick us up at the airport, feed us great food, and then we tell them their best friend was a murderer. And after we slap that pile of sorrow on them, we stay the night and drink their booze.'

'I know. But we did what we had to do.'

Gino grunted, lifting and stretching out his legs to greet the ottoman in front of him. 'I told you we should have driven up here. But, oh no, you had to take a plane.'

'We couldn't drive in this crap either, Gino.'

'We could go real slow. As it is now, we're stuck here sitting on a hot computer and a freak show terror plot which could be moving forward by the second.'

Magozzi stared into the fireplace that still held the dying embers of the earlier fire. He could envision himself living in a place like this one day, old and retired and bird-watching with little binoculars as he drank his morning coffee. Not a bad place to get snowed in.

Gino stretched and yawned. 'Man, I feel beat up. I think I'm going to hit the rack. How about you?'

'I'll be right behind you. I'm just going to give Grace a quick call to check in first.'

'Where's my briefcase?'

'Still in Claude's truck.' Magozzi tossed Gino the keys. 'Don't slip on the ice. If you're gone for more than five minutes, I'll come out to make sure you didn't get mauled by a bear.'

Gino went pale and unholstered his weapon. 'Shit.'

While Gino went to retrieve his briefcase, Magozzi pressed speed dial. Grace's cell phone didn't even ring, just rolled straight over to voice mail. He paused, wondering if he should leave a message, remembering Grace's admonition not to call any phone but her throwaway cell. *That's the only number you can call, Magozzi. I'll keep it on twenty-four/seven. Someone will always answer.*

Magozzi closed his eyes and thought about it for a moment. Grace never messed up; never failed to follow through. If she said she'd answer the phone, then she'd answer the phone . . . unless something was wrong.

He felt his heart skip a beat and the hair on his arms stand up. He scooted to the edge of his chair, put his cell down on the coffee table, and stared at it. Take it easy, Magozzi. Don't jump off the edge here. She could be in the bathroom. She could have left the phone downstairs when she went to bed. The battery could be dead. It could be any one of a million things.

Someone will always answer.

'Screw it.' He jumped to his feet, snatched up his cell, and called Harley's landline in the Monkeewrench office. Again, no answer. He felt tiny roots of panic form in his stomach, then spread and grow when he tried Annie's cell next, then Harley's, then Roadrunner's.

Gino straggled back in, lugging their bags. 'Man, you should stick your head outside and listen to the owls. Sounds like they're having a rave and I think one tried to . . .' When he saw the look on his partner's face, he truncated any further conversation about owls. 'What's wrong, Leo?'

Magozzi's hands felt hot and sticky on his phone. 'I can't reach any of them. All their phones go to voice mail.'

He watched Gino put his bag down and return calmly to his chair. That was something uniquely Gino – high-strung and difficult as a purebred cat most times, unless there was a crisis looming in any arena of his life – then he turned into the Dalai Lama. 'Did you try their home phones?'

'Yeah. I'll try again.'

Gino watched him punch in number after number, then look up in dismay.

'Nothing. This is all wrong. Grace promised someone would always answer the burner phone.' He paused and looked straight at Gino. 'For Christ's sake, they killed Kardon looking for Smith. Maybe they're spreading the net.'

Gino puffed out a long exhale and reached into his pocket for the monster bottle of Tums he'd been popping all during the plane ride. He took out two and passed the bottle to Magozzi. Chili had been a really bad idea. 'Okay,' he said quietly. 'I get where you're going and why you're going there. But remember, the marina was the first place anyone would look for John, and we haven't heard a peep from any of the next logical places they'd go to – like the Feds in DC or the people at his condo. If they're spreading a net, they've got a few other places to look before they jump all the way up to Minneapolis and Monkeewrench . . .'

Magozzi was breathing too fast. 'Goddamnit, Gino. There's a jihad on John Smith, and we've got a nationwide terrorist plot, and terrorist activity all over Minneapolis. You were the one who said we were in the middle of something. What if we are? What if John Smith is the catalyst?'

Gino looked down at his hands and tried to pull his scattered thoughts together. They'd been so focused on Joe Hardy and the Little Mogadishu murders, and that pesky new information about a group of assholes planning to blow up the country, that he'd never really tried to put it together. People trying to kill John Smith had been out there on the periphery; a totally separate can of worms that had crept in just because of Grace's connection to John and how that affected Magozzi; but damnit, the people who had tried to slash Smith's throat on the boat had been Middle Eastern, probably acting on the jihad. Hello, terrorists. 'Okay. I'm with you, buddy. Take a breath, then do what you have to do.'

Magozzi stared down into his glass and smelled the peaty fumes as they rose upward to his nostrils, beckoning him to be a real man and drink up. He liked the cinematic notion of downing a drink with steady hands before taking on an important, possibly destiny-altering task. The only problem with that scenario now was that adrenaline was screaming through his blood with the intensity of lava and his hands were shaking like a Chihuahua in a snowbank. Not exactly movie hero material.

His paralysis wasn't lost on Gino, who finally said, 'Call McLaren. He's at the office holding down the night shift. He'll take care of it.'

Magozzi finally mobilized, downed some whiskey, because that's what John Wayne would have done, and made his call. McLaren answered after two rings. 'Johnny, this is Leo . . .'

'Hey, Magozzi! I heard you and Gino had to trek it up to Siberia . . .'

'Johnny, I need a favor, and I need it fast.'

'Sure, anything. Sounds serious.'

'It is. We think somebody's after Monkeewrench – presumed armed and very dangerous. They should all be together at Harley's, but none of them are taking phone calls. I need you to send some men over there to check it out. They'll need ladders, lights, flak jackets – I want every floor looked at from the outside and if there's any sign of foul play, tell them to break a window, knock the goddamned door down, whatever they need to do.' The words had tumbled out in a fast rush of panicked breath, and he hoped they'd made sense, because there wasn't time to explain any further.

'Jesus. Do you want me to send SWAT?'

'Whatever manpower St Paul can afford to give. They need to cover Grace's house, too. Have Minneapolis handle Annie's and Roadrunner's places.'

'Got it. I'll make the calls and get it to Dispatch ASAP,

then head to Harley's myself. You want me to call you back at this number?'

McLaren was a guy who didn't like to be taken seriously on his downtime, but when the chips fell, he was the best man for any job because he always got it done. That gave Magozzi some peace to cling to in the midst of this particular shit storm. 'Yeah. Thanks, Johnny.' He hung up and put his head in his hands.

'What?' Gino asked.

'Johnny's taking care of it.' Magozzi finally looked up. 'They're gone, Gino. Or they're dead. Like Kardon.'

Gino shook his head. 'Give that up, Leo. Monkeewrench knows how to protect themselves. There might be a houseful of bodies down there, but I guarantee none of them are theirs. Come on. You know Grace. You know the rest of them. No one's going to catch them with their guard down.'

'Yeah, I suppose.' Magozzi desperately wanted to believe it, almost had to believe it.

'Leo, don't go to the darkest place right now,' Gino said firmly, reading his partner's face. 'Just try to figure out how you're going to survive until McLaren calls back with an all clear. And it won't take long – Johnny knows what this means to you. He won't leave you hanging.'

Magozzi survived the gap in time by drinking the rest of his whiskey while he built and stoked a new fire over the waning coals in the grate. And Johnny didn't let him down. True to form, he called back within the hour, as soon as he had news to share.

He put him on speaker so Gino could listen in, and possibly take over if the news was bad. There was a lot of background noise – men, squawking police radios, and whoops of sirens, which made it hard to hear, so Johnny had to shout.

'I'm at Harley's along with some squads, off-duty SWAT guys, and a couple fire departments. Law enforcement loves Monkeewrench, so when I put out the call, anybody who was free showed up. It's clear.'

Magozzi swallowed a lump in his throat that went down like a bag of cotton balls. 'How clear?'

'The place is empty, no sign of foul play, and the doors are locked. Alarm systems armed and uncompromised.'

Magozzi and Gino breathed a collective, tentative sigh of relief.

'What about their other places?' Gino asked.

'Same,' McLaren said. 'Nothing bad happened down here, but just in case, Minneapolis and St Paul stepped up patrols for the night. Nothing suspicious now, but we're covered, and I'll plant myself in front of Harley's until I hear anything different from you, or until the Homicide desk lights up and I have to scoot.'

Magozzi leaned forward and took a deep, shaky breath. 'Thanks, Johnny. You're the man.'

'Of course I am. And I damn well better get a full report on what the hell is going on when you get back.' He paused, and an anxious sigh emanated from his end. 'You'll let me know if you hear from them, right?'

'You're our first call.'

41

Annie was not pleased with the back roads. Not one bit pleased. They were narrow, bumpy, and very dark, because towering pines started to crowd the road the farther north they drove, choking out what little light the moon cast through the growing cloud cover. It was like driving into a black hole, and it reminded her of a very scary time not so long ago when an army had tried to hunt her down and kill her in a similar, ghostly pine forest in Wisconsin.

There were reasons why certain places remained mostly uninhabited, and she had absolutely no desire to discover those reasons for herself. 'We're just as likely to find a Tiffany's as we are a phone if we stay on this bridle path to nowhere, Grace.'

Grace was beginning to think Annie had a point, her friend's loathing of the wilderness notwithstanding. 'I'll pull off at the first place we can get out of view, then we can take a closer look at the map.'

'Out of view from whom? We haven't seen a car in at least an hour.'

'Is that a sign up ahead?' John asked quietly from the backseat.

Grace slowed the Rover to a crawl and the headlights illuminated a faded, listing road sign that probably would have tipped over into the ditch long ago without the bolster of the thick, vining brambles that strangled the post.

If there had ever been any lettering on it, time and the elements had erased it, but she could still make out two faded pictographs: the universal symbols for toilet and phone. 'A rest stop.'

Annie felt her shoulders tense up into twin knots. 'That beat-up ol' thing looks like a post-Armageddon prop out of a doomsday movie to me. And there are bullet holes in that sign, Grace. Bullet holes mean people with guns, who obviously shoot signs for fun. What else do you think they shoot for fun?'

Grace considered the pockmarks on the old sign, which were rusty and most certainly an historical artifact left by bored kids from days past. Unfortunately, the wayside rest and its promised phone service were probably historical artifacts by now, too. Places like the one advertised on the decrepit sign used to be welcoming, scenic havens for weary drivers traversing the vast, unpopulated countryside; a peaceful and pretty respite where you could stretch your legs, eat a sandwich, and take in Mother Nature before getting behind the wheel of the family station wagon again. But that had all changed a long time ago, with freeways carving much faster routes to desired destinations. The off-the-path places had faded poignantly away, back into the fields and woods where they'd nestled so usefully for decades.

'It's probably been abandoned for years,' John said. 'But we have to try.'

Grace took the turn, and the tar abruptly ended. The Rover bounced along a dirt track for what seemed like an eternity, and she tightened her grip on the steering wheel. The trees grew thicker, and boughs started scraping the sides of the big truck that was at least a foot wider than the road.

'Oh dear Lord,' Annie murmured, her hands mounted firmly on the dashboard as she tried to stay in her seat. Even Charlie was whining.

The path finally opened up onto a small, overgrown parking area littered with empty beer cans. There was a pathetic cluster of broken-down picnic tables, an old water pump that must have sufficed as a drinking fountain way back in the last century, and a concrete block outhouse. An old pay-phone box stood like an unlovely museum piece right next to the picnic area and Grace felt the utter loneliness of the place seep into her bones.

Harley grunted. 'No way that thing is going to work.'

Grace unholstered her gun and scanned the area, turning back and forth in her seat for a three-sixty view. John caught her eye and nodded.

'I'm going to check out the phone. John, you take over in the driver's seat and keep it running. Harley, up front. Annie and I need some rest.'

'I'm coming with you to the phone,' Harley said, no leeway in his voice. Charlie beat him out the open door.

Grace got slowly out of the truck. The air was much colder this far north, and a bitter wind hissed through the pine boughs. Other than that, it was quiet and dark.

The phone wasn't far from the Rover, and Grace stopped midpoint and scanned the woods, which seemed to rise up in the distance. Some kind of ridge. The flat topography of the farm country they'd been traversing was beginning to undulate in gentle swells, courtesy of an ancient glacier, she supposed. Clouds were moving in fast, but she could see a distant glow of light glancing off the cloud's plump, snow-filled bottoms, just beyond the ridge. Moonlight? A house? Or a car? Maybe kids drinking the night away in this forlorn place.

'Do you see something?' Harley whispered tensely, his own sidearm out and ready.

She shrugged uncertainly and pointed to the light.

He relaxed. 'Moonlight,' he said. 'The woods play tricks. You have no sense of distance, no point of reference up here.'

Grace felt any lingering doubt melt away and closed the distance to the phone with three long strides.

Life was as random as the spin of a roulette wheel and held no miracles; there was no such thing as fate or destiny; Grace firmly believed that. And yet when she picked up the cracked plastic receiver of the phone and heard a tone, she felt like she'd just experienced divine intervention. 'I can't believe it,' she whispered to Harley. 'The damn thing works. Give me some change.'

Harley scowled and started digging through his pockets. 'Who has change anymore? I haven't used anything but an ATM card for fifteen years.'

Grace looked at the ancient relic and remembered her days on the run as a child, when she'd make daily rounds of the city's pay phones to scrounge up loose change left in the coin return slots. On good days, she'd collect enough to buy toast and a warm seat in a diner, where she'd steal coffee creamer and ketchup packets that she made into soup with hot water from the bathroom faucet.

She jammed her hand into the slot and withdrew it with a victorious expression – two quarters. Kids were obviously too lazy and privileged nowadays to even bother to raid a simple source of free money anymore.

'Good job, Grace,' Harley said in a hushed voice as she plugged the change into the phone and dialed Magozzi. She talked quickly, listened, and then felt Charlie push against her leg. After she hung up, she bent to pat the dog and felt the rigidity of his body. He was sitting down, pressed hard against her, but his eyes were turned toward the ridge she'd been looking at earlier, and the light in the clouds above it. He whined once, then rumbled a low growl deep in his throat.

42

Mukwa was turning into a persistent visitor – tonight he came to the Chief to show him a dark, silent, wintry forest. He then led him farther into the forest to a small clearing, where a thin spear of moonlight filtered down through the sparse, leafless canopy to illuminate the forest floor, which was covered by a crepe-thin sheet of crackling ice. Above, skeletal, crystallized branches winked and sparkled, fancily adorned by an ice storm.

Somewhere nearby, 'waboo' – rabbit – stuck his twitching nose out from beneath a barberry bush to test the night air, then hopped out cautiously from under cover to forage for food. That was strange, because waboo wouldn't normally leave his hutch at night because of the many dangers, so this little bunny was hungry.

As his soft, furry paws mounted the ice on the forest floor, it snapped and crackled under his insignificant weight, and waboo froze in place, knowing the sound would alert predators. His hunger had driven him to judge poorly.

In the near distance, shadows began to materialize and draw closer.

'Wiisagizi maa'ingan.' *Mukwa spoke for the first time since Khe Sahn.*

Coyotes. The tricksters.

The Chief woke up to the tinging of ice pellets still chattering against the window, and let out a heavy sigh, wishing Mukwa had shown him what had happened to waboo.

Gino had no idea how long he'd been sleeping – one minute he'd been talking to Magozzi, trying to distract him from the missing Monkeewrench gang, even though McLaren had reported back with positive news. And then the next minute he felt a burning crick in his neck and a hand on his arm, shaking him gently awake. He opened his eyes and saw a blurred figure with black hair standing in front of him who he hoped was Magozzi and not a bear. 'Uh . . . how long have I been out?'

'A couple hours, maybe.'

'Sorry I zonked on you.' Gino swiveled his head to loosen his hamstrung neck.

'I zonked, too, woke up when Grace called.'

That woke Gino up instantly, which did nothing for his eyesight, because Magozzi still looked like a bear. 'Are they okay? Where are they?'

'They're okay, and they're on their way here. I gave them directions.'

'They're coming *here*? What's going on?'

'She wanted to keep it short so they could get back on the road. They were calling from some old wayside pay phone. All she had time to tell me was that Monkeewrench got a call from someone pretending to be DC FBI, asking about John. Smith called them a few minutes later. He had a tap on their line, said the call wasn't from DC, it was from Minneapolis, and they had to get the hell out fast.'

Gino frowned. 'So somebody really is after them?'

'That's what Smith thinks. He's with them and he's got information he says we need immediately, so I told them to come here.'

Gino rubbed his eyes, thinking that if he could clear his

vision, his thoughts would follow along. 'What in the hell?'

Magozzi shook off the question like an unwanted touch. 'We'll find out soon enough. The only good news is she's positive they weren't followed. They've been driving most of the night and barely saw a car once they got out of the city.'

Gino struggled his way up into sitting position and worked on retrieving his wakeful bearings.

'What's happening, Detectives?' A deep, sleepy voice came from the hallway as the Chief walked out wearing camouflage from head to toe.

'It's a long story,' Magozzi said. 'But we do have some visitors meeting up with us here. As soon as they arrive, we'll be on our way. Maybe you could point us in a direction? Something off the reservation?'

The Chief crouched in front of the hearth and started tossing more logs and paper kindling into the fireplace. 'Why off the rez? Your visitors got something against us skins?'

'Skins?' Gino asked.

'Tell me what's really going on.'

The Chief deserved the truth, so Magozzi gave it to him. 'Our friends are in trouble. And the last thing we want to do is bring trouble here to you.'

The Chief looked at them curiously. 'What kind of trouble?'

Great question, Magozzi thought. 'I'll give you the short version. They're with an ex-Fed who has a jihad out on him and they think there's somebody after them. And if there's any chance of danger, which we have to assume there is, no way we're going to jeopardize you or your people.'

Chief sat down on the hearth. 'We know how to handle trouble up here. No place safer. Now why don't you tell me this long story so I can get an idea of what we're dealing with here.'

Magozzi and Gino sighed collectively, then took turns telling Smith's story, and in the telling, they both realized the story wasn't so long after all. The sum total of their knowledge was that Smith and maybe anybody who ever knew him had bull's-eyes on their foreheads. They'd left out the detail about Grace killing Smith's would-be murderers, of course, and the Chief knew they were holding back something, but he didn't push it. Good cops knew how and when to prise out information, and as they spoke with him, it became evident that the Chief fell into the good-cop category, because he asked all the right questions.

'Okay, let's see if I got this straight. Two Middle Eastern guys try to kill a retired Fed who's sailing with your friend Grace, and I can pretty much surmise what happened to them because you left out the ending of that particular tale.'

Gino and Magozzi kept their expressions impassive, which had probably been more telling than a shared glance would have been. But the Chief ignored it and continued.

'Then the marina owner got killed, you're thinking for information on Smith's whereabouts, and that maybe your friends are next because of their association with him.'

'Right,' Gino said.

'Which means you think your friends aren't the only company we're about to get.'

Magozzi shrugged uncomfortably. 'Grace swears they weren't followed. But I don't know. I've got a bad feeling about this.'

The Chief studied their faces with eyes that looked like shiny black stones in the low light of the room before returning his attention back to the hearth. 'You're tying this all up with the terrorist angle, right?'

Gino and Magozzi just looked at him.

'Jihad, Middle Eastern assassins on a boat in the Caribbean, big-time terrorist plot . . . hey, guys. I'm an Indian, not an idiot. This Smith character is tangled in this web in a big way. How am I doing so far?'

'That's about the long and short of it.'

Chief grabbed an iron poker and started coaxing the fire. His dark skin looked like old, burnished wood in the glow of the coals. 'So why didn't he stay invisible? Being with your Monkeewrench friends right now is putting them in even more jeopardy, am I right?'

Magozzi frowned down into his lap, one of the many places he habitually looked for answers, even though he never found them there. 'Apparently he thinks they're in danger with or without him.'

The Chief nodded absently. 'Sounds like this is going to be one big ball of yarn to unravel.'

'I hope not,' Magozzi said, feeling exhaustion and worry start to nip at his nerves, along with the incessant clatter of ice on the windows.

The Chief remained silent and immobile for a long time before finally wagging his head, an ironic smile punctuating his mouth with deeply engraved parentheses. 'John Smith. You can't make this shit up.'

'What do you mean?' Gino asked.

'John Smith, on his way to an Indian reservation. That name has a real tight association with Native people. Does Pocahontas ring a bell?'

Magozzi and Gino looked at each other, suddenly recalling high school history classes. John Smith, Jamestown settler back in the early 1600s, saved from slaughter by an Indian princess, or so the story went. Maybe history would repeat itself.

The Chief seemed satisfied that they'd comprehended the irony of Smith's name and his current situation. 'I'm going to throw on a pot of coffee – too damn early for man or beast to be up and about. Sun's not even close to a rise yet.'

Gino looked at the Chief's camo again. 'Are you and Claude hunting this morning or something?'

'That depends.' He stood on his sequoia legs and gestured for them to follow. 'Come on, follow me out to the kitchen. I want to show you something.'

The Chief led them through the kitchen to the utility room, which had all the usual trappings – hot water heater, washer and dryer, extra cleaning and paper products, flashlights and candles. 'If you need spare toilet paper, this is the place to come,' he chuckled, moving to the back of the room and unlocking a heavy door. 'And if you need spare firepower, this is the place to come.'

Gino and Magozzi looked wide-eyed at the impressive array of impeccably tended hunting rifles and shotguns – one model or another appropriate for any animal that inhabited these forests, Magozzi figured. Boxes of corresponding ammunition were stacked neatly on shelves next to the gun racks.

'Wow,' Gino said. 'This *is* a four-star hunting resort.'

The Chief nodded proudly. 'We're well equipped. The serious hunters bring their own hardware, but a big part of our business comes from corporate parties and weekend warriors who want to play survivalist for a couple days before they go back to their suits and ties and Starbucks lattes. Most of those types have never even held a gun before, so we give them gun safety first, target practice next, and if they pass, we let them check out a weapon and some ammo for their stay. I'm leaving these doors unlocked for you both.'

Gino scratched at the bumper crop of whiskers that had repopulated his jaw overnight. 'That's really nice of you, Chief, but I don't think we're going to have much time for target practice.'

'I'm not talking target practice, Detective.'

Gino and Magozzi wandered back into the living room and watched the ice pellets turn to a light snow while the Chief made coffee.

'The Chief's nervous,' Gino finally said.

Magozzi checked his watch, wondering how far out Monkeewrench had been when they'd called from the wayside. 'We just told him we have a carload of people who are on a terrorist hit list showing up at his front door. Of course he's nervous. Aren't you?'

'Well, yeah,' Gino conceded, then lifted his head abruptly and started sniffing the air like a hound. 'You smell that, Leo?'

Magozzi inhaled the acrid fumes of marijuana filtering from the breezeway between the kitchen and living room. 'Great. Just what we need – a stoned host with a closet full of guns.'

'That's not pot, Detectives.' Claude's voice startled them as he emerged sleepy-eyed from the hallway, wearing camo similar to the Chief's. 'That son of a bitch is smudging again. It's only sage, but that shit smells worse than the worst ditch weed I ever smoked, and it lingers for a month, I swear.'

Chief walked into the living room cupping a smoldering river clam shell. 'Everybody take a handful of smoke and wave it on yourselves.'

Claude rolled his eyes but did what he was told.

Gino coughed. 'Why? And what's smudging?'

'It's a purification ritual and it keeps bad spirits at bay.'

'Well, I'm all for that,' Gino said, following Claude's lead. 'So this is sage?' Gino finally asked, his eyes watering as the smoke wreathed around his body.

'Yep. It's medicine. A purifying herb.'

'Are you sure it's not pot?'

The Chief gave Gino a condescending smile. 'No more than the smoldering incense your priests smudge with on their way up the aisle. Most religions have more in common than you think. We're different, and we're the same. There's a comforting synchronicity in that, don't you think? Like we all came from the same place; we're just different tribes. You two should go to bed, grab an hour or two of sleep while you have the chance.'

43

Ten miles north of the wayside, a gentle rain began pattering against the Range Rover's windshield. Twenty miles farther north, the rain abruptly turned to sleet, and then ice pellets. John was driving now. He slowed considerably when the traction control kept kicking on and off as the tires began to skid on the ice-slick road. He kissed the shoulder twice, eased the wheel to the left, and almost spun into a three-sixty.

'Do you want to stop and wait this out?' Grace asked him.

'No. We can't. But it's white-knuckle driving. We're going to have to take short shifts. Harley, you're up.'

John moved to the rear and Harley replaced him without complaint or comment. He was a seasoned veteran of winter driving, but even he couldn't manage the Rover much better than John in such miserable conditions, which were getting worse by the minute. Skill, four-wheel drive, and fancy electronic traction and braking systems were useless when you were navigating a skating rink.

Forty minutes into his shift, Harley had slowed to a crawl, but even then, the truck danced all over the road and ice was accumulating on the windshield faster than the defroster could melt it. He finally flicked on the emergency lights and pulled over, grabbed the ice scraper, and went outside to clear it.

Grace shifted up to the driver's seat and watched Harley work in the ambient glow of the headlights, frozen chips flying up from under his scraper blade to land in his dark beard and hair. When he finally came back in through the rear door, he was shivering and frosted with ice.

'Move over, John,' he grunted, shaking the tiny icicles off his beard. 'You get the hump this shift.'

When everybody was settled, Grace eased the Rover back onto the road and kept the right wheels on the gravel shoulder.

'Are you sure you're okay to drive, honey?' Annie asked from the passenger seat. 'You didn't sleep a lick.'

Grace sighed. 'Couldn't.' She'd jumped a lot of psychological hurdles recently, but apparently three months on a sailboat in the Caribbean couldn't completely eradicate a lifetime of paralyzing paranoia. She still didn't trust anyone to drive, to keep watch, to see all the warning signs she'd trained herself to notice and react to over the years. She'd had a respite from that on the boat, but it had all come flooding back with John's voice on the phone saying, *Get out. Right now.*

Within the hour, all three men were snoring noisily in the backseat.

'Harley!' Annie hissed, actually reaching back to poke him in the stomach. 'Close your mouth, for God's sake. You sound like a dying hog.'

Harley shifted his weight and grunted, but never came fully awake.

'Men,' she grumbled. 'They fall asleep the minute they sit down and the hell with whatever goes on around them. No wonder they can sleep in foxholes. Women watch and worry, men snore.'

Grace smiled. 'Maybe they're the lucky ones.'

'They're the stupid ones. They sleep through the baby crying and the burglar breaking glass in the front door. If the woman didn't shake them awake, they'd snore through Armageddon.'

'You sound a little bitter.'

'I'm sleep-deprived from staying awake to make sure Harley and John didn't drive us into a tree . . . wait a minute. Is that the lodge?'

Grace glanced right. 'Must be.'

'Well, bless me, that's a good-looking building with nice landscaping and decent architecture and you can see all those lights in all those big, beautiful windows. They've got electricity, Grace, and probably indoor plumbing. So I say screw a cabin where we've probably got to cook dead animals in a pot over a fireplace and go to the bathroom on a tree trunk, which is, I need to tell you, a skill I have never perfected . . . hey. You drove right past the entrance.'

'Magozzi said go to the cabin, so that's where we're going.'

Annie saw the Rover's headlights illuminate a carved wooden sign that advertised Cabin One with an upward-pointing arrow. After ten long minutes on a rough, two-track dirt road that was apparently maintained by gophers, they emerged from the thick woods into a small clearing. Grace brought the Rover to a stop in front of a large log home with a brightly lit wraparound porch that looked like it belonged in a very wealthy suburb for lumberjacks.

'Well,' Annie said happily. 'This doesn't look quite as awful as I expected in spite of my innate prejudice against log structures, which just says you were too lazy to saw the tree trunks into nice smooth boards. On the upside, there are no carcasses hanging from tree branches, no yahoos on the porch with long rifles over their shoulders. People with money stay here. I like that.'

Grace cracked her window, the film of ice that was coating it shattering to the ground, then turned off the ignition.

'Good Lord, would you listen to that? I haven't heard owls hootin' like that since Mississippi.'

'Pretty,' Grace admitted, relieved to see daybreak finally penetrating the woods. 'But a little spooky.'

'Mournful songs,' Annie murmured, listening to the soft hoots breaking the still night air, then hugging her shoulders. 'Cold,' she shivered, rubbing her bare arms. 'Close the window and let's get inside.'

The men in the backseat snorted their way into wakefulness. 'Where the hell are we?' Harley groaned. 'And why aren't we moving?'

'We're there,' Grace said, watching the front door open and four men step out onto the porch. 'And there are your yahoos, Annie.' She saw Magozzi first. He was carrying his shoulders the way he did when he was on adrenaline watch.

Gino stood next to him, legs spread as if he needed a wide base to stay upright. Flanking them were two much older men.

Chief watched the ice-coated Range Rover sliding sideways to a reluctant stop a short distance from the steps. He was thinking that they were all part of a nostalgic configuration: a line of men standing motionless, expressionless, waiting as others approached. Chief remembered a page that repeated time and again in his own history.

The tribal elders always stood quietly in the chamber, their faces unreadable as members appeared before them to receive their wisdom. They seemed invincible, above emotional involvement. He'd been eleven the first time he'd been admitted to the chamber, scared to death by the aged faces of men and women who had lived so many years.

For the first time in all his life, he now felt like an elder, and realized that on this day, that was what he was. He hadn't sought the role as leader; fate had chosen him, and the mantle of responsibility lay heavily on his shoulders. In Vietnam, all the Chimooks had called him Chief just because he was an Indian, something he'd never minded one bit or considered racist, because back home, he was only a brave. But he had eventually earned the title, more so after his appointment to the Tribal Police.

Like the other men standing beside him, he watched the front passenger door of the Range Rover open, spilling cracked ice on the ground. But unlike the others, his gaze was impassive and uncluttered by human emotion.

The woman who emerged first was relatively short, but quite amazingly plump. To his eye, this voluptuous visage was a sign of wealth. Slender young women might stir a young man's lust, but the amply endowed promised pillows of comfort for grown men ready for the long, peaceful rest that warmed their older years. Better yet, the woman wore her weight like a badge of honor, so confident in her own skin that she moved with a come-hither sensuality that invited all to adore her.

He watched her sashay a few steps from the truck and cock a hip. She wore a strange dress made of feathers, which he saw as a sign, and moved with utmost confidence on high-heeled boots she balanced perfectly on the slick, icy surface of the drive. She was as self-assured as Noya, fully aware of her power.

'Which one of you gentlemen is going to come down here and escort a lady?' she called out with a southern lilt that sent Claude tripping over his own feet to race down icy steps, arm chivalrously offered.

The next creature out of the truck was a bizarre-looking dog so genetically jumbled he could have been a feral rez dog. Chief saw that as a sign as well. The dog raced from tree to tree in exuberance, city paws slipping on the ice. That was the wondrous thing about the wolf's cousin. Dogs were first and always dogs, never pretending to be anything else. He stopped suddenly at one tree, leg raised comically, and turned his head to focus on Gino and Magozzi.

He made a beeline for the two men, slipping and sliding up the steps and finally leaping to place front paws on Gino's shoulders, his whole body wagging a nonexistent tail.

The remaining occupants stepped out of the Rover. First was a stunningly beautiful woman who had to be Grace MacBride, and it was obvious she wielded absolute power over Magozzi. The change in the man's posture and respiration was like a neon sign to anybody who cared to look. Following her were two men so different in stature, color, and carriage, they could have been from two different planets. The big, bearded man was a sturdy soul, while the tall, thin man was a lost one, so ambiguous in every way, Chief wondered if he was a Two Spirit.

Grace's eyes were on Magozzi as she stopped at the bottom of the steps and looked up. Eventually her gaze moved to the two old men they were putting in danger just by being here. 'We won't stay here, Magozzi.'

John nodded briefly to Gino and Magozzi and ignored the tall man who was totally preoccupied with Annie. Then John's eyes rested on the Chief, who wore this place and this land on his face. 'John Smith,' he said to introduce himself. 'I trust Magozzi and Gino told you that having us here is not safe for you. We'll only stay long enough to tell the detectives what they need to know.'

'Chief Bellanger, Tribal Police. This is our safest place, and now it's yours. Welcome.'

John shook his head, then glanced at Magozzi. 'Is there someplace we can talk?'

'Inside,' Chief said. 'Everybody. We know what's happening, we know the risks, and we can't let you take these women away from a place where they can be protected.'

John frowned at Magozzi. 'You told them?'

'We told them everything we know.'

'Was that wise?'

'There was a good reason. They might as well hear whatever you have to say.'

'Boozhoo,' Harley said, moving his bulk onto the porch like a boulder displacing stones.

The Chief cocked his head. 'You speak Ojibwe?'

'Just enough to get myself a free meal. I had friends up at Bad River a while back.'

'Then you have friends here. Everyone inside, please.'

Roadrunner tried to fit his size fourteens on the steps and angled all his appendages to mount them. He looked like a praying mantis climbing a hill and dropped his head in front of the Chief, totally screwed by confusing protocol as usual, timid as always. 'I'm Roadrunner.'

Chief nodded and took his hand, frowning down at the crippled fingers. 'Looks like you tangled with some kind of machinery. Farm accident?'

Roadrunner blinked. 'Foster father with a hammer.'

Chief tightened lips that were barely there to begin with, then looked Roadrunner in the eye. 'Did you kill him?'

'No. I ran away.'

'How old were you?'

'Eight.'

Chief nodded. 'Very smart. Of course you're older now. You could pay him a visit with a hammer of your own.'

44

They sat at the big table in the cabin's dining room, Magozzi, Gino, the Chief, and Claude on one side; John and the Monkeewrench partners on the other. Harley and Roadrunner shoveled food into their mouths; Grace and Annie picked at their plates, the way women do when adrenaline was suppressing appetite.

Chief directed his attention to Grace. 'You weren't followed?'

'No. We were careful.'

'Then why are you so worried?'

She thought about that for a moment, examining a piece of dry toast that seemed harmless. 'I don't know. Just a feeling.'

Chief was watching her with those dark, impenetrable eyes. 'You feel a presence?'

Grace raised her brows, took a bite of toast that turned to sand in her mouth.

'You're certain you weren't followed, but you sense danger,' he persisted.

Grace laid her toast next to the untouched eggs on her plate. 'I tend to overreact.'

Chief's dark brows reached for each other as he studied her, but his thoughts were someplace else. 'Rabbits find their burrows when a storm is coming,' he said, standing up. 'Birds fly.' He left the table and went out the front door while the others watched him, mystified.

'He's got a spiritual bent to him,' Claude explained. 'He sees signs in everything.'

'He's also a cop,' Gino added. 'He's onto something. Where's Charlie?'

'Still outside, running the kinks out, watering stuff,' Harley said.

A few moments later Chief came back inside, holding a tiny black box. 'Someone's tracking you,' he said perfunctorily. 'This was under your truck, attached to your chassis. It's one of the new transponders. You didn't see a tail because they never got close enough. This thing tracks from two miles, minimum.'

Annie felt a spidery shiver creep up her spine. All that watchfulness, all their precautions, and all the time someone had been just a few miles behind them, waiting for an opportunity.

While Chief went to another room to make some phone calls, Grace spoke quietly to the others. 'We have to leave now.'

Harley stood up and tucked his chair under the table. 'Right.'

Annie stood, fluffed her dress, and smiled at Claude. 'It's been far too brief, Mr Gerlock.'

'Sit down,' Claude said. 'All of you.' Not one of them sat down, and Claude wasn't used to that kind of defiance. Normally when he gave orders, everyone jumped.

On the other hand, no one ever ordered Grace to do anything. She squared her shoulders and stared him down. 'This is our trouble, not yours. We're leaving now.'

Claude shook his head at Grace, his expression immutable. 'You're not thinking clearly. They could already be here, hiding out there, just waiting for you to move. The reservation is over a hundred square miles. Lots of places you could ditch a car and disappear into the woods on foot.'

Grace almost smiled. Poor man had made a little mistake. 'If they're on foot in the woods, we can be off the reservation before they get back to their cars. And without the tracking device, they'll never find us.'

Chief came back into the room and hesitated; he knew a standoff when he saw one. 'What's this about?'

Claude tipped his head toward Grace and rolled his eyes. 'Little Miss Speed Demon thinks she can blast out of here before anyone chasing them can get back to their cars.'

Something about the Chief changed as he walked up to Grace and looked her in the eye. He was just a little bit shorter than she was, but in that moment it didn't appear that way. 'Then you'd better think again, Miss McBride. These people aren't amateurs. They tracked down Agent Smith, they tracked down the marina owner in Florida, and now they've tracked you down. You think they're sitting on their hands in the middle of the forest toasting marshmallows? We're setting up a tight perimeter around the cabin and we have people guarding the road between the cabin and the lodge, but the minute you get past that, they're going to be waiting on the side of the road out of here and your Rover will be full of holes before you get another twenty yards.'

Magozzi waited for Grace to tie into the Chief, but she

remained silent. Maybe she was going to fool them all and be reasonable. 'He's right, Grace,' he said, and Gino nodded his agreement.

She sat back down at the table and the others followed suit, relief obvious on their faces.

Chief looked over at John. 'Agent Smith, we have lives on the line here and it's about time you started talking. We need to know everything.'

John told the rest of them what he'd already told Monkeewrench in the car: about tracing serious terrorist chatter on the Web to their points of origin and anonymously passing on home addresses to law enforcement. 'Somebody who received my tips apparently decided to see to it that these suspects were taken out before they could do any damage. That's why they're after me. They found out I was the source of information that was getting their people killed.' He looked over at Gino and Magozzi. 'I never put it together until I read a news report about your Little Mogadishu homicides – those men were terror suspects on the lists I sent out.'

Magozzi and Gino both stared at John, speechless, while the final puzzle piece finally dropped into place. 'Holy shit,' Gino breathed. 'Somehow, Joe Hardy got his hands on your list. That's why he went to those two houses.'

John said, 'It's not just one guy who's doing this. Ten more of the men on that list have been murdered. But who's Joe Hardy?' John asked. 'Name sounds familiar, but I can't place it.'

'The news was all over that one,' Gino said. 'Reporting that Hardy killed the two Somalis in the second Little Mogadishu house.'

'Oh yeah. The hero that takes down the two trying to kill him.'

'Turns out, that's not the way it went down,' Magozzi said. 'Joe killed all four of our Little Mogadishu vics. Premeditated, and we were thinking that he had knowledge the men in those houses were terrorists when the Feds didn't, and decided to take them out himself. Still fighting the war, maybe. That's why Gino and I came up here. Claude and the Chief were Joe's best friends. He was up here with them the night he was killed and left his computer. The Feds wanted a look at it to see if they could find out who fed him the information. Turns out it might have been you. You could be the source we were hoping to find.'

John was shaking his head. 'That list only went out to law enforcement. Was Hardy on the job?'

'Hell no. He was two years off his last tour, dying of cancer, and no friends on the force as far as we know.'

'So how did he get the names?'

Chief cleared his throat. 'Who knows? Maybe someone you sent it to talked. Maybe even put it on the Web. These days everything ends up there eventually, and that's the kind of thing that would go viral. At any rate, if an unfamiliar vehicle comes onto the rez, my deputies have orders to stop it and detain the occupants until we can take a closer look. So for the time being, as long as you all stay put in the cabin' – he nodded to Monkeewrench and John – 'you should be just fine.'

Magozzi glanced at Gino and got the nod of permission. 'Uh, Chief, we may be talking about more than one vehicle. A lot more. This isn't a couple of radicalized students trying to make a name for themselves like the kids on John's boat. It's a major operation. And John isn't the only target anymore. Anyone who's had contact with him is. That means all of us, and all of your people.'

Claude actually rose from his chair to parry that one. 'You mind telling us how you got there, son?'

'They're not after John just because he's getting their people killed. He's getting people killed who were supposed to be participants in a multistate terrorist attack set to go down in three days.'

That shut everybody up.

Chief walked to the window and looked out at the weather. 'What kind of hardware are we talking about?'

'Automatic weapons for sure; maybe more than that. This is all-out war for them. John, do you still have a copy of that list?'

He nodded numbly and pulled a thumb drive out of his pocket.

'Agent Dahl at the Minneapolis Field Office. He's running the show down there. E-mail him that list right now.'

'Computer's in the den,' Chief said, getting up from the table. 'But we're going to need some help. I'll check in with my FBI liaison to give them a heads-up on what might be happening here and ask if we can get some backup.'

'Gino and I will check in with Agent Dahl in Minneapolis. Is there a landline in the living room? My cell is dead.'

'Yeah. Side table next to the fireplace.'

Agent Dahl answered on the first ring. Of course Magozzi was calling his cell number so he could have been home in bed, but he didn't think so. He could hear multiple conversations and the clatter of computer keyboards in the background. 'Agent Dahl. Magozzi here. We've got a situation in Elbow Lake.'

'More important than a multistate terror attack?'

'We think it's connected.'

Dahl was quiet for a moment, then said, 'Tell me everything.'

Magozzi did, ending with, 'Monkeewrench and Smith were followed up here. We found a tracking device.'

He heard Dahl shout at the other people in the room, and the background noise stopped abruptly. 'Listen to me, Magozzi. You saw the weaponry in that Little Mogadishu house. And that probably wasn't the only cache. Whoever is tracking Smith is going to be armed with a whole lot more than your service pistols can handle, and besides your people, you've got a local population of innocents you need to keep safe. Find a place you can defend and dig in until we can get some teams up there through this storm.'

Half an hour later, Chief came in to stoke the dying embers while Magozzi was relaying his conversation with Agent Dahl to Gino. 'He got John's e-mailed list, he's all over it.'

Chief layered oak logs, then kindling, then paper into the huge fireplace and struck a match. 'I hope you asked him about getting some support up here. My guy in Duluth said nothing's moving out of their city.'

Magozzi nodded. 'I did. Minneapolis is getting this storm, too. Flights are grounded all over the state, shutting everything down, and they just closed I-94, I-35, and

Highway 10 – semis jackknifed all over the place and the ditches are filled with spinouts. Dahl is pulling together some teams that will be ready to move whenever the weather clears, but for the time being, we're on our own here. How many men can you put in the field?'

Chief pushed against his knees with a sigh, rising to his feet. He felt the right one crunch a little, making him wince. 'I've got a lot of men, but not so many I'd want to put in this kind of situation. High on macho, low in skill. But I've got ten more men with recent combat experience in addition to the fifteen deputies already surrounding the cabin. All of them were on the front lines in either Afghanistan, Iraq, or both, and can do some damage with firearms if it comes to that. I'm going to meet the extra ten at the lodge for a briefing and deputize them all to keep everything legal. Trouble is, we don't know how many we're up against.'

Gino looked up from his seat on a cushy chair, thinking beautiful thoughts. The terrorists hadn't followed Monkeewrench. They weren't up here at all. They were all going to have a nice meal, stay inside out of the weather, and then maybe watch an instructional movie in the media room, like *Dances with Wolves.*

Magozzi took a seat on the hearth. 'Can we hold the cabin until the Feds get here with backup?'

Chief took a moment, looking around the living room as if he were considering his reply carefully. Magozzi hadn't known him long, but he'd already noticed that the Chief did this often – pretending to assess your question, giving it weight, when the truth was, he'd known instantly what his answer would be. The man was a scary politician.

'Lots of windows here,' Chief said. 'They'll strafe those nonstop, making it impossible for anyone inside to get a clear shot outside. We can't defend this place by sitting tight. We have to do it out there, in the woods.'

45

Chief and Claude dressed in their blaze orange winter gear and left by the cabin's back door, hefting their personal rifles, both outfitted with scopes that could magnify a mouse into Godzilla from half a click away. They traveled stealthily through the woods in complete silence, like any hunters would, but the quarry they sought wasn't the four-legged type; not today.

The trees and shrubs and grasses were encased in crystal shells of ice. Had they not been so focused on keeping their hides, they would have been completely distracted by nature's pageantry. The morning's relentless sleet was now giving way to wet, thick snow, and that gave the Chief pause. Snow made it easy to track your enemy, but it also made it easy for your enemy to track you. His people knew better than anybody on the planet how to move through snowy woods without leaving a trace, but the city cops worried him. He'd have to find a place to keep them stationary.

When they were finally satisfied that there was no imminent danger within range of the cabin, they veered up over a berm and started walking the ice-glazed road to the lodge, treacherous already and getting worse with the addition of accumulating snow.

'We're too damn old to risk breaking any bones, Chief,'

Claude complained, choosing his steps carefully and keeping his voice low. 'Besides, we're exposed out here. We should have stayed in the woods.'

'The deputies are watching this road. Besides, we're just hunters heading to the lodge,' he replied. 'If there are intruders here, they probably don't want to reveal their position shooting a couple of old yahoos stupid enough to wander around in blaze orange. And they probably didn't figure on us finding their tracking device or tying this all together, so they have a false sense of security right now. This gives us a chance to scope things out a little, but I'm not seeing anything, are you?'

Claude didn't, and for all the other things that age had diminished, he still had the sharp eyes of the sniper he'd once been. 'False sense of security or not, if they're smart, they won't move until dusk.'

'Don't know if they're smart or not, but either way, we'll be ready and waiting for them.'

Claude took a deep, cleansing breath of crisp air, but he still couldn't shake the anxiety that was tightening his chest. 'Lord, this is one hell of a crazy mess we've suddenly got on our hands. A lot of innocent lives on the line. You sure we're doing the right thing here?'

'No choice, Chimook. Not anymore.'

'What are you going to tell your men?'

Chief blew out a moist breath that turned into fog. 'I'll tell them it's a police action – which it is.'

'But they'll ask some questions, and they deserve some answers. So how's it going to go down when somebody like Moose or Eugene Thunderhawk asks why they should risk their lives for some troubled white folks they don't even know? And really, why should they?'

The Chief paused for a moment, regarding a clump of young aspen trees that looked about ready to snap under the weight of their icy burden. They'd lose some trees during this storm. 'These people are terrorists, which makes them our common enemy. That makes us a tribe, and warriors fight for their tribe. You know that firsthand, Chimook. Besides, the Somalis are into this up to their eyeballs and we've got a past with those bastards, and when they kidnapped those Sand Lake girls right off the reservation, they declared war.'

Claude lowered his head, finding a loose stone in the road that had somehow escaped an icy entombment. He kicked it and watched it skid across the slick road, leaving an erratic trail through the mounting snow. 'I still can't believe Joe did that,' he finally said. 'What the hell was he thinking?'

The Chief didn't react at all, just lifted his hand and froze in place. He put a finger to his lips, then pointed.

Claude felt his heart speed up, wondering if they were walking into an ambush of cold, pissed-off, fully armed terrorists, but he saw nothing but a rabbit a few yards ahead of them, its fine gray fur frosted with snow. Its twitching ears heard them even though they were standing stock-still, and it pounced hell-for-leather across the road into the ditch to make its escape. 'For crissakes, it's just a rabbit,' he finally said. 'This place is lousy with 'em.'

The Chief nodded and continued walking toward the lodge, the rational part of his brain knowing what Claude had just said was true – this place was lousy with rabbits.

But the other part of his brain couldn't help but think of waboo from his dream, crunching across the ice on the forest floor, freezing in place because the coyotes were moving in on him.

46

Grace and John were standing on the front porch, both nearly unrecognizable in heavy jackets borrowed from the cabin's closet of outdoor wear.

'We shouldn't be out here, you in particular.'

'We haven't had a moment,' John said without looking at her. His eyes were trying to penetrate the thick woods, searching for the Indians the Chief said were surrounding the cabin.

'I know,' Grace replied. 'I miss the boat.'

'I'm sorry, Gracie. I can't tell you how much.'

'Not your fault. Isn't that what you kept telling me? Some things are beyond our control. Let it go.'

He looked down at the thin ridge of ice on the railing. 'You were always good at throwing my own words back at me. I can't see anyone out there, can you?'

Grace ran her fingers through her hair, still damp from the shower. The short cut had been great in the Caribbean, but not in Minnesota.

John turned his head to look at her. Her lips always moved when she was counting. He wondered if anyone else in the world knew that.

'Twelve,' she said.

John chuckled. 'Unreal. I couldn't see a one.'

Grace turned and placed her hand on his cheek. 'I'm not used to the beard.'

'Me either. How did it go with Magozzi?'

'He thought we slept together.'

John looked like a cat who'd just swallowed the world's biggest canary. 'You've got to be kidding. That's awesome.'

The cool thing about the cabin were those spiffy windows that blocked out heat in the summer and cold in the winter. They also gave you a clear view outside, while making it difficult for anyone to see inside. Magozzi had learned that early this morning when a twelve-point buck had paused at the living room window and looked directly at him when he was standing behind the sofa.

'Look at that,' he whispered when Chief had come up behind him, making about as much noise as dandelion fluff falling on soft grass. 'He's looking right at me.'

'He doesn't see you,' Chief said. 'As long as you don't move, all he sees is his own reflection.'

Magozzi was standing in the same place now, watching Grace and John on the porch. He couldn't hear what they were saying but he saw Grace put her hand on John's cheek and felt something inside contract a little.

Later, Magozzi found John Smith alone in the den, working the computer, printing out pages.

'These are for you and Gino,' he said. 'Copies of every list I sent out, and where they went. There are hundreds of names and addresses. I'm trusting you to follow through in case something happens to me.'

Magozzi took a deep breath. 'Nothing's going to happen to you. You're going to be inside the cabin with your skirt over your head like the rest of the girls.'

John looked up at him, his gaze steady. 'Get it off your chest, Leo.'

'Don't call me Leo.'

John didn't say anything, which made Magozzi feel a little foolish. Not foolish enough to dampen his rage, though. 'What I want to know is how the hell you could do this to her. To any of them. You took them away from a safe place and dragged them out on the road with you when you knew goddamn well terrorists were targeting *you*, and that anyone with you was going to pay the same goddamned price Kardon paid. You set them up so you'd have company.'

John shook his head. 'It happened too fast. At that point, all I knew was that the people who were after me were in Minneapolis and that they knew where Monkeewrench was. They could have been at the front door in minutes. I was trying to save them.'

'Well, nice fucking work, Smith. You've just put a lot of really decent people in the crosshairs.'

John put his head in his hands and talked through his fingers. 'You think I don't know that?'

If the FBI tried to wring all the emotion out of the agents they employed, they'd missed the mark on this one. The man's voice was tortured, and Magozzi got his first inkling of what it might be like to carry the weight of so many lives on your shoulders just because you'd tried to do something good for your country. Kardon dead. Joe Hardy dead, and now all the people up here at risk.

Magozzi found a chair and sank into it. 'Look at it this way, Smith. If it hadn't been for you and your little extracurricular computer hacking, we never would have uncovered the attacks they have in the works. You probably saved a lot of lives.'

John looked up with a miserable expression, reached into his pocket, and handed Magozzi a tiny key. 'DC First National Bank, K Street. You and Grace are on the list to access my safe-deposit box. She gets everything I have. The condo, the boat, my bank accounts. Can you handle that?'

Magozzi hesitated, then took the key. 'You'll be fine,' he said. 'You'll be safe here. Just stay in the cabin.'

John smiled. 'That's not going to happen, Leo.'

Magozzi knew where to find Grace. While everyone else was trying to get some rest in the many separate bedrooms of the cabin, she was in the kitchen, washing dishes, putting away food, as if they all would be here tomorrow to eat it.

He paused at the doorway and nodded to Charlie, as if the dog would understand the gesture. He hadn't left Grace's side since they'd arrived, and if Magozzi had to count on anyone to protect her, it would have been that sorry mongrel dog, who understood more than anyone gave him credit for.

Charlie was sitting in one of the kitchen chairs, watching every move she made. He looked at Magozzi when he appeared in the doorway and woofed a soft greeting.

Grace turned around, drying her hands on a dish towel. 'Hello, Magozzi.'

Magozzi exhaled softly. 'Are you okay?'

'As okay as anybody can be in these circumstances. Claude gave us all a little lecture about how to handle firearms and hide behind chairs.'

Magozzi chuckled a little and tried to remember the last time he'd done that. 'Did you tell him you all used gnats for target practice?'

'He's a sweet old guy. We didn't want to scare him.'

Magozzi walked over to Charlie and ran his hand from the wet nose down to the wiry ruff of his neck, remembering his history with Grace that was really a short period of time, but seemed like the sum of his life. The dog had warmed up to him faster than Grace, hiding under chairs at first, then finally jumping up and laying fuzzy paws on Magozzi's shoulders while he licked his face, making Magozzi feel like he belonged somewhere. And like he'd earned it.

God, he loved this dog like he loved this woman and he didn't know what to do with emotions that strong. He looked at her briefly because that's all he could stand, then he turned around and left the room.

47

Chief and Claude returned from the lodge in midafternoon and called everyone into the dining room.

Chief stood at the head of the table, his face emotionless. 'One of my deputies found two abandoned sedans on a hunting trail. He went a little farther into the woods and found two SUVs parked out of sight, in a clearing. They ran the plates – they're rentals.'

'Hunters?' Gino asked hopefully.

'Better not be. All the vehicles had empty ammo boxes – NATO rounds, sweet shot favorite of terrorists.' He looked at John. 'Guess whose credit card and personal info they used to rent the cars? John Smith, Washington, DC.'

John jerked back in his chair. 'How the hell would they get that?'

'You said yourself they were in your computer. Now they're here.' He let that sink in for a minute while he took note of their reactions. Most of the Minneapolis lot were working hard at keeping a game face on, but Roadrunner showed his nerves, rocking a little in his chair, lips compressed and white.

'This is the way things will happen,' Chief said. 'We need a fallback contingent here. It will be the last line of defense if things go south. Monkeewrench and Agent

Smith' – he looked at each of them in turn – 'this is you. You will stay inside the cabin.'

Grace and John immediately started to shake their heads, mouths open to protest, but before they could speak, Chief silenced them with a glance. 'You have no voice here. This is my land, these are my people, and now this is my war. Is that understood?'

Gino was looking down at his lap like a schoolkid who didn't want to be called on.

'Detectives,' the Chief said, 'you two will man the tree stand closest to the cabin. You will stay down. You will not talk, and you will not move no matter what you hear. Your job is only to cover the cabin if anyone gets through.'

Harley stood up and tried to look imposing. 'You've got John, Grace, Annie, and Roadrunner in here, crack shots every one of them. You need another man in the woods.'

Claude glanced up at him from his chair. 'Sorry, son, we're running a little low on guns.'

'I brought my own.'

'Yeah? More peashooters?'

Harley smiled, crooked his finger, and led Claude and Chief out to the garage. He opened the back hatch of Grace's Rover and lifted a green tarp to reveal the weapons Roadrunner had hurriedly stashed there before their sudden flight out of the city.

Claude looked at him in disbelief, and perhaps with a little apprehension – it was hard to tell in the dimly lit garage. 'AKs? What do you do with this kind of firepower back in the city?'

Good question, Harley thought, suddenly doubting what

may have been an unwise display of bravado. He'd spent over half his life training with every kind of firearm under the sun, had spent countless thousands of dollars collecting them and hundreds of hours on the shooting range. He'd never once used a gun against an animal, and certainly not another human being. To him, they were instruments of recreation and skill, not of death. 'It's always been a passion,' he finally said. 'A hobby.'

Chief folded his arms across his expansive chest, which rivaled Harley's in girth. 'I'm guessing that out in these woods, it isn't going to be fun and games. Are you sure you want to do this?'

Harley suddenly felt nasty tendrils of fear strangle his knees, making them wobbly. Maybe this was what he was supposed to be feeling, or maybe he was just a chickenshit dilettante who wanted to play war with real soldiers in theory, but was finally realizing that any targets out there wouldn't be paper, they'd be blood and bone. This *wasn't* a game – the Chief had been dead right about that. 'I want to do this,' he finally said firmly. 'But to be totally honest, I'm kind of scared shitless.'

Claude gave him a sympathetic smile and a pat on the shoulder. 'Join the club. Anybody who picks up a gun and knows he might have to use it to defend himself is scared shitless every single time. The only thing worse than looking down the barrel of a gun with a mind to use it is looking at the business end of somebody else's.'

Harley felt all the blood in his body drain to his feet. He'd been in plenty of bar fights in his day, had even deflected a couple knives and had the scars to prove it, but the business end of somebody else's gun was thankfully nothing he'd ever seen before. Although that could change in a hurry. 'You still get scared, even after a couple tours in Vietnam?'

'Of course we do,' said the Chief, hefting one of the AKs. 'Being scared is what keeps you sharp.'

Claude nodded. 'And what keeps you alive. War sucks. The only reason we do it is because we believe in what we're fighting for.'

Harley let out a shaky breath. 'I'm fighting for my friends.'

'Best reason of all,' Claude said. 'Don't worry, we've got your back, son. Nothing's going to happen to you.'

'Are the AKs fully auto?' Chief wanted to know.

'Yeah. Help yourselves. I've got three of them. You guys know AKs?'

'Better than any woman,' Claude said. 'We used to poach these off enemy corpses in 'Nam and throw out our M-16s because you could drag these fuckers through a rice paddy filled with mud and water buffalo shit and they'd never jam. Most reliable combat weapon ever made, in my opinion.'

Chief pulled out the AKs, then regarded the other guns in the Rover's cargo hold. 'You mind if we bring all these weapons into the cabin for backup, Harley?'

'That's why I brought them. I'll give you a hand.'

Claude watched the two men off-loading guns and thought it was uncanny how they damn near matched each other pound for pound and inch for inch, except Harley had the benefit of fewer years and more muscle. They also both had black hair, swarthy complexions, and the high cheekbones prevalent in the Native folk of these parts. They could have passed as brothers. Hell, maybe they were even related. Blood quorums were hard to trace in any race, more so with Native Americans because of their long history with the white man, where a lot of pairings, both voluntary and involuntary, had gone undocumented for centuries.

'You just going to stand there and watch us do all the heavy lifting, Claude?'

'That was my plan. You two big boys get the guns. I'll bring in the extra ammo.' Claude looked at Harley, still curious about his resemblance to Chief. 'You got some Native blood in you, son?'

Harley was a little surprised by the query. 'You're not the first person to ask me that. But the truth is, I never knew my family.'

'Of course you've got Native in you,' Chief said. 'No Chimook in his right mind would hang with riffraff like those Bad River yahoos unless there was some common DNA.'

The quip was a welcome release valve for all the anxiety, giving the three of them a reason to chuckle in spite of their imminent future in the woods with guns, fighting very bad men who wanted nothing more than to see their brains splattered across the forest floor. But the uneasy, distracted laughter died quickly, and they refocused on their task, silent now.

Chief dressed Magozzi and Gino in camouflage outerwear poached from the front cupboard, then led them to a tree less than fifty yards from the cabin's front door. Gino was freezing to death three steps off the porch. By the time Chief stopped in front of a trunk Gino later learned supported a fifty-year-old oak, he couldn't feel his face. The ice had turned to snow not so long ago, but there was a slight breeze that dropped the windchill way below Gino's comfort zone.

He'd had a vague image of what a tree stand would look like, and as far as he could see, this tree didn't have one. Just a faux ladder of spindly two-by-fours climbing up the trunk. His eyes followed the tiny slices of wood that would never, ever support a man, up, up, until the hood of his parka fell back, exposing his head to the falling snow.

Oh, shit, he thought, looking up to what looked like half a tree house constructed by demented Boy Scouts with absolutely no conception of weight load and gravity. Damn thing had to be at least twenty feet off the ground and there was no frigging railing. Magozzi was already scrambling up the makeshift ladder like a monkey, guns slung over his back. Gino just stood at the bottom, feet frozen to Mother Earth, strongly shaking his head. He felt Chief's bulk pushing him closer to the tree's trunk, and then a pair of big hands grabbing his buttocks, pushing him upward.

'There you go, Detective. Wow. I haven't seen a backside like that since I accidentally caught a glimpse of myself in a three-way mirror.'

Gino scowled over his shoulder at the Chief. 'We're not allowed to talk, but you can make wisecracks about my finer parts?'

Chief grinned up at him. 'Man, sometimes you just can't hold back. It's a ladder, Rolseth. Hands and feet up to the top.'

Magozzi was on his belly, peeking over the side of the ice-slick floor of the tree stand, watching Gino's perilous ascent. The man just wasn't good with heights. Hell, he hired kids to clean out his gutters in the fall, and when he and Angela had moved into the house, he'd only painted halfway up the walls because he wouldn't go near a ladder. Angela, seven months pregnant with The Accident at the time, had finished the job. 'Almost there, buddy,' he whispered over the edge, reaching out to grab the neck of Gino's parka and pull him up the rest of the way.

Gino collapsed on his belly, then rolled over onto his back. 'Give me a gun so I can shoot you, you bastard. First the plane and now this? You've been trying to kill me since we left City Hall.'

'Stay on your belly, or you're going to slide off the edge like a giant hockey puck.'

Chief hissed up at them from the base of the old tree, admonishing them to shut up, then disappeared into the trees.

48

Moose had been fifteen years younger and eighty pounds lighter the last time he'd met a two-legged creature in battle, but he still had his good eyesight and had kept his skills sharp. Hunting had fed his family during some lean years, and it was still a great matter of pride that kept him in the woods for a large part of the year. It wasn't sport. It was ritual, a sacred tradition, nurtured by a respect for the animals the Great Creator had provided for the Original People.

He'd done some guide work for the lodge over the years, but no more. Better to live off the land than assist incompetent once-a-year white hunters in the torture of gentle spirits who populated the earth. Bow-hunting season had turned him against the well-paid guide positions the lodge offered. He'd never understood the appeal of this most challenging form of hunting to Chimooks who knew nothing of its history.

Bow season starts earlier, Chief had once explained to him. *And it enhances their self-image of machismo even when they do it poorly.*

But Moose hadn't been able to watch the heedlessness of unskilled hunters, shooting their expensive compound bows with their manufactured arrows into the hips or stomachs of gallant bucks who ran for miles in insufferable pain before collapsing and dying from their wounds.

Moose took a deep breath and tried to push that from his mind and concentrate on what was to come. The world, as far as Native American tradition was concerned, was divided into two parts: those who respected all life and those who did not. Apparently, the enemy now intruding on the reservation were those who did not revere life, and for that he was grateful. It made them undeserving of life, and it was permitted to kill them.

He looked out over the frosty forest beneath his tree stand, then sank cross-legged to the plank floor and stroked the smooth arch of the bow his great-grandfather had made by hand nearly a hundred years ago. Moose made his own arrows, laboring over them until they were perfect. The flight had to be true, the arrowhead sharp and clean, because only a heart shot was acceptable. Death had to be instantaneous and as painless as possible to be a good death. In all his years, Moose had never wounded an animal or a man, even in war. His shot, whether from rifle or bow, had always flown true, and he was proud of that.

After hours motionless in the chill of dusk, his legs began to complain. He rose slowly, painstakingly to his feet, his movement almost indiscernible. After another half hour of standing motionless, he saw a movement out of the corner of his eye. A last errant ray of the setting sun glinted off the short barrel of an AK-47.

He could see the shadow-man form moving now, hear the crunch of heavy boots against the skim of ice on the forest floor. A true warrior would never allow his movement to be seen so clearly; would never take regular steps that announced the presence of a man walking. If noise came from your footstep, you stopped and waited endlessly, patiently, so your prey or your enemy would dismiss the sound instead of focusing on it.

The Chief's words came back to him. *This is a police action. Capture, do not fire unless you are fired upon, is that clear?*

He loved the Chief and respected him, but sometimes he wondered if the old man hadn't spent too many years following the laws of the FBI, forgetting his own heritage.

He was perfectly still on his perch twenty feet above the ground, and therefore invisible. The man walking below him had no idea he was there and consequently would never fire upon him.

Moose went down on one knee to steady himself and pulled the bow taut, arrow ready to fly. Stupid man never looked up. Desert training camps, Moose thought with contempt. No trees in that desolate land that the Great Creator had never blessed, so he had no sense of danger from above. He would just keep walking toward the cabin.

It irked Moose that his purpose here was to protect foolish white people. In his heart, he hated all of them, but he hated the Somalis more. He'd lost a niece to the sex trade the Somalis exploited to fund overseas terrorist groups, and there was a debt to be repaid, an honor to be upheld. He remembered Chief's admonishment to fire only in self-defense, but he also remembered the Chief saying that some of these intruders would certainly be Somali.

He pulled the bowstring that critical last inch while a smile tugged at the corner of his compressed lips. *Turn around.* He sent a mental command to the man moving ever farther away, but the man didn't respond.

Moose deliberately moved his deerskin boot against the plank floor of the tree stand, making a scratching noise as dried pine needles crackled underfoot and rained down from the stand. The man-shadow spun in place and raised his weapon, but didn't fire. Stupid, Moose thought, rubbing his foot against the floor again so the idiot could at least guess at a target location. The man fired at the treetops, shattering with branches with a volley from his AK-47, startling an owl. Moose nodded reverently to the departing owl, then released his arrow.

Thwuunk! His arrow pierced the man's heart, and he crumpled instantly, spilling blood into the snow.

Moose released a held breath softly. It had been a good kill, respecting the taking of life from a fellow warrior, even if he was a fucking Somali. And best of all, it started the war.

Eugene Thunderhawk was in a tree stand of his own, a quarter of a mile from Moose, when he heard the initial burst of fire, and then the scattered burst of automatic gunfire coming from many directions. Not braves. Braves never fired until their target was in the crosshairs, and then, seldom more than one shot. The automatic setting was for amateurs.

Eugene didn't think a whole lot of guns. He had a scope rifle on the stand with him, but the sad truth was he was a piss-poor shot. He'd done a turn as a dead-eye sniper in Afghanistan right after 9/11, but returned home to hunker over computer printouts of ledger sheets and wasted years keeping the tribal books until macular degeneration started corrupting his vision. Now he trusted himself only with the knife.

In the shell of the very school where his ancestors had been forced to dress in white men's constrictive clothing and forbidden to speak their native language, he had listened to a white teacher postulate that if man went back to hand-to-hand combat, wars would end. He'd never understood that. Indians faced their enemies in battle, paid respect to the sacrifice of life by looking into the eyes of the man they were killing. Otherwise there was no honor. It was unthinkable and cowardly to kill from a distance, and in Eugene's case, now, with his failing eyesight, it was also irresponsible. He had to be very close to make sure he was killing his enemy and not his brother, thus the knife.

He wondered how many braves were crouched in tree stands with clean shots at the unwary who crept beneath them. It seemed a little unfair, like shooting unwitting fish in a barrel. Eugene wasn't able or willing to do that. He would meet these despicable disrespecters of life face-to-face, and gently but gladly slit their throats.

He was a simple accountant, his glasses were thick and distorting, but his aim was true when he leaped down on the man beneath him and slit his throat. Blood spilled onto his hand in a rush of red. He picked up a handful of snow and wiped the liquid of death away. Less than a second later, he heard a burst of gunfire and felt a sharp heat penetrate his back through his shoulder blades.

As he was falling, with the last beat of a shattered heart, he gave himself up to what he would become, thinking it was much better than being an accountant.

49

It was a short volley. A good distance from the cabin, but the sound of it traveled across the stillness of the snow-muted forest with terrifying clarity.

Roadrunner, stationed in the kitchen at the back of the cabin, jerked to immediate attention with a force that threatened to snap his slender frame like a stick in the hands of a giant.

He'd spent most of the day in crushing anxiety, but the reality of the danger hadn't hit him until he heard the gunfire. Now the terror was real, settling around his heart, squeezing with inexorable force.

He held a shotgun in both hands, its weight heavy and unfamiliar. He handled small arms very well and, surprisingly, never left a bull's-eye untouched on the range. But that had been like a video game, his little .22 barely heavier than a joystick, and seemingly as nonlethal. The heft of the 12-gauge was a burden, the much longer barrel awkward, and the knowledge of its potential destruction profound.

Roadrunner closed his eyes and shuddered and, for the first time in his life, wished for a drug that would obliterate dread.

John had been in the Chief's bedroom on the north side of the cabin, backed up next to the wide window, 9mm in his hand, safety off. He was no fighter, no superhero, much as he wanted to be. But this time the only people in his life he cared for were threatened, and he'd never felt steadier.

His heart sank when he heard the gunfire, but he didn't tremble and he didn't hesitate. It had come from the west side of the cabin, where Grace and Annie were stationed. In a flash, he saw the big windows, Annie in her silly feathered skirt trying to manhandle the shotgun Claude had placed in her hands; Grace, solid and strangely invincible with calm sureness that had killed two men in an instant on the boat.

His heart seemed to swell with his love for these people. It was such an alien feeling to carry this late in his sorry life, and it filled him with a quiet joy. He rushed out to the kitchen where Roadrunner stood trembling and very brave.

John smiled at him and put his hand on the thin man's bony shoulder. 'The gunfire came from the front, Roadrunner. Grace and Annie are alone in the living room. There's no one in the world I would trust more than you to take care of them. I'll watch the back.'

Roadrunner took a shallow breath and tried to find something to exhale. 'I won't let you down.'

'I know that.' John's smile broadened, and something behind it made Roadrunner certain that everything was going to be all right.

Annie always surprised you. Her generous form was simply not made for speed and alacrity, and you couldn't possibly look at that fashionista's perfectly coiffed bob and meticulous makeup and imagine that her response to danger would be quick and certain. But when that first burst of fire sounded outside in the woods, she kicked off her pumps and dropped immediately to a crouch beneath the windowsill, feathered skirt be damned. Those harrowing days in the Wisconsin wilderness had honed her like a sharpening steel.

'Stay down, Annie,' Grace said, inching toward the heavy front door with its triptych of small windows toward the top.

'Duh,' Annie replied, racking the shotgun she held, careful not to compromise her manicure. 'It wasn't that close.'

'I know. Chief's men are between us and the fire. They're the target now.'

Annie dropped her head and Grace had the feeling she was praying for those courageous men out there protecting them, even though she'd never known Annie to be one for prayer of any kind.

They both turned when Roadrunner slinked into the room in a crouch. 'John's covering the back. He wanted me out here with you.'

Grace turned her head to again peer out the tiny windows in the door, her brow close to wrinkling in a frown. It didn't make sense. The back of the cabin was relatively safe from the gunfire in the front. John should have come to the living room himself, leaving Roadrunner in the back. She thought about that for a second, then took a breath and dashed back to the kitchen.

Empty. Silent.

She looked out the window and saw a familiar form darting from tree to tree. John Smith, retired FBI, patriot . . .

'John,' she whispered, loving and hating him at the same time, because he didn't know how to do this.

There had been a lot of times in her life when Grace had felt her heart pounding against her chest like this, but all of those times had been fueled by fear for her own safety. This time it was different. This time it was fear for someone else, someone she loved, and that made all the difference.

She ran headlong into the icy forest, crystal-covered twigs snapping in her wake as she followed John's tracks through the snow.

Too much noise, she thought, listening to the sound of her own heavy breathing sucking cold air into her lungs, to the pounding of her feet into snow where ice cracked beneath. This was not the old Grace MacBride, who crept breathlessly around corners, whose footfalls were soundless. She was not looking for potential danger, not even fearing it; she was just running heedlessly toward something important.

She heard the fire of an automatic gun ahead but never slowed, and just before a rise in the earth blocked her view from what was beyond, she saw John's tracks scuffle long marks into the snow, and then the scarlet droplets piercing the white.

She hesitated for the first time, focusing on the droplets, thinking, *Cherries in the Snow.* Her mind flashed back to the dressing table of one of a long line of foster mothers, to the gold tube of lipstick with its colored cap that looked like a strawberry ice-cream cone. She hadn't liked lipstick then, or even understood its purpose, but on the bottom of that tube, a white paper label identified the color as Cherries in the Snow and she had thought the name quite beautiful.

But it didn't look so beautiful now. There was no more gunfire ahead, and maybe it wouldn't have mattered anyway. Grace was beyond external stimulation, lost in that place in her mind that had a clear sense, a horrible dread of what she would find over this tiny lift in the forest floor.

Funny, she thought, that her legs weren't tired from her run through the trees – they were simply stiff – blocks of wood attached to her feet that showed no grace in their leaden movements.

One step, two, three, and then she was on top of the slight rise, looking down. She stood perfectly still for a second, two even, deep breaths moving in and out, as she felt the slow creep of frost come up from the snow, through her boots, inch by inch up her body to her face until all nerves were dead. There was a lot of blood. Too much to leave life behind.

I don't have to go down there. I don't have to see reality at close quarters to know it is reality.

But remarkably, her frozen legs moved against her will, taking her to what she didn't want to see. John was face-down in the snow, recognizable only because of his clothes and his long gray ponytail slung sideways, soaking up the spilled blood as if to take it back into the body that was absolutely, deathly still.

Grace knelt automatically, ripped off her glove, and pressed two fingers into the neck where the carotid should answer. She waited a long time for a single pulse that would never beat again, and then stood up and looked down at the body one last time, her face stiff and expressionless, feeling so much, so intensely, that it was like feeling nothing.

In her memory, she saw John with his strong legs braced on the teak deck of the boat, squinting against the Caribbean sun as he lowered the flag, silly gray ponytail tossed by the evening wind.

That was John. That was what she remembered.

50

Gino and Magozzi had been lying motionless on their bellies for almost two hours. The sun had almost set, and the serious chill of nightfall was settling around them.

Gino was thinking this gig was almost as boring as a stakeout; worse, actually, because it was frigging freezing, and there was no food. He was obsessing over thoughts of a sausage pizza, mozzarella oozing over the sides, when Magozzi tapped his shoulder and jerked his thumb upward. Sit up, the thumb said, and Gino got it. On your belly, the body absorbed more cold. They needed to sit up to put their legs between the icy plank floor and their internal organs.

Gino had just forced himself into a sitting position when they heard the first shots crack through the forest, and suddenly, this horror story of a situation became real.

He was no stranger to fear. Anyone who thought cops got used to danger was flat-out crazy. Every time you got an armed suspect call, your heart rate skyrocketed and you tried to remember where you'd put your will. That was fear. This was different. This was the kind of sheer terror that paralyzed you, tied your stomach into knots, and drenched you with sweat. He glanced quickly at Magozzi and wondered if his own eyes were showing that much white.

You could wave the flag and support the troops until

the cows came home, but not for one second could you ever understand what they lived through until you had a real taste. And this hadn't even been a taste, just a glimmer, because soldiers lived it every single day.

Neither he nor Magozzi had ever served in a war, and their time on the street hadn't prepared them for this. This was no juiced-up druggie out there waving a .22, this was a goddamned army of goddamned terrorists who had come here for one reason only – to kill.

They both inched to opposite ends and looked over the edge of the tree stand, weapons at the ready.

Can you tell the difference between a Native American and a Middle Eastern terrorist? The Chief's words came back to Magozzi, who thought, God, I hope so.

Gino was frozen on his side of the stand, shotgun in his hands. He held that position for a solid half hour, and he was starting to feel like part of the forest around him. There had been a lot of scattered gunfire, and there was no way to know what was happening out there. And then suddenly, there was silence. Absolute. Seemingly endless.

Fifteen minutes of shallow breaths and sweat beading on foreheads in spite of the cold. They heard the footsteps approaching long before they saw the man. Magozzi squinted through the trees, spotted the shape coming closer in the near dark, then looked through the sights while his finger trembled on the trigger.

'Don't shoot,' Harley's voice called out a millisecond before Magozzi pulled the trigger.

Magozzi dropped his head and his gun and began trembling violently. 'Jesus Christ, Harley. Jesus Christ, I almost shot you.' His voice shook like an aspen leaf in a high wind.

'Come on down. It's over.'

Magozzi moved down the ladder first, legs still shaking. Gino followed much more slowly, trying to manage his fear of heights. 'Where are Claude and the Chief?'

'They're okay. They're out searching the woods.' His voice sounded faint and deeply diminished.

Magozzi jumped to the ground, felt it jar his legs, and wished he hadn't. It was hard to make out Harley's face in the shadows, but there was no mistaking the blood spatters on his cheeks.

'Jesus, Harley, are you okay? Were you hit?'

Harley shook his head in a slow, wooden movement, then swiped at his face. 'This isn't my blood.'

51

Roadrunner and Annie were in the cabin's living room, still manning their posts at the front windows, when they saw Magozzi, Gino, and Harley approaching from the woods.

'Oh, thank God,' Annie whispered, rushing to unlock the front door. Her heart skipped a beat when she saw the blood smears on Harley's face, thinking you never knew how you really felt about someone until they were hurt. 'Oh Lord in heaven, Harley, are you all right?'

He swallowed and nodded. 'Fine.'

She took his arms gently, in case the big lug was lying, and tugged him inside. 'Get in here and sit down. Roadrunner, get a cloth and some disinfectant . . .'

'I'm not hurt, Annie, relax.'

He was telling the truth. She could see it in his eyes. But her heart was still pumping hard, because she understood instantly that if he wasn't hurt, someone else was. And life for Harley was going to be a lot different from now on. She took a breath and stood aside as Gino and Magozzi filed in. 'Is it over?' she asked them.

'It's over,' Magozzi said. 'Where's Grace?'

Roadrunner propped his shotgun against the wall. 'She and John are in the kitchen, watching the back.'

'No need to watch anymore.' Magozzi led the way to

the kitchen to pass on the good news and then froze in his tracks. The room was empty.

Roadrunner and Annie started calling out for John and Grace until Magozzi said sharply, 'Wait. Be quiet.'

His eyes were closed as he listened, and then they all caught their breath, finally identifying the scratching sound that had caught Magozzi's attention.

A closed door led to a mudroom that opened onto the back of the cabin. Behind it, Magozzi found Charlie, scratching frantically at the door that led outside. 'Oh Jesus.' He looked out the window in the door and saw two pairs of tracks in the snow. 'They went outside.'

The second he opened the back door, Charlie shot outside like a rocket. All of them raced after him, unable to keep up with the dog's pace, but easily followed the scattered snow he left in his wake.

When they came upon drops of blood mingled in the mess of tracks ahead of them, Magozzi ran even faster, his heart pounding.

He stopped at the top of a small rise in the forest floor and looked down, breathless.

John was lying facedown in the snow, motionless. When Magozzi saw Grace sitting next to him, holding his hand, his heart started to slow. Charlie sat next to her, his nose reaching for her face, but never touching her, perhaps understanding the way that dogs sometimes did, that this was a time for restraint.

'God in heaven, no,' Annie murmured, following Magozzi as he moved quickly down the hill toward the terrible tableau. Like Charlie, he collared all the emotions that wanted to break free and simply slipped off his parka and laid it over Grace's shoulders.

'Thank you,' she said softly, looking at Magozzi, not John. 'I had to follow him.'

Magozzi swallowed hard. 'I'm sorry, Grace. Really sorry.'

Gino was on his haunches, automatically checking for John's pulse. There was too much blood in the snow and not enough in John's gray hand to indicate life, but it was something you did on the job. You had to make sure.

Roadrunner, Annie, and Harley closed the circle around Grace and John, and then all of them watched as Charlie left Grace's side and walked slowly, cautiously, around John's head to the other side, claiming the space. He sniffed at John, jerked back, sniffed again, then laid down next to the body and put his head on John's back.

He snuggled close, then released a great sigh.

52

There were a lot of somber faces at the cabin's dining room table that night. For a time, no one spoke about what had happened in the woods: not the stunning death of John Smith, or the terrible loss of Eugene Thunderhawk, a brave man who would still be alive if they hadn't come up here. Grace wondered how many more bodies she would leave in her wake in this lifetime, innocent people who had died simply because of an association with her.

It was all too much, too big, too crushing to even acknowledge openly, and at least for now, trying to put words to it seemed diminishing and utterly pointless.

And maybe none of them would ever talk about it, Magozzi thought, stealing glances at Grace, who sipped a cup of tea with downcast eyes. Individual terrors and heartbreaks were sometimes better left to settle to the bottom of the psyche, like toxic sediment in a polluted pond.

Chief's wife, Noya, had arrived after sunset and fed them all a rich soup, wild rice salad, and stacks of Indian fry bread. They ate in silence, exhausted, sad, trying to process the events of this day.

'Thank you for the meal, Old Woman.' Chief wrapped his arm around her waist in a rare display of public affection that made everyone else feel alone. He looked around at the others, at the guilt on every single face. Apparently none of them believed that things happened for a reason or that there was another life after this one. He thought that must be a terrible way to live.

Noya stood and put her hand on Chief's shoulder. 'We have to go,' she told him.

The Chief pushed himself to his feet and looked at the solemn faces around the table. 'We have respects to pay to Eugene Thunderhawk's family,' he said. 'I'll be back in the morning.' He hesitated, pressed his lips together, and frowned. 'One more thing. We need to know where to send John's body. Where is his family?'

'Right here,' Grace said quietly, and the others at the table nodded. 'There's no one else. We'll take him back to Minneapolis and bury him there.'

Before he left the room, Chief took the chair John Smith had sat in earlier that day and turned it backward.

He wasn't there anymore, Grace thought, and part of her life was gone.

The helicopters awakened them all shortly after sunrise. They heard the steady thumping of the rotors as the choppers were setting down at the clearing near the lodge. Chief brought Agent Dahl to the cabin door an hour later, a cadre of his agents fanning out behind him, and behind them, at an enforced distance, dozens of journalists and photographers.

Dahl greeted Gino and Magozzi, who introduced him to the others. He tipped his head back toward the media in apology. 'This is big news, worldwide. The powers that be thought it would be wise to let them cover what happened up here.' He looked at the people gathered in a ragged semicircle around him, at their red eyes and long faces, and thought they looked shattered. 'I am so sorry for your losses. I want you to know the Bureau considers Special Agent John Smith and Eugene Thunderhawk heroes in this war against terror, and they will not be forgotten.' He looked at Magozzi. 'Is there a place where you, Detective Rolseth, Chief Bellanger, and I could speak privately?'

After the four men were settled in the den, Agent Dahl inched forward in his chair and braced his forearms on his thighs. 'I don't think I'm talking out of school when I give you a summary of what the Bureau has learned so far.'

Gino reached for a butterscotch hard candy in a dish on the coffee table, then remembered getting one of those evil things caught in his throat at the fourth-grade Halloween party. 'Just relax and let it melt,' the stupid school nurse had told him as he was choking to death. He put the candy back in the bowl and looked at Agent Dahl. 'We looped the Chief in on everything we knew.'

'I'm guessing you've all been a little too busy to catch the news, but the fact is, everybody in the country has been looped in,' Dahl replied. 'The Director himself held a prime-time press conference last night detailing the terror plot and the target cities.'

'Whoa,' Gino whistled. 'That doesn't sound like the Bureau.'

Dahl shrugged. 'New Director. He has this crazy idea that keeping the public fully informed of the dangers might help our image. I figure he'll be gone within the week.'

'Too bad,' Chief said.

'That's what I think.' Dahl looked at Magozzi. 'After we saw the plot detailed on that computer, I called all the target cities personally and got a little surprise. When the locals went with warrants to the addresses on John Smith's list, they found the occupants dead. All recent kills, no guns, no suspects. At this point, it looks like a lot of people had access to that list, including Joe Hardy. We're theorizing some kind of network, pretty well organized, but right now it's only a theory. We have absolutely no evidence to support it.'

Chief leaned back in his chair and blew a silent sigh out through pursed lips.

Magozzi cleared his throat. 'John ran a check on the people on his list and found the same thing. Up to that point, he didn't know what was happening. He only sent that list to law enforcement. He had no idea it had gone farther than that. He was trying to do the right thing.'

Dahl nodded. 'And he did do the right thing. He saved a lot of lives.'

'That's what I told him,' Magozzi said.

'We're hoping that Joe's computer might give us something more to go on.'

'In his bedroom.' Chief jerked a thumb over his shoulder. 'The computer's in his duffel bag, but there could be some personal things in there his wife would like returned.'

'I'll see to that personally,' Dahl promised.

Magozzi rubbed the back of his neck, still sore from his time in the tree stand. 'So some kind of an organization is bumping off terrorists before they can kill American citizens. You sure you want to follow this trail?'

Dahl pushed himself to his feet. 'Not really. But that's a personal sentiment, not the Bureau's.' He glanced at the Chief. 'Great work taking so many of them alive, Chief Bellanger. We took them into custody when we arrived. They're already on their way to the Cities for questioning. We'll autopsy and ID the ten who didn't make it and see what we can learn.' He hesitated, suddenly uncomfortable. 'I didn't want to say this in front of the others, but with John Smith dead, at least his friends will be safe. Toward that end, we're going to see to it that his death gets heavy coverage in the media. The downside is that our source of information is gone. We've already put every address on the list under surveillance, but there will be more to take their place, and we still don't have any idea how John was able to find so many that slipped through the cracks.'

Magozzi raised his eyebrows. 'I think Monkeewrench might be able to help you with that.'

53

It hadn't taken long to arrange John Smith's funeral. There were no relatives to notify, no newspaper notices to post, just the core group of people who'd known him best and who would attend his burial.

Harley, oddly enough, had taken care of everything. 'We're going to bury him in Pattern Lake Cemetery. It's right next to the golf course where we picked him up.'

'They still have available plots there?' Annie asked. The proximity of golf courses to cemeteries was a big attraction to the male Minneapolis population. Annie thought that was weird, and more than a little disturbing.

'I gave him my plot,' Harley replied.

Annie gaped at him. 'You have a plot?'

'Of course. Doesn't everybody?'

There was a bitter crispness to the morning air the day of John's burial that made you feel like the sky was about to crack overhead and spill fractured pieces of blue onto the ground.

Grace led the procession as Gino, Magozzi, and Monkeewrench followed her on a carefully shoveled path that curved through an older section of Pattern Lake Cemetery. She hadn't said much to anyone since she'd found John facedown in the snow, and those who knew her well knew better than to question her. She'd done her mourning for John in private, and all that remained now was sorrow that had settled over her gently, like falling feathers.

Everyone thought she'd fall apart now; that she'd slip back into that horrible paranoid isolation that had defined her life for over a decade. What they failed to realize was that John had changed all that.

In the distance, Magozzi saw another service taking place with at least a hundred people gathered to pay their respects to someone who had obviously been well loved. It made him feel badly that John Smith had only their sad and small contingent of people who had cared about him.

Magozzi saw the mound of earth ahead, covered with a white tarp so they could all pretend there was no frozen dirt there waiting to be shoveled onto a box that held someone they knew. Standing beside the tarp was a minister Roadrunner had asked to speak at the internment. Funny. Roadrunner knew a minister. Life was full of surprises.

A little closer, and Magozzi saw a cluster of men and women in dark suits and coats, standing quietly beside the ready grave, waiting. He recognized Agent Dahl, and many of the agents who had come to Elbow Lake to clean up the mess of an unheralded war. The FBI was paying homage to one of their own, and yet still, the mourners were few.

When they had all gathered at the graveside, heads bowed and thoughts unspoken, the minister read a Bible verse Magozzi remembered from his grandfather's funeral so many years ago. It echoed in this cold, empty place, and then he heard the drums – soft, muted thumps of cushioned drumsticks pounding in perfect synchronicity against deerskin drums, counting the cadence.

They all turned around and saw the procession coming behind them, led by Claude and Chief in full dress Marine uniforms, and then the other reservation veterans, wearing the uniforms of many branches of the service. These men were the standard-bearers, marching like West Point cadets in the perfect, rigid exactness of a drill team, bracing the flags of the United States of America and the bands of the Ojibwe Nation in the holders at their waists. John had never worn a uniform, he was not entitled to military honors at his burial, but in his own way he had fought for his country all his life. Apparently, these men who had traveled five hours to be here understood that.

Grace felt the drumbeats deep in her chest and swallowed hard as the number of people around John Smith's grave multiplied.

He should have had a flag, she thought, standing at rigid attention as John's casket was lowered into the ground. It hurt her that he didn't.

She looked around for Magozzi as they left the cemetery, and saw him kneeling to place an American flag in the mound of earth covering John.

It was the first time she had cried in a very long time.

54

Agent Dahl sat at his desk long after the majority of Federal workers had left the office. He thought of all those people, home with their families, getting a sound sleep because they weren't privy to the kind of information he was.

His assistant rapped lightly on the door, then entered. 'Do you need me, sir? It's November first.'

Dahl glanced at the digital clock display on his computer. Three minutes after midnight. October thirty-first was history. 'No, Neal. Go home. I'll see you in the morning.'

'Thank you, sir.'

Dahl looked at the scribbles he'd made on the pad beside his phone. On October twenty-ninth, the Director of the FBI had held a much-publicized press conference, warning of random, unconnected terrorist attacks planned for specific cities all over the country.

Every one of those cities had been on edge for the two days since, the news coverage had been nonstop, and the level of security had been amped up everywhere. He'd watched a lot of the coverage, and had been saddened by the film of uniformed officers marching down the center of Main Street USA. These were necessary defensive measures, but to him it had looked a lot like martial law.

Then again, maybe that was why nothing had happened

on Halloween. It was common for terrorists to change plans when they were discovered. It didn't mean the plans had been canceled, only postponed.

He put his elbows on the desk and rubbed his eyes. This didn't end here.

Epilogue

Claude and Chief were out on the cabin porch, feet propped up on the railing, chairs tipped back precariously on two legs. Claude wondered which one of them would fall first and break a hip. Women always thought men did stupid things because they never considered the consequences, and that was just false. Men knew they could get killed in war and fall off chairs; they just didn't give a shit.

Claude was back in the worn, comfortable cowboy boots that had walked miles on Texas soil; Chief was equally comfortable in the soft, pliable moccasins that belonged in this land and nowhere else. The woods were quiet and peaceful once again, reclaimed by the wildlife as if nothing unusual had happened here.

It was the same with the two men – a battle was a battle, and once it was over, there was no point in discussing it because you'd already lived it.

Claude studied their four legs braced on the railing and felt a deep sadness because there should have been six. 'I miss Joey. And I'm a little pissed at him, too. We were supposed to hit those Little Mogadishu houses next week, not last week, and we've always been a team. He cut us out of the picture.'

Chief laced his hands over his belly and sighed. 'Maybe he didn't think he'd make it to next week. And maybe he thought he'd spare us some risk.'

Claude took his feet off the railing and planted them on

the porch deck, righting his chair. It was a simple gesture, but one that transitioned the mood from relaxation to business in a single motion. 'Did you put the word out that the Feds are surveilling all the houses on Smith's list?'

'I did. The news will spread fast in the Native community; the other vets are harder to reach. It might take a couple days.'

Claude folded his lips together and thought a minute. 'Maybe just this once, we could reach out with e-mail. Be a damn shame if one of our boys walked into a Fed stakeout.'

Chief sucked in a deep breath and righted his own chair. 'We can't risk it. In the beginning days when we fought each other, your people wrote dispatches we intercepted, and my people sent smoke into the air that disappeared. Today the world communicates on computers. How do you fight such a thing? You refuse to use the white man's talk, just like the old days. You talk only to people you trust, and you write nothing down. You know this, Chimook.'

'Yeah, I do. But it's slow and worrisome.'

'We'll get it done.'

'Well, the FBI damn well better follow through on this. It's their turn to fight the war.'

Chief's shrug was eloquent. 'If they don't, we'll still be here.'

read more

P. J. TRACY

DEAD RUN

It should have been a simple journey – a drive from Minneapolis to Green Bay, Wisconsin. But a couple of unplanned detours lead Grace MacBride, Annie Belinsky and Police Deputy Sharon Mueller deep in the northern woods, far from civilization and a mobile phone signal. Then the car breaks down.

The nervous search for a landline and a mechanic leads the women to Four Corners, a sleepy crossroads town. And a place they soon wish they'd never stumbled on – because something terrible happened in Four Corners . . .

Filled with the same crackling dialogue, pace and rich, vivid characters as *Want to Play?* and *Live Bait*, *Dead Run* firmly establishes P. J. Tracy as one of the most exciting thriller writers in the world.

'A fast-paced, gripping read with thrills and devilish twists' *Guardian*

'Outrageously suspenseful' Harlan Coben

'A thrilling page-turner with a nail-bitinge finish' *Sunday Telegraph* read more

P. J. TRACY

LIVE BAIT

When elderly Morey Gilbert is found lying dead in the grass by his wife, Lily, it's a tragedy, but it shouldn't have been a shock – old people die. But when she finds a bullet hole in his skull, the blood washed away by heavy rain, sadness turns to fear. It looks like an execution . . .

Soon a whole city is fearful as new victims are found, killed with the same cold precision. All elderly. All apparently blameless.

Detectives Magozzi and Rolseth race to uncover a connection and their best hope of doing so may be Grace MacBride, beautiful, damaged survivor of an earlier killing spree. And the answers, it seems, are buried in a terrible past.

Filled with the same crackling dialogue, pace and rich, vivid characters as the author's debut, *Want to Play*?, P. J. Tracy's *Live Bait* is an electrifying thriller that explores the chilling extremes of evil and retribution.

'Slick, enjoyable thriller. P. J. Tracy is about to become a household name' *Daily Mirror*

'Her second offering doesn't disappoint. Vivid scenes, realistic characters and humorous dialogue' *Time Out*

P. J. TRACY

PLAY TO KILL

Play to kill . . .

When Minneapolis homicide cops Gino and Magozzi fish a body out of the Mississippi, they think it's just another day, another corpse . . . until a film of the victim's murder appears online alongside other films, also featuring brutal killings. Pretty soon they're asking themselves whether the murders are linked and, if so, whether this is the work of a lone killer . . . or several?

Desperate to find a connection between the gruesome films before more are uploaded, Gino and Magozzi turn to computer maverick Grace MacBride for help. But as the bodies and videos stack up, the team creeps closer to a terrifying truth with consequences for them all.

. . . kill to play?

'A fast-paced gripping read with thrills and devilish twists' *Guardian*

'Outrageously suspenseful' Harlan Coben